THE SPARKLING RAIN

THE SPARKLING RAIN

ELIZABETH O'HARA

POOLBEG
FOR CHILDREN

Published 2003
by Poolbeg Press Ltd.
123 Grange Hill, Baldoyle,
Dublin 13, Ireland
Email: poolbeg@poolbeg.com

1 3 5 7 9 10 8 6 4 2

A catalogue record for this book is available from the British Library.

ISBN 1-84223-026-3

Typeset by Patricia Hope in Goudy 11/14.5
Printed by
Cox & Wyman,
Reading, Berkshire

www.poolbeg.com

About the Author

Elizabeth O'Hara lives in Dublin. She is the author of *The Hiring Fair*, *Blaeberry Sunday*, and *Penny Farthing Sally*, as well as many books for adults. Her work has won several prizes, including the Bisto Book of the Year Award and The Readers' Association of Ireland Award.

Acknowledgements

Thanks to Westfield Flying School for information on small planes, to Siobhán Benoit for information on the French judicial system, and to Doireann Ní Bhriain and the Imaginaire Irlandaise festival for inviting me to the Cevennes.

For Hanna

1

Chestnut Cottage

The Moody family lived in an old farmhouse in a valley in the Cevennes mountains in the south of France. Their house was four hundred years old. Once it had been called *Les Arbres* and later *Les Chataigniers*, a name which had been etched onto a battered wooden plaque on the gatepost. But the Moodys had taken down the old plaque and replaced it with a shiny stainless-steel plate saying *Chestnut Cottage* because Mrs Moody could pronounce that more easily, although the postman and most of the neighbours could not – they continued to call the place by its original name.

The cottage was a very large house, with thick stone walls, small deep windows, and a roof of red tiles so steep that it was almost vertical. In spring the walls were covered with mauve wisteria, which filled the air outside the door with a rich perfume. On the 21st of March every year, swallows began to arrive in the valley after their winter holiday in Africa, and during the summer dozens of them nested in the eaves of the cottage, and swooped and soared through the branches of the trees. In autumn, vines twisted around the windows, dripping purple grapes against the glass. During the winter snow piled up in the corners of the garden, and for months fat snowmen stood on guard at the gate. The garden itself was full of secret nooks and crannies, criss-crossed by uneven stone paths and shaded by ten great chestnut trees, so that you could always find a cool spot there, even at the height of summer when the temperature soared and the sun tortured the stones.

Inside the house was cool in summer, cosy in winter, and full of quaint old furniture and surprising little secrets. Its star feature, and the one of which Mrs Moody was most proud, was a secret panel of gleaming chestnut wood in the hall. Behind that panel a local minister had been hidden once for four weeks, in the days when people who adhered to the Protestant faith were hunted down and killed by the French army in this part of France – Languedoc, where people had been renowned for their independent thinking since the Middle Ages. When the minister was caught, he had been burnt to death in the garden. Mrs Moody loved to recall this and claimed that she could still see the marks of the fire, and hear the minister screeching with pain in the middle of the night. She was also fond of recalling that, on another occasion, on the road outside Chestnut Cottage, ten men and women accused of heresy had had their eyes put out and their noses cut off – and had been forced to march for miles and miles through the land of the Cathars, as an example of the fate in store for anyone who disagreed with the religion of the majority. The people of Languedoc thought for themselves and were outspoken. Even their language was different from that of the establishment. They said "*oc*" instead of "*oui*", and that was just the start of it. For being different, independent and honest, they were hated and punished by those whose job it was to make everyone conform to their own ways.

But that was a long time ago, centuries before this story begins. Now Chestnut Cottage was inhabited by the Moodys, a family somewhat different from most others and somewhat the same: Mrs Moody and Mr Moody and their three children. Mrs Moody's first name was Lily, short for Elizabeth, and she was forty-five years old. Mr Moody's first name was Jack, short for John, and he was fifty, although he didn't look it. Their children had names that had not been shortened at all, namely Brian, Clara, and David. They were always called Brian, Clara and David. It is very difficult to find a short form for Brian, and it is not often that you find one for Clara (What would it be? Clar? Ra?). David could have been called Dave or Davy, but he was not. David: that is what he was called, in France where he lived, in Ireland where he had come from, and everywhere else as well.

Brian was the eldest child in the family. Almost sixteen, he was a tall, quiet boy, who had for the past two years learned to prefer his friends to his family. When anyone asked him what interested him, he said "football"; he played centre-back for his school team and was one of its best players. In secret he liked to write poems and had a thick spiral copybook that was slowly filling up with sonnets and short lyrics, many addressed to girls with whom he was in love. But he had not been in love with anyone at all for at least six months and, at the moment, many of his poems wondered why this was happening. What had gone wrong?

His darkest suspicion was that girls did not like him because he was not good-looking enough. In fact, he was extremely handsome: his hair was thick and dark and his eyes were shining and green as leaves in early summer. But he had a grievous flaw: ears. His ears were big; they stuck out like handles, and were the bane of his life. Whenever he had a spare moment his thoughts wandered quickly in the direction of his ears, and he wallowed in worrying about them. On his darkest days, they drove him to the edge of despair, and sent his thoughts on a journey to a cold bleak country where life seemed not worth living. Fortunately, Brian seldom visited this terrible place. He was learning, slowly, to turn his back whenever he spotted the signposts in his head encouraging him to go there. Anyway, he was usually much too busy to get depressed. He attended boarding school in a town on the coast, the town of Merle, and from Monday to Friday studied and played hard. Every weekend he came home to Chestnut Cottage, taking the train on Friday after school and returning on Sunday afternoon.

Clara was the middle Moody child, and she had been fourteen in March. She was experiencing a growing spurt, and as a result was thinner than she had been ever before – for most of her life she had been a chubby little dumpling. But now she was suddenly slim. Her hair was red, and tumbled in a mass of curls and ringlets and tangles over her shoulders, or, more often, was tied in a wild-looking ponytail on the back of her head. She had unobtrusive ears but a lot of freckles, even in winter. These freckles did not bother her one bit – she thought they looked cute and friendly. Her hair was a brighter shade of red than was strictly desirable, and she hoped that one day it would darken to a rich and elegant auburn. Then she would look just perfect. But in the meantime she was happy to dash around in old clothes and forget about the finer points of beauty. She lived at home in Chestnut Cottage, and loved to play in the river, climb the mountains, and, whenever she possibly could, fly in an aeroplane. Her ambition was to be a pilot with a big commercial airline. It was a vague ambition, and she had given no thought to how it could be achieved. But already she could fly a small plane, and planned to take out her private pilot's licence as soon as it was legal for her to do so. Her mother had taught her to fly.

David was the youngest. He was ten, a stout, sturdy boy with a round baby face which showed no sign of changing. His eyes were a bright brown and very large and his skin looked as smooth and golden as a table of polished pine, a complexion which complemented his head of blond curls charmingly. And "charming" was a word people often used when referring to David, a word which is always spiked with question marks. The fact is, David was a charming boy whenever he felt like being charming, and as bad-tempered as lumpy porridge the rest of the time. His main interest in life was computer games; he planned to design and make his own when he grew up. Like Clara, he lived at home in Chestnut Cottage.

The family had been in Chestnut Cottage for almost eight years; they had moved in when Clara was six, and were thoroughly at home in France at this stage. Before, they had lived in Ireland, where Mr Moody worked as a wine importer. But eight years ago his business had necessitated the move to France.

"Why?" Clara had asked, at the time, when she had been dismayed at having to leave her friends behind in Dublin.

"It's easier for Daddy to live where they make the wine," said her mother, Mrs Moody. "He has to spend so much time there anyway, checking out vineyards and tapping the bottoms of bottles and things. We'll see more of him if we all go to France. If the vineyard won't come to Mohammed bring Mohammed to the vineyard."

But they didn't see more of Jack. Soon after they moved into their new home, he began to go on business trips, just as he had when they lived in Ireland, and continued to spend long periods away from his family. The farmhouse they had bought for its character and beauty was so high up in the mountains that no vines worth talking about grew nearby: the grapes which nudged the windows of Chestnut Cottage were small, sour, and purely decorative. The vast flat acres of vineyards where Mr Moody bought his barrels of wine lay many miles away to the south, on the lower sunny slopes of the land of the Cathars, and on the flat wide plains that stretched to the Mediterranean. Jack Moody spent a lot of his time down there, wheeling and dealing with farmers and merchants, and he also spent a lot of time abroad. The Moody children and their mother only saw him now and then.

Clara and David were enrolled in the village schools, but they seldom attended classes. Mrs Moody didn't consider them important. She often told the children not to bother going to school today, for one reason or another: it was too fine a day to waste indoors, or it was too cold to go out, the road was too icy, or she suspected they were about to catch a cold.

So, unlike other children, Clara and David did not daydream about the school burning down, or the teachers going on strike, or heavy snows making the road inaccessible. They didn't have to. Most of the time, they didn't go to school anyway. It was a delightful state of affairs. They would almost have liked school, if they hadn't been so out of touch with lessons. They knew no grammar, or history, or mathematics. Their knowledge of geography was sketchy, to say the least. They knew that Paris was the capital of France and Dublin the capital of Ireland, but if you asked them "What is the capital of Norway?" they would have hesitated, and if you asked "What is the capital of the United States" they would have shouted, all too promptly, "New York". Even their French was not as good as it should have been, since they seldom met French children, and Mrs Moody couldn't be bothered learning any language apart from English, which, she said, had always been good enough for Shakespeare and the Moodys and so should be good enough for the French. Why they insisted on speaking their incomprehensible language she did not know.

In addition to being fairly ignorant, the Moody children were very badly behaved, especially according to the accepted, inhumanly high, standards of schools. Being silent for hours on end seemed pointless to them. They found it very irritating to move to one place when one bell rang, and to another when another bell rang, even if they had no wish to move at all. Most of the lessons taught in school they found dull and useless. And sitting in one place for several hours on end was an anathema to both of them. David couldn't do it at all, and Clara found it very, very difficult and quite unnatural.

But they were very skilled in subjects which were not

found on the school curriculum. On the days, the many days, when Mrs Moody decided that they should mitch from school, she did not sit idly by. Far from it. She often got them to dress up, usually in curtains and tablecloths, black tights and white sheets, and they acted out plays. They knew *Hamlet* and *Macbeth* and *The Merchant of Venice* and several other Shakespearean plays off by heart. Since there were only two actors (Mrs Moody thought of herself as the director), Clara and David knew all the parts, they had played them so often. When they did *Hamlet*, Clara was Hamlet and Claudius and Polonius and Horatio and Gertrude, and David was Ophelia and Rosencrantz and Guildenstern and the Ghost of Hamlet's Father. Among others.

Dark winter days were Play Days. Bright spring or summer days, however, were Nature Days. On Nature Days, the Moodys set off up the mountains, with their backpacks strapped to their shoulders, and their mountain boots laced on their feet, and tramped around, identifying flowers and trees and animals, or, more often, the tracks of wild animals. They tried to name all the flowers and animal prints they came across, and wrote these names down in little notebooks with brightly-coloured covers. The notebooks were carefully kept by Mrs Moody in a drawer in the kitchen. Sometimes she gave Clara nature books and got her to copy out the names from the printed books into the notebooks, very neatly, drawing many red lines horizontally and vertically in between her lists of this and that. "For a rainy day!" Mrs Moody would say, and wink.

Very fine days, of which there were quite a few, since this was the South of France, after all, were Thalassa Days. *Thalassa* is the Greek word for "sea", or at least that's what

Mrs Moody thought. She liked the word because once, in ancient times, the Greek army, on a long journey, fleeing from their enemies, finally reached the seashore and felt safe, whereupon they yelled at the top of their voices: "*Thalassa, thalassa, thalassa!*" A bit on the repetitive side, and not brilliantly original, Clara thought, but she could understand their excitement. On Thalassa days the Moodys put on stripy T-shirts, found their swimming gear in unlikely corners of the house, filled soft straw baskets with baguettes and juice and cheese and chocolate, and took the train down to the coast. When they reached the busy shores of the Mediterranean, Mrs Moody always shouted "*Thalassa, thalassa, thalassa!*", much to the embarrassment of the children. They tried to hide behind other peoples' umbrellas and look as if they did not know Mrs Moody while this ritual was being enacted. Luckily, since the beach was as crammed with people as a peak-period railway station, it was easy to hide. Once Mrs Moody had expressed her appreciation of the sea in this mortifying way, the worst part of the day was over. After that, they went swimming in the Mediterranean. Mrs Moody was a great swimmer. They raced one another from one cove to the other. All the Moodys could have been champion long-distance swimmers if they had felt so inclined, but they did not. Their joy in swimming was not competitive. They had never been in a swimming-pool in their lives. Mrs Moody ranked swimming-pools with school. She did not believe in them.

Best of all, Mrs Moody liked to fly. She did not own an aeroplane, but she hired one out as often as she felt like it from a small aerodrome on the plains of Languedoc. Her private pilot's licence had been obtained years ago, and she flew the children all over the south of France and further afield. She had given Clara lessons, even though Clara was too young to take out a pilot's licence. It was illegal, too, for Clara to fly a plane, but this was not the sort of detail likely to bother Mrs Moody much. "We're above the law!" she would say, as Clara piloted herself and David around, shakily, swaying and swooping alarmingly, like a young and inexperienced magpie, over green vineyards and red farmhouses. "Can we land, can we land?" David had often shrieked, terrified and close to vomiting, during the first wobbly days. By now Clara was a competent pilot and usually did not wobble too much, at least not on calm days. In two or three years, she would take her licence and at some vague time in the future, when she had finished school, apply to an airline for a place in a training programme. Not that she was in any hurry to do so – life at Chestnut Cottage was usually so much fun that she sometimes felt she would never want to leave it.

There were, however, occasional problems.

Mrs Moody sometimes disappeared. She did not travel abroad and stay away for weeks on end, as Mr Moody did. Indeed, she usually did not accompany him on his travels at all. But sometimes, on the rare occasions when Clara and David were in school, making fools of themselves thanks to their appalling ignorance of the most elementary academic facts, she forgot she was a mother with children to mind and just wandered off. She would go on long, long walks alone in the mountains, have a Nature Day all alone, sketching scenes which appealed to her as raw material for the paintings which she liked to make when the mood struck. Or she hopped into the car and drove fifty miles to the nearest cinema, and spent hours there, watching all the movies one after the other. Sometimes she took out her favourite plane, an old rickety Cesna 150, and flew away to Italy or Spain and bought some special treat for dinner in a marketplace a hundred miles from home. She would turn up eventually with a bag of pasta, hand-made in Modena, or sausage from Bologna, or marzipan from Barcelona. The children tried to impress upon her that they could easily do without these delicacies. Pasta from the shop in the village tasted much the same to them as pasta from Italy and they loathed marzipan, much preferring the bags of fizzy brightly coloured sweets they could buy at home. But their mother always said, "Nonsense! This is the real thing!"

* * *

Today, a warm day in spring, Clara woke up to find her room full of golden sunshine. She glanced at her watch. It was ten o'clock. She sat up and yawned, wondering whether to go back to sleep for another while or get up. She looked around her room – it was a large attic room, and had a sloping roof with a skylight through which she could see a sky of clearest azure. The room was painted white and had several bright pictures on the walls, which Clara had made herself. Pine presses contained her clothes, and she had a big pine desk and a bookcase with a glass door. Often Clara's room was a mess: she was a very untidy girl. But this morning it was neat as a button. Madame Bonne, a woman who came every day to Chestnut Cottage to help out, had obviously been at work recently.

After contemplating her room with dreamy grateful eyes for a few minutes, and listening to music which wafted upstairs from the radio in the kitchen, Clara jumped out of bed and threw on her dressing-gown. When she came downstairs, she found Mrs Moody in the kitchen, listening to choral music by Palestrina and painting a picture on the big table.

"We're too late for school again, Mum!" Clara said, cheerfully. She felt guilty about being such a bad school-attender, and at night she usually made up her mind that she and David were going to improve their ways and go regularly. But in the morning she often felt quite different about it.

Mrs Moody looked up from her picture.

"It's far too nice a day for school," she said, with a smile. "Today is a Nature Day if ever there was one! As soon as David comes down I want you and him to run out there and play and play all day."

She returned to her picture, humming along with the choir as she daubed red and yellow paint on what seemed to be a picture of a burning haystack, but which Mrs Moody would certainly call *Wedding Day* or *The Children at Play* or something equally inappropriate. Clara shrugged happily and went to the fridge to find some food for breakfast. While she drank orange juice, she went to the window and looked out at the front garden, which faced east. There the sun was dancing on the flowering chestnut trees and the swallows twittered and fluttered like leaves. "You're right," she said to her mother, who was concentrating so hard on her work that she did not hear her. "It's a Nature Day all right." She went to the foot of the stairs and yelled "David!"

2

The Valley of the Springs

David and Clara spent the whole day wandering around the mountainside. They identified at least two wild flowers and saw the footprints of a wild boar, a dog and a cat, all of which Clara noted carefully in her little notebook, as instructed by Mrs Moody (she was not too sure about the wild boar, but she put it down anyway). Lunch was partaken of, rather late, on the bank of one of the rivers which tumbled down the hillside into the valley, making a great racket as it went. Clara and David had to shout to make their voices heard over its rambunctious roaring. After lunch, David and Clara played one of their favourite games, leap-frogging from rock to rock in the river. It was a risky game, because there were always some rocks which looked firm, but were as shaky as loose teeth. If you fell into this river at the wrong place, you could be swept downstream and over a waterfall in no time at all.

David did fall in – he almost always succeeded – and

Clara had a few anxious moments as she watched his little body being swept along on a strong current. But luckily David's progress towards his destruction was impeded by another rock. He held onto this and Clara managed to pull him to safety.

"I'm wet!" said David, somewhat unnecessarily. Water dripped off him as if he were a garden sprinkler. "And cold!"

"It's time to call it a day," Clara said, in the resigned tone she frequently had to adopt when on escapades with her small brother.

* * *

When they reached the house, the kitchen and living room were empty. Mrs Moody was not at home. Clara was not surprised, although she was disappointed, but David was very angry.

"Where is Mammy?" he screamed. "I want her! Where is she?" His teeth were chattering and his brown skin was puckered with goose pimples.

"She'll be back soon," said Clara. "She's probably just out for a walk." But she was nervous. She realised it could be hours before their mother returned. She might forget to come back until tomorrow. It had been known to happen.

"I want her now! Mammy, Mammy, Mammy!" screeched David, at the top of his voice, a voice which could reach a very high pitch indeed. He could scream like an ambulance in full spate when he felt like it.

His resounding roar was met by an almost equally loud sound: *thumpety-thump, thumpety-thump*, on the stairs. A large animal, an elephant or a rhinoceros, seemed to be making its way down the Moody staircase.

"Madame Bonne!" Clara said, with relief. She hugged David. "Everything will be all right, Madame Bonne is here!" she said. Her words worked like a charm. David stopped screaming and poised himself to welcome Madame Bonne. He wiped his face with his hand, smearing it with mud and other dirty substances, and stared grumpily at the kitchen door.

Madame Bonne came into the kitchen.

Madame Bonne was a woman, Clara thought, as she had often thought before, for whom the word "motherly" might have been coined (just as Mrs Moody was a woman to whom that word could never be convincingly applied). But the word "motherly" suited Madame Bonne down to the ground, as well as other related words, such as "warm", "reliable", "clean", "good cook", and "buxom". She was shaped like a big fat pillow, always dressed in a dark navy dress of a style which might have been in fashion about fifty years ago, and a navy blue overall dotted with tiny red flowers. She had leathery skin, brown and creased and oily like a bat's, and very long, arched, black eyebrows. Her eyes were large and brown and missed nothing, and her black hair was pulled back into a severe bun at the nape of her neck. Madame Bonne seldom smiled. But she cleaned the Moodys' house so that it not only shone like a new pin, but was always pretty, fresh and cosy. She filled their bread-bin with fresh, delicious bread, and put flowers in the vases that had escaped being accidentally smashed by Mrs Moody. She washed and ironed Clara's and David's clothes, so that there was always something clean and pristine in their drawers, waiting to be worn with pleasure and pride, when they were in the mood for that sort of thing.

"*Mon pauvre petit!*" she said, in a whistling tone, when she caught sight of David. "What has happened to you?"

Clara explained. Madame Bonne dispatched her to get towels and dry clothes for David. Within minutes, he was wrapped in a voluminous bath-towel, standing in front of the warm stove, his hair being rubbed vigorously by Madame Bonne.

"*There's fennel for you, and columbines! There's rue for you and here's some for me!*" David was saying, sadly. Usually when he was wrapped in a towel he was playing the part of some woman in a play, or of a figure from classical antiquity. Almost drowning had reminded him of Ophelia in *Hamlet*, one of his favourite roles. "*There's a daisy! I would give you some violets, but they withered all when my father died.*"

"*Hein?*" said Madame Bonne. "I would give you some hot chocolate? Would you prefer that?"

"Yes," said David without a moment's hesitation. Madame Bonne's hot chocolate was one of the finest things in creation.

"Get dressed then," said Madame Bonne. "Both of you, sit by the stove and get warm."

Clara and David obeyed her. David pulled on jeans and a jumper. Then the brother and sister sat by the stove, singing Ophelia's song, while they waited for the hot chocolate.

3

Village School

It didn't take David long to recover from his wetting in the river. The next day, Clara woke him up at seven in the morning. Her mother, who had come home late the night before, was asleep. It would, it had occurred to Clara, be a suitable day for going to school. They hadn't been for about a week so she thought it was probably time to put in an appearance.

"I'm tired!" David said.

Clara had ambivalent feelings about school. She enjoyed not being there, but not being there had its drawbacks, and she was aware of them too. David had no such doubts. He didn't see the point of school at all.

"Never mind that!" said Clara. "Just get up and come on!"

In the dark kitchen, Clara flung open the casements. Already the sun was playing through the leaves on the trees, and all around the house swallows were singing their joyous chirpy song. Clara made a pot of coffee, and they sat at the big table drinking hot milky coffee from bowls and eating crusty bread. Hot dinners were in short supply in the Moody household, but the fridge was always stocked with cheese and sausage, jam and bread, milk and juice, thanks to Madame Bonne's efforts.

"It's Friday!" said Clara. "A good day to go to school, because the weekend is just about to start."

"Goody! Brian will be home this evening!" said David.

"Yes," said Clara, looking forward to seeing Brian again. She enjoyed hearing about his adventures in school.

"Will Dad come too?"

"Maybe," Clara shrugged.

"Keep your fingers crossed," said David. "I think he will be home this weekend. He hasn't been here for ages."

"That's true," said Clara cautiously. In fact, her father hadn't been home for about six weeks. She had no idea where he was, and neither, as far as she could gather, had her mother. Clara was beginning to wonder if they would ever see him again: the gaps between his visits were ever-increasing in duration.

"I think he'll bring me something really good this time," David continued happily, filling up his bowl with hot milk, which he loved.

"Yeah!" sighed Clara, not sharing his optimism. She finished her coffee and put the bowl in the dishwasher.

"What do you think it'll be?" he asked.

"Well. What would you like?" Clara played along with David's fantasy, not knowing what else to do.

"Mm," David stared thoughtfully out the window, allowing his mind to wander over all the delightful possibilities. "Maybe a new mountain bike?"

"Ah come on!" laughed Clara. "Get real!"

"A new game for my computer then. I think that's what he'll get. There's a great new game about a safari, he'll see it at the airport – it's much better than the old ones. The graphics are the best they've ever made on any game."

"Well, let's hope that's what you get then," said Clara, taking his bowl and stacking it in the dishwasher. "If he comes, that is," she added, sadly, not wanting David to be too disappointed.

"He will," David nodded firmly, smiling with his mouth closed. His wide brown eyes were bright with anticipation.

"Let's go then," said Clara. "Have you got all your stuff?"

David's stuff consisted of his lunchbox, his schoolbag, and something called a "cyber pet", a toy which was fashionable at this time in the south of France, and possibly all over the world. It was a small plastic chicken that had to be "fed", and otherwise nurtured, by means of a simple computer programme. You fed it by pressing buttons on its tummy. If David didn't attend to it, it indicated that it needed attention by bleeping. If he did attend to it, it rewarded him by staying quiet.

Now he pulled his cyber pet from his pocket, and looked affectionately at its plastic face. "Yeah," he said, smiling, and happily pressing buttons.

They walked along the country road in the cool morning sunshine. All around them lay the white flowering chestnuts, and other trees: ash, hazel, beech, birch. The air was crystal clean, tuneful with birdsong and the sound of many rushing streams and tinkling springs. *Les Sources* – "The Springs" – was one of the names this area had, because so many rivers rose in the mountains round about. It was here that they began their journeys down to the Mediterranean. And here they were at their brightest, strongest, liveliest.

As they walked, the bells of the church down in the village rang out. The whole valley was full of music, the music of bells and birds and running water. Clara felt her heart turn a somersault of joy. In spite of everything, she felt lucky to be alive, and to live in such a wonderful corner of the world. David felt the same pleasure. He liked the sunshine and the bright green colours, and his sister. His cyber pet was fed and watered and tucked safely into his pocket. He held his sister's hand, and they skipped along the road together, all the way to their two schools, which stood at either side of the narrow village street.

School progressed in the usual way. Their teachers expressed astonishment that Clara and David were in attendance.

"I had believed you had left the region," Clara's teacher said. Her face indicated that such an occurrence would have pleased her. "But since you have decided to grace us with your presence once again, I suppose you have not?"

"Oh no, I'm still here!" said Clara. Acting innocent was the best tactic, she had discovered, when dealing with the sarcasm of teachers.

"Has the school-attendance officer visited you recently?" the teacher asked, with a sly smile.

"Oh yes," said Clara. "We had a visit from him just a few days ago."

The school attendance officer came to Chestnut Cottage almost as often as the postman. Whenever he came, Mrs Moody gave him coffee and cakes made by Madame Bonne especially for unwelcome guests. The cakes were indescribably delicious and had the effect of making the most difficult person soften up, lose all sense of proportion, distort their judgement, and believe that all was right with the world, the sun was shining, no problem that could not be solved existed on earth or elsewhere. When the officer had eaten two of these cakes, he believed that Madame Moody was the most beautiful wise woman on the face of the earth. She convinced him that her system of education, keeping children at home and sending them to school on the odd day, was the answer to France's educational problems. He went away from Chestnut Cottage composing a report to the Minister for Education in his head, convinced that if he used the principles formulated by Madame Moody that he would be promoted on the fast track to the highest position available to a French school-attendance officer. He would be School Attendance Officer in Chief for all of France. He swelled with pride as he dreamt of the glory which would follow, as soon as he relayed the Moody Principles to his boss: Teach the Children Nothing; Let them Do What They Like; Play with Them all the Time; Get Up Late Every Morning; Have Fun Whenever Possible; Throw All Rulebooks Out the Window; and finally, Mrs Moody's trump card, Always Keep a Nature Notebook. She always produced these notebooks when the inspector had eaten three cakes. They invariably impressed him as indisputable evidence of her genuine educational zeal and exceptional competence as a teacher.

Usually it was about twelve hours later when the officer realised he had been duped once again. This realisation began to dawn on him as the effects of Madame Bonne's cakes began to wear off. Life seemed greyer and drabber for a while then. The officer understood that it would not be a good idea to pass on "the Moody Principles" to his boss. In fact, he understood, not for the first time, that Mrs Moody was at least half mad, and that her principles would cost him all prospects of promotion and possibly his job if he ever breathed a word about them to anyone, even by accident. His dreams shattered, as the final crumbs were digested, and he sent a stiff letter to Madame Moody, threatening to take the children away and put them in a home if she did not send them to school more regularly. He wrote this with some despair: he realised that the threat would never be fulfilled. He would never be able to take her children away from Madame Moody, because he would never be able to refuse her terrible and irresistible cakes.

"Sit at the front of the class," the teacher told Clara, and David's teacher was saying exactly the same thing to David. "Maybe you can manage to learn at least one thing while you are here."

David and Clara spent a long dull day sitting at the front of their respective classes. Clara managed to learn one thing. She learned that Tallinn was the capital of Estonia, information which would be useful to her, she knew, if she ever took part in a television quiz. She knew that if she actually went to Estonia, and she had no plans not to, since her ambition to be an airline pilot meant that she would probably visit many places, she would probably find out that Tallinn was its capital shortly before she landed in it, which in her view would be more than adequate for her requirements.

David did not learn a single thing. His capacity for not learning was prodigious. He sat at his desk with his hands over his ears, blocking out the sound of the teacher teaching and occasionally sneaking food to his cyber pet. Cyber pets were forbidden in the school, but the teacher turned a blind eye to David's. He was never going to learn anything anyway, so what was the point in fussing about his cyber pet?

David and Clara, and their teachers, were extremely relieved when three o'clock came, and they could all go home.

And when Clara and David arrived at Chestnut Cottage, David's prayer was answered. As they walked along the road by the hedge that surrounded their garden, they heard the voices of their father and Brian, laughing and talking. And when they raced in the gate, there sat their mother, dressed in a velvet tunic of midnight blue, with moons and stars appliquéd on it, her black hair plaited into about a hundred small plaits and wound around her head, silver ear-rings and bangles and necklaces dripping from her in profusion like water from a waterfall. Opposite her sat Brian and Mr Moody.

David could hardly contain his delight at seeing his father and mother together. It was a sight for sore eyes, and one David's eyes had not enjoyed for seven weeks.

"Dad!" He rushed into the arms of his father. Mr Moody rose. He was a tall man with thinning reddish hair and small, crinkly green eyes. He had a red moustache which made him look like a character from a nineteenth-century novel, even though he dressed in ordinary modern clothes, unobtrusive, unlike Mrs Moody's clothes. Mr Moody had to sell things to people and couldn't afford to look eccentric. For some reason people trust salesmen who look exactly the same as everyone else. The slightest difference from the norm puts them off, and suggests unreliability. Mr Moody knew he was overstepping the boundaries of the acceptable with his red moustache. He would have been much richer if he shaved it off. But there was a limit to the sacrifices he was willing to make for the sake of money. Like Mrs Moody, he had a strong individualistic personality and suppressing it had been the bane of his life. But unlike Mrs Moody he had been forced to do it, most of the time, to earn a living and support his family. However, he allowed himself occasional days off, when he was as eccentric as he chose to be. And he allowed himself the moustache. Recently, he had given himself a little more leeway in other areas, too. As yet, nobody in his family knew about these transgressions.

Now, he caught David in his long arms and swung him into the air. David screamed with delight.

"Hi there, son!" he said, his face as happy as David's. "Great to see you!"

Clara watched the scene from her vantage-point at the gate. And for years after she held that image in her mind, like a photograph in a family album: her father, with his roguish smile, swinging David, his curls flying, in the air. David was wearing his red shirt again today, and it contrasted with her father's white polo neck and smart, expensive tweed pants. Her mother, looking outrageous but beautiful, sipping coffee quite sedately at one side of the old rough wooden table. Brian, his long skinny legs stretching far in front of him on the grass, his black hair tousled, his blue denim shirt opened at the neck. David laughing, her father smiling broadly, Brian and her mother looking on, their expressions joyous and serene. Behind them, the old, kind walls of Chestnut Cottage, and the cushioning, buxom, blossoming froth of the chestnut trees. Grey and green and white and pink. A happy family in a lovely setting.

Clara sometimes saw herself in this photo, as she was then – a thin girl with her hair tied back in an untidy ponytail. She was wearing blue jeans and a white sweatshirt – the only splash of colour was her red hair and green schoolbag, its strap biting into her shoulder. Sometimes she saw herself in the photo, and sometimes not – either way she hovered on the edge, observing her own family, outside, not part of it. And why was that?

She did not ask that question on that May afternoon in the garden. Like Brian and her mother, she watched her father with pleasure. They were all delighted to see him. They basked in his presence, they opened their hearts to him, like daisies in the sun. And nobody more than David, who adored his father more than anyone in the world – more than Madame Bonne. More, even, than his beloved Clara. It was uplifting to see his joy.

When her father released David, and he perched on the wooden bench beside him, Clara walked somewhat sedately over to the table. Her father gave her a long, quiet hug.

"And how is my beauty queen?" he said. "Getting more spectacular by the minute!"

"Hi, Dad," Clara said quietly. "Good to see you."

She gave Brian a hug as well, and held the hug longer than usual. For some reason she was close to crying: it had been such a long time since the whole family had been together like this, all five of them sitting in the garden, having coffee in the afternoon after school. Like a perfectly normal family, the kind of family she often longed to belong to.

"What can I get you?" asked her father.

"Oh, I'll get it myself," said Clara, since this is what she always did anyway.

"No, no, no, no! What? Coffee, juice, milk?"

"We usually have orange and biscuits when we come in," said David. "And crisps."

"OK," their father said. He patted David on the head and linked him, and the two of them went into the house.

"Like my outfit?" asked Mrs Moody, stroking her skirt of deep blue, with its silver stars and orange moons.

"Yeah. It's lovely," said Clara. Sometimes, just sometimes, she wished her mother could live in the lower key. Sometimes she wished she would wear jeans, or a track-suit, and behave like most other mothers.

"Yesterday I flew to somewhere, somewhere nice in Italy," Mrs Moody wrinkled her forehead and thought hard. "Maybe it was Rome. There were lots of ancient buildings there anyway and a lot of very heavy traffic. It was probably Rome."

"Did you notice a very big dome as you flew over it?" asked Brian. "Or a little man with a tall shiny hat walking around on a stick?"

"No," said Mrs Moody. "Maybe it wasn't Rome. But anyway. I picked it up in a wonderful little boutique down a dark alley. It was so dark and lonely that I was scared to walk along it alone, but I decided to be brave, and didn't it pay off!" She laughed happily and patted herself on the shoulder.

"Yeah." Clara wanted to say no, but Brian caught her eye. "It's a lovely outfit," she added, lamely.

"Let's all go shopping tomorrow!" her mother offered, taking a sip of coffee. "You all need new things. Summer is a-cumin with luve to town! It's time to get new gear, folks – on your bikes!"

"Well," Clara was doubtful, "it's a long time since Dad was home. Shouldn't we stay here and relax?"

"Nonsense!" said Mrs Moody.

"I could do with a new pair of jeans," Brian patted the jeans he was wearing, which were well-worn. "But couldn't we just drive somewhere, in the car?" He hated flying. Being in a small plane terrified him and made him feel horribly sick, and he never ever accompanied Clara or her mother or their expeditions.

"I'll drop you at the station on the way to the aerodrome," said Mrs Moody airily. She had no patience with Brian's attitude to air transport. "And I can pick you up on the way home. OK?"

"OK!" said Brian with a helpless shrug. He knew just what his mother thought of his fear of flying: she viewed it with deep contempt.

"That's settled then!" said Mrs Moody.

Jack Moody overheard the end of the conversation as he returned with a tray of snacks for David and Clara.

"What's this about a trip? I've just got home and you're planning a big trip!"

"Just a shopping trip, love," said Mrs Moody.

"Ah sure don't mind me!" said Mr Moody, ironically. "I'll be grand here all on my own."

"No, no, you'll come too," said Mrs Moody.

"Yeah right!" said Mr Moody.

"Ah, go on, darling!" she said.

"Shopping? Not on your life," he said. "You can bring me on a sightseeing flight on Sunday if you like."

"Of course I can!" said Mrs Moody. "Shopping tomorrow, flying on Sunday. Sunday is my favourite day for flying. *Nearer, My God, To Thee!*"

"All those Sunday afternoon learners though!" warned Clara.

"It'll be great!" said Mrs Moody. "We'll all go up. We can go somewhere really nice."

"Like Tallinn?" said Clara.

"Tallinn? In Estonia," said her father. "Why would you want to go there? It's very far away."

"Just joking," said Clara.

Mr Moody put the juice and biscuits on the wooden table. Clara started to eat.

"So where have you been this time?" she asked.

Her father looked quizzically at her.

"I've been to the other side of the world!" he said. "You wouldn't believe me if I told you."

"Tell us anyway," Brian looked challengingly at his father. He was laughing, but his eyes narrowed and his skin reddened. Clara hoped he wasn't going to start fighting with Mr Moody: this sometimes happened. Brian disapproved of his mad family, even though he was fond of them. He wished his parents were more normal, more conformist, and more mature. Sometimes he felt that he was the most grown-up person in the household, even though he was only fifteen, and he resented that.

"China," said Mr Moody abruptly.

"China!" David squealed. "Wow!"

"They don't make wine in China, do they?" asked Brian, frowning.

"They do actually," their father answered. "But not wine that I'll be importing. No, I was there on other business."

"What sort of business?" Brian couldn't let the subject drop.

His father grinned. "Financial business. I've shares invested in the stock market in Hong Kong."

"And you had to go out there to check on shares? What are stockbrokers for?" Brian spoke very quietly. He stared at Mr Moody, like a detective on a television series cross-examining a suspect. Clara suspected that Brian modelled himself on one of his favourite screen snoops.

"Oh, leave your dad alone," Mrs Moody broke in, surprisingly. Usually she lapsed into a daydream when a family dispute arose. "You know he needs to keep an eye on everything himself. And at least he's home now."

"Thanks be to God!" Mr Moody stretched and changed the subject. "You know, we made the right choice when we bought this place. There is nowhere as nice as it in the whole wide world."

"No," said Mrs Moody hazily. Mr Moody gave her an affectionate kiss. Clara and David looked on, delighted at this moment of family harmony. Brian's face was more suspicious.

"Did you get me something?" asked David, when the kiss was over. He had been patiently waiting for a present to be produced for about an hour, and thought it was time to issue a reminder.

"Of course I did!" Mr Moody jumped up and lifted David into the air.

"What?"

"You go into my bedroom and you'll find a white bag lying on the bed. That's for you. And the brown bag is for Clara." He paused and looked at his elder son. "And the pink bag is for Brian."

Brian laughed, but it was obvious to everyone that he was

not amused. David dashed upstairs, disappointed that he was probably not getting a mountain bike, since it was unlikely to come packaged in a white bag, but full of expectations. As he had hoped, he got some computer games, the latest, with better graphics than any previous issues. Clara got a silver pendant in the shape of a helicopter, and Brian got a very fancy-looking fountain pen, "Made in China".

4

Shopping by Air

The following day, Saturday, Mrs Moody was true to her word. She got up at the unusually early hour, for her, of nine o'clock, and she and the three children piled into her big car and set off for the aerodrome. Mr Moody insisted on staying at home.

"I'll potter," he said, stroking his moustache lovingly. Today he was wearing very old baggy corduroy pants and a huge lumberjack shirt. On his head was a black beret. His clothes were making a statement and the statement was: "It's Saturday! Don't bother me!" He asked if he could prepare anything for dinner

"Oh, we'll be back long before dinner!" said Mrs Moody. "I'll look after that."

"Will you make shepherd's pie?" asked Jack. "I've been longing for that for weeks, as I ploughed through Chow Mien," he paused, trying to think of another Chinese meal. "And Chop Suey," he added, dissatisfied with his own lack of originality. "And Sweet and Sour Pork," he tacked on, in desperation. Brian looked at him with deep suspicion.

"Of course," beamed Mrs Moody. "We have shepherd's pie every Wednesday, usually, but we can have it again, for your sake."

The children suppressed a giggle. They hadn't had a cooked meal, apart from those they got at lunchtime in school, for months. "I could face shepherd's pie again this evening. And maybe tomorrow we can have spaghetti bolognese?"

"Brilliant idea, I'll make that!" said their father.

"See you later then!" called Mrs Moody. She tooted the horn. The children turned and waved at Jack, who stood in the gateway, framed by the trimmed laurel hedge, blowing kisses at them. He looked good-humoured and solid and dependable. It really was a pity that work did not let him spend more time with his family! Life was fun when he was away, but it became more stable when he was at home. Clara was absolutely certain that if Mr Moody were at home more often they would attend school regularly, for instance. She knew he would be horrified to find out that they were never there. Mrs Moody kept the letters from her friend the Inspector hidden from him. As far as Mr Moody knew, his children led an ordinary uneventful life and this is exactly what he wanted. Clara knew her father desired nothing but the very best for his children. That he was never at home to make sure they were getting it was not his fault at all; she believed he had to be abroad constantly, and would have dearly loved to stay with his children and wife. But he couldn't. He was too busy and successful, and his job had to come first, for everyone's sake. "*C'est la vie!*" he liked to exclaim, shrugging his shoulders, throwing up his hands. "*C'est la vie!*" That was his way of saying that he had no choice in the way he lived his life.

Clara sometimes suspected that he liked to be away from home, in spite of what he said. But she really loved him. They all did. Clara knew that there was a tension in her life which dissolved when her father was at home. When he was around, she felt safe. Mrs Moody behaved better then, and life at Chestnut Cottage was fun, but secure. When he was not at home, it was often fun, but very seldom felt safe.

Mrs Moody speeded down the mountains and dropped Brian off at a village railway station before proceeding to the aerodrome. They parked the car and walked over to the bungalow where the owner sat in an untidy office, surrounded by filing cabinets and coffee cups. Mrs Moody went in and made the necessary arrangements, while the children sat on the grass outside, watching the planes, which were perched here and there on the big field of the aerodrome like awkward toy birds, white and yellow and blue. Planes took off and landed all the time, in a seemingly haphazard fashion, and there were two or three flying around in the sky above, their long wings flat and light as those on paper planes.

Soon Mrs Moody emerged from the office, dangling a key and four headsets.

"We're taking the *Saratoga Piper* today," she said, and the children cheered.

This was a substantial, comfortable plane, with plenty of room and deep upholstered seats. Soon they located their plane. Mrs Moody gave it a quick examination, checking that the wings, the flaps, the tyres, the engine and all parts of the exterior were in order, and then they climbed into the cockpit. David sat in the back seat, while Mrs Moody and Clara placed themselves in the pilots' seats, in front of the control panel.

"You do it!" Mrs Moody said, putting on her earphones.

Clara nodded. She settled in comfortably in front of the control column and the panel full of winking, shining discs and clocks and gauges. She knew exactly what to do.

"Take off in that direction," said her mother, pointing to the edge of the aerodrome. "Then fly east due south. We'll go over to Italy and try to find that marvellous little shop again."

Clara turned on the ignition and started the plane. She turned it out of the field and drove slowly to the head of the runway. She spoke to the man in the office, and told him she was preparing for take-off. No other plane was landing, so he gave her the all clear. She drove down the runway at a moderate speed, turned into the wind, and lined up for take-off. Again, no other plane was ahead of her. She took out her checklist and checked that all was in order – fuel mixture, lights, gauges. At a signal from the aerodrome, she sped along the runway, gathering speed until it seemed the plane could go no faster. At that moment she tipped the control column downwards and lifted off.

"Aaagh!" screamed David, who always screamed at this moment.

Clara guided the plane smoothly upwards into the air.

"Well done!" said Mrs Moody, when they were a thousand feet above the ground, moving swiftly along. It was a clear day, without a cloud in the sky, and below them the fields and vineyards, roads and villages were spread out like a map, with every detail clearly visible.

A little rush of wind made the plane shudder, and David screamed again.

"Stop it!" said Clara crossly. "It's nothing." She tipped down the control column and ascended slowly, until they were three thousand feet up.

"Turn south now, and take the coastal route," said Mrs Moody. "It's much easier. I never get lost if I do it that way."

Clara nodded, and veered south. Her eyes were on the sky, the patch of sky in front of the nose of the plane and beyond the wing tips, but she was also looking at the landscape beneath her. To her it seemed much more beautiful from above even than when you were down in it. She loved the perspective which flying gave her on the places in which she lived. It was not that this perspective diminished those places; it simply made them clearer, and showed how they fitted together, how the system of fields and roads and rivers, houses and churches and villages, meshed together and formed an intricate, logical pattern which was lovely to see.

"It's fantastic, isn't it!" she yelled. Mrs Moody agreed, but David said nothing. He was sitting in his seat, with his eyes closed, wishing the journey would finish.

Soon they were flying over the port town of Merle and out over the Mediterranean.

"Just keep going for about an hour or so," shouted Mrs Moody. "We'll land then. Isn't this wonderful!"

Clara cruised along through the clean blue air. She was so experienced that she could fly in these conditions almost without thinking about it. There were many planes in the skies, big commercial craft on their way to the airports of Montpelier, Nice, Pisa, and others that were dotted along the coast of France and Italy. But these were flying high above Clara, and did not cause her any problems. As she flew, her spirits lifted higher and higher. She looked below, and saw France spread out like a tablecloth – roofs and steeples, roads stretched like dark blue ribbons through green fields, craggy peaks covered with snow in the background. The speckled blue sea sprinkled with ships and boats and yachts. The blue sky, an image of perfection, ahead and around and above.

"Prepare to land!" Mrs Moody yelled.

A small airport, like the one they had left, became visible below.

Like the other aerodrome, it was uncontrolled – there was no air-traffic controller. Clara looked around, for other planes. There were none immediately visible in the skies, and the runway below was empty.

She hovered over the airport. Two planes were hovering with her, both small private planes like her own. She watched them going down, taxiing along the runway, stopping. Then she began her own descent.

This was the most difficult part of the entire operation, and usually Mrs Moody handled it. But she insisted that Clara take the plane down today. Nervously, Clara tilted the control column up, causing the plane to descend. She tilted it gradually, and slowly, slowly, she brought the plane down. David closed his eyes and put his hands over his ears. But the touchdown was so perfect that he didn't notice it. Clara taxied along, and drew to a halt on the grass at the side of the runway.

A few minutes later, the Moodys were tumbling out of the plane.

"Where are we?" David asked.

"Italy," said his mother. "This is where I landed yesterday."

"We're outside Nice actually," said Clara, who was observant about these things. She had seen the sign for Nice airport ten minutes earlier.

"All we have to do is catch a bus outside the gate here, and we'll be in town in ten minutes," said Mrs Moody.

Shortly afterwards, the Moodys were trotting around Nice, doing their shopping.

Mrs Moody behaved impeccably, as she led Clara and David from shop to shop. She encouraged the children to try on outfits, watching with interest, genuine interest, as they selected items which she thought were too boring for words. Clara tried on dozens of the most ordinary clothes in the world: jeans and T-shirts, blouses and skirts. David tried on two track-suits, and then refused to do it any more. His mother bought him the track-suits, and also two new pairs of trousers, shirts, and jumpers. She even remembered to get socks and underpants, items which were frequently in short supply at Chestnut Cottage. Then David ran off to a toy-store, arranging to meet Mrs Moody and Clara in an hour.

Clara and her mother, to Clara's surprise, spent a happy morning together. At the end of it, Clara had in her possession a pair of designer jeans, three new tops of cotton and velvet, a white silk shirt, and two new short denim skirts. They finished with a visit to a shoe store, where she got a pair of trainers and a pair of sandals, with gold and white straps.

"Now! All set for the summer!" said Mrs Moody, pleased with herself.

"How about you? Aren't you going to get anything for yourself?" asked Clara.

"Not today. Today is your day," her mother smiled.

Clara's heart leaped. Today is your day. It was Her Day. It was seldom her mother ever said that. Indeed, she had never said it before. It wasn't in the Mrs Moody script – it was a Perfect Mum line. What a good one it was! Clara thought of the whole day, packaged in bright paper with a big ribbon, presented to her. Wonderful! Clutching her big, elegant paper bags, she accompanied this delightful mother of hers across the crumbly cobbled square to an outdoor cafe. There they had a good lunch, sitting in the sunshine, watching the doves flutter over the red roofs of the town.

"We can go to the sea soon!" Mrs Moody said, looking up at the blue sky, longingly. "*My mind is tossing on the ocean; There, where my argosies, with portly sail, like signiors and rich burghers of the flood, do overpeer the petty traffickers*. I'd love to go for a swim!"

"Oh yes!" breathed David. "Let's go next week. I'm sure it's warm by now."

"It doesn't really get warm until June," Clara said.

"It's still much warmer than the sea in Ireland," responded David, who could barely remember Ireland, but he had heard all about it. "I want to go for a swim now!"

"I thought you'd have had enough of the water to do you for a while!" laughed Clara.

"The sea is different from that river!" countered David. "I love the sea. I love it!"

"Why don't we go some day next week if this weather keeps up!" their mother suggested. "We could drive down to the coast and spend the day. Have a picnic!"

David and Clara looked at one another and giggled silently. Their mother sipped her coffee, smiling her Perfect Mum smile at them all.

After lunch, they walked around the city, and then they caught the bus back to the airport. This time, Mrs Moody took the captain's seat and flew them back home, flying higher and faster than Clara had. But she was a great pilot, and they arrived back safely. Brian was waiting for them, sitting sadly on a bench outside the village station. He had bought his jeans, but had had a long and lonely day. On the drive back to the house, he was silent and wrapped up in his own thoughts, which were gloomy. His ears, his father, his mother: nothing seemed quite right. He was filled with sadness, and with a premonition of disaster.

Clara noticed, but David slept, oblivious to everything, and Mrs Moody chattered madly on, about shops and planes and clouds and birds and sandwiches. Her conversation was bright as tinsel and irritated Brian beyond belief. He wanted to scream. But he did not. He sat in the back of the car, clutching his plastic bag. He suffered.

* * *

It was six o'clock when the Moodys arrived back at Chestnut Cottage.

"Jack! We're home!" sang Mrs Moody, as soon as she walked in the door.

There was no reply.

"Where is that man?" she asked, good humouredly.

David, grumpy and cold after his nap, looked around the house, but Jack was not to be found.

"Probably gone for a walk!" said Clara, putting her arm around David's shoulder. David was shivering, with a mixture of apprehension and tiredness. He had bought a present for his dad, a plastic Tyrannosaurus Rex, and he wanted to give it to him straightaway. He knew it was just what his father needed.

"He'll be back soon," Brian said, pointing out that Jack's car was in the garage. Brian had pulled himself out of his blue mood. He prided himself on his ability to be calm in a crisis. "Take it easy, everyone! Why is everyone in this family so worried all the time! I don't get it!"

An hour passed, and Jack did not return. "Where can he be?" Mrs Moody lit a cigarette, a habit she had when worried. She did not smoke often, but when she did she smoked hundreds, one after another, all day long without stopping. She always kept a supply in a drawer in the kitchen dresser.

"He's not far away," said Brian. But he looked concerned. "I'll go out and look around."

Clara looked at him questioningly. Where could you start to look in this place?

"Dad's car is in the garage," David kept saying. "He can't be far away. His car is in the garage. That means he hasn't gone to China or anywhere. He's not far away."

"Divil a bit of him," said Mrs Moody, reverting to what the children supposed was the dialect of her youth. She did this sometimes when she was feeling cross. "He'll show up soon enough. And I'm going to sit right here and smoke like a chimney until he walks in through the door."

"What about the shepherd's pie?" Clara asked.

Mrs Moody looked astonished.

"Shepherd's pie? We had a big lunch. Surely you couldn't eat again?"

"I could," said Clara. It was about six hours since they had eaten lunch.

"Well, make the shepherd's pie yourself then, dearest," said her mother, with a smile. She opened her novel, lit another cigarette, and ignored the children.

"Take it easy, sis," Brian said. Worry was etched into his pale forehead. "Losing your rag isn't going to help us find Da."

The telephone rang. Everyone jumped. Brian was the one to pick it up.

"It's for you, Ma," he said, handing her the cordless phone.

"Yes?" said Mrs Moody, stamping her cigarette out on the floor and putting on her best telephone voice.

Clara and her brothers watched, reading their mother's face. It did not look happy. On the contrary, it was obvious that whatever their mother was hearing was bad news.

"*Oui*," she said again. "*Oui, oui. Je comprends.*"

After a minute she put down the phone.

"Jack has been arrested," she said in a neutral tone of voice. "He's in prison in Merle."

5

Smuggler's Cottage

"Why?" asked Clara, when she had recovered from the shock. "Why has he been arrested?"

"Drug-smuggling." Mrs Moody sat at the table and put her head in her hands. All the energy had faded from her face. Under her cap of jet-black hair, her skin looked white, wrinkled and old. "That's what he said. Drug-smuggling."

"Drug-smuggling!" Clara cried. "But that's impossible." She could hardly grasp what her mother had said. She felt cold and empty, as if someone had picked her up and poured her out, leaving nothing in the skin, none of the person that was called Clara.

"Alleged!" Mrs Moody wagged her finger in the air, with a sudden show of her natural spirit. "He may be innocent. Let us not forget it."

"Dad has been smuggling drugs? But Dad imports wine," said David. He was the one member of the family who still looked normal. He hadn't realised the enormity of what had happened. "Where is he now?"

"He's in Merle, in the jail there," Clara explained patiently, putting her arm around David's shoulder.

"But what about our dinner?" David asked, looking from face to face, his brown eyes wide as plates.

Brian sat as still as a statue and said absolutely nothing. Clara glanced at him and was terrified by what she saw. She clung to David and hugged him tighter. "Don't worry about dinner!" she muttered, pointlessly. "Don't worry, everything will be all right."

Then Mrs Moody began to cry.

She wept big tears, not even bothering to put her hand in front of her face. Mascara rolled down her cheeks, streaking her face with black smudges. Her chest heaved and she began to tear at her black hair, the way Ophelia does in the play.

"I knew this would happen," she wailed. "I knew it, I knew it, I knew it!"

The children were embarrassed, but Clara's ears perked up. A second ago her mother had said that Dad was probably innocent. If so, how had she always known "this would happen"? Brian snapped awake, too, and was obviously sharing Clara's thoughts. He glanced at her, curious, but he said nothing. Clara was the first to put the necessary question.

"You knew?" she asked. "You knew that Dad would be arrested sometime?" She glanced at Brian again. He was alert now; he no longer looked like a marble monument. They both waited.

"I knew it, I knew it, I have always known it!" their mother whined, incoherently.

Clara sighed; this was not very useful information. Mrs Moody was drifting off into a state of stupidity, to a world of her own. Clara had seen this happen before. Mrs Moody could float off, like a leaf, to a place where nobody could find her, just as in reality she flew away to places even she did not know the names of.

Clara didn't want this to happen, because she knew from experience that when Mrs Moody drifted too far off, there was no chance of retrieving her. She might as well be at the other side of the world. So she grabbed her mother by the shoulders, shook her gently, and asked in loud, clear tones that could not possibly be misunderstood: "Mother, did you know that Dad was smuggling drugs?"

Mrs Moody stopped pulling her hair, and she stopped weeping. She stood up from her chair and walked across the room to the window. The white trouser suit she had worn for the shopping trip was crumpled and stained, and her hair straggled to her shoulders in a dry tangle. For a minute she stared at the garden, her back to the children. Then she turned to them, and laughed harshly.

"He never told me a thing," she said. "Come to France, live on the top of a mountain! Goodbye, I'm off to Singapore, Hong Kong, Timbuktu. He kept his business life to himself. So I'm as wise as you are, darlings!"

Her face became sad and serious again.

"I'm as wise as you are, darlings, I'm as wise as you are!"

Clara felt relieved. She wanted to get up and give her mother a hug, but something held her back. She sat in her chair, with her arm around David, and hoped that Brian would ask the next question. He didn't, however. He looked less transfixed than he had at first, but his face was still rather stony. Clara felt impatient.

"You mean, Mam, that you don't know? That Dad probably

is innocent?" Clara asked, and a tiny trickle of hope seeped into her heart.

Her mother stared at her, the manic expression returning to her face.

"I know nothing!" she said. "I'm told nothing. I'm kept in the dark." She pounded the windowsill with her fist, alarming David. Clara clutched him. "But I can put two and two together. I didn't come down in the last shower. I wasn't born yesterday. I'm the full shilling. I'm not a complete and utter fool!"

Clara felt despairing. David began to whimper. Mrs Moody walked to the far side of the room, oblivious to everything except the thoughts in her own crazy head.

"How do you think we could afford all this?" With a dramatic sweep of her arm, Mrs Moody indicated the big stone-flagged room and its lovely antique country-style furnishings. "It's far from villas in the South of France that myself or Jack Moody were reared. Oh yes indeed and it is! How do you think we could afford all this? All this I say?"

Clara shrugged, feeling weary. Her mother was impossible. She would go on speculating and complaining, but in fact she hadn't a clue whether Jack was innocent or not. There was no point in trying to have a rational discussion with her.

"She doesn't know one way or the other," Clara whispered across the table to Brian, and to David she said, "We'll get something to eat soon."

Mrs Moody went to the dresser and took a bottle of wine from the rack on the dresser.

"Ochone, ochone agus ochone oh!" she said, looking around for the corkscrew. Clara saw it on a table and handed it to her. *"They're all gone from me now!"* Mrs Moody continued, as

she inserted the screw into the cork. "*They're all gone from me now,*" she repeated, as she twisted it in. "*And there's nothing more the sea can do to me!*" she shouted, pulling the cork out with a grand flourish.

"*Ochone, agus ochone oh!*" she said, quietly, pouring the wine into the glass. "Look at that – *the beaded bubble winking at the brim, the deep claret of the deep south, the wine-red sea, oh me oh my I think I want to fly!*"

Clara glanced anxiously at Brian. He looked horrified. It occurred to Clara that he wasn't as accustomed to Mrs Moody and her ways as she and David were, because usually this sort of scene was not enacted at weekends. Mrs Moody behaved in very strange ways during the week, when she was alone with Clara and David, but when Brian was around she tended to play a slightly more normal role. So now it was as if his worst nightmares were being enacted in front of his eyes. Mrs Moody, her glass in hand, sat down on the big sofa near the window, lit another cigarette, and settled down to smoking and drinking. Puff and sip, sip and puff.

David turned to Clara.

"Clara," he said, in a calm but serious voice. "I want to ask you something."

Clara nodded and told him to go ahead.

"You won't go away to school now and leave me here?"

"Of course not!" Clara replied hotly. "I would never have done that, ever, no matter what anyone said. Never!"

David looked relieved. He slipped off his chair, and said calmly, "I'll go and feed my pet. I hope he's not dead."

"He's not," said Clara. "You feed him and tuck him in for the night."

As soon as David left the room Clara picked up the

telephone directory. She dialled the number of police headquarters, explained who she was, and said she was making enquiries about her father, Jack Moody.

"Mr Moody has been arrested on a charge of drug-smuggling," a policeman told her. "He is in prison here at the moment and will face trial in due course."

"But he's innocent!" Clara cried.

"That will be decided when he is tried," said the gendarme.

Brian nudged Clara. "Ask about bail," he said.

Clara asked. "What about bail?"

The policeman answered in his cold voice: "The charge is very serious. In these cases, the accused is not allowed out on bail."

Clara shook her head at Brian. Brian swore.

"Can I see him?" Clara asked despairingly.

"Who are you?" asked the gendarme. But when Clara told him again, he said: "You should telephone tomorrow."

Clara felt her heart sink. It had now sunk so far there was hardly anywhere deeper for it to go. But it seemed to find a new place, new depths.

"Oh God. Can I talk to him?" She tried to keep calm.

"That is not allowed," said the gendarme, quite unmoved by her distress.

"But he's innocent," Clara repeated. "He's totally innocent. He's never imported drugs."

There was a brief pause before the gendarme said, "Please ring this number tomorrow afternoon."

"If anything changes let me know. Tell him we telephoned. You've got my telephone number?"

"Goodbye," the man said, not answering her question, and rang off abruptly.

Slowly Clara replaced the receiver.

Mrs Moody was on her tenth cigarette. It was astonishing to watch her smoke so fast. Her hands went like pistons, transporting her cigarette to and from her mouth. As soon as one cigarette came out another went in. Not a second was lost. She was like some steam-driven machine in an old-fashioned factory, an impression that was enhanced by the clouds of smoke which floated above. She took a break for a few seconds to make a statement, in a voice which was by now somewhat slurred: "He should have stuck with the wine. I told him. But he had to expand. He wasn't satisfied with making a good living – he had to be the big guy."

Clara went over to her mother. She put her arms around her and spoke kindly and gently, as if her mother were a child.

"Dad's in jail, Ma," she said. "We should try to go and see him."

"Tomorrow and tomorrow and tomorrow," said Mrs Moody. "I'm so tired." She stared at Clara as if she had never seen her in her life before. *"My little body is aweary of this great world."* She paused again, and stared out the window. Then she added, rather sensibly: "And I'm too upset to do anything sensible tonight. Let's sleep on it. Sleep knits up the ravelled sleeve of care, you know that, Clara. Macbeth never said a truer word. Rustle up some nice nourishing potato crisps and some Coca-Cola for yourselves. Then why don't we all go for a nice sleeve-knitting sleep?"

With that, Mrs Moody struggled to her feet and staggered upstairs to bed.

6

Behind Bars

The next day was Sunday. Mrs Moody telephoned the jail but got no information and was not allowed to talk to their father.

"We'll have to go to the prison and talk to Dad," Clara decided. "This is hopeless."

Mrs Moody put her head in her hands and said, "Frankly, I couldn't bear to see Jack in prison. It would be just too much for me in my present condition."

Clara looked despairingly at Brian.

Brian sighed, stiffened his back, and turned his head and looked out the window. He wanted to forget about this and go back to school. Usually he took the train on Sunday evening and was back in his dormitory before bedtime. Couldn't he do that now, and leave all these terrible people behind to deal with their own problems? It was too much for him.

"I don't see the point, Clara," he said, turning back to

her with a tiny sigh. "Let's just wait and see what happens."

Clara stared at both of them with a mixture of anger and disbelief.

"OK," she said. "Do what you like. But I'm going to see him. I have to find out what is really going on."

"You've always been so full of energy!" said Mrs Moody, maddeningly. "Ever since you were a tiny little girl. You go and see Jack and sort it all out. Then come home and tell poor little helpless us."

She smiled slowly, slowly left the room, and went slowly upstairs.

Clara marched out of the living-room and went to the kitchen. She sat in the window seat and gazed at the garden. It was a grey overcast day, and the garden looked gloomy, just as she felt. That neither Brian nor her mother would lift a finger to help her father astonished her. She could not understand their reluctance to do anything. She could not understand their lack of curiosity, their lack of impatience, their enormous, treacherous, passivity. What Clara wanted to do was race down to the jail, break into it, and rescue Jack. She wanted to scream at whoever it was who had accused him in the wrong; she wanted to do more than scream, she wanted to kick them and punch them and if possible shoot them.

Above all, she wanted to take some action.

Clara had been sitting in the window for a quarter of an hour dreaming of how she would rescue her father and punish his accusers when Brian came in. He walked slowly and looked sad.

"I've phoned school and told them I won't be back for a few days," he said, grumpily. "So I can go to the prison with you tomorrow."

He spoke in such a resigned, martyred tone that Clara's anger flared up again.

"Don't bother!" she said, shortly. She decided to say no more than that, just leave him to figure out that she was disappointed. But she couldn't restrain herself and after a few seconds she added, "I'll do it myself. Obviously you don't care about Dad. Why knock yourself out? Just go back to your bloody school and forget about me and David."

Brian's eyes widened in surprise. He had felt he was making a major concession. He had felt like a saint. Shocked at her reaction, he moved closer to Clara.

"I do care about Dad!" he said, with a little more passion. "Of course I care."

"So why don't you want to do anything then?"

Brian shrugged and threw up his hands. He sat down and stared at Clara, trying to find something – some words to express what he thought and what he felt. But he couldn't find any. He looked so lost and shocked and sad that Clara began to feel uneasy. She reached out and patted his arm.

"I'm sorry," Brian said then. "I'm sorry."

Then he did something he had not done for years. He started to cry.

Clara became alarmed.

"It's OK," she said, nervously. She hated all this crying. "It's OK, Brian." Brian crying was not something she could have anticipated. She wanted him to stop, and go back to being grumpy and dense.

But Brian did not stop crying. He had started and he could not be stopped. He sobbed and sobbed and sobbed. There was a lot to cry about. He sobbed because his father was in jail, and his mother was mad and drunk; he sobbed because he could not go back to school where a normal ordered life was always in progress, where sanity and predictability waited to welcome him and absorb him into its comforting, dull routines. He sobbed because a girl he had asked out two months ago had refused his invitation and hurt his pride beyond belief, although he had not quite known that at the time. He sobbed because his ears were too big. He sobbed because he had always known there was a fault-line in the Moody family and that one day it would split open and destroy them all and now this was happening. He sobbed because the world was a dangerous and unpredictable place. He sobbed because he hadn't let himself sob for five or six years.

"It's OK, it's OK," Clara said, because she did not know what was going on inside Brian's head, because she did not know what else to say, or what to do. "It's OK, it's OK," she repeated inanely. It was what she said when David cut his knee, or sulked because his mother had gone off somewhere without telling anyone.

David came plodding into the kitchen, and Brian was still crying. Intent on his own aim, which was to get some food, David gave him a sidelong, unconcerned glance. He still wasn't very disturbed by what was going on around him. It was as if he hadn't taken it in, or couldn't take it in. As long as he had Clara to look after him, he felt secure anyway.

"What's wrong with you?" David asked, but in a calm, unconcerned tone, giving Brian a faintly surprised look, as he went to the fridge and opened it with a sharp swift pull.

"Ah nothing," said Brian. But it was his signal to stop. He had been crying profusely for about ten minutes anyway, and he was almost cried out, if that is possible. He pulled away from Clara and rubbed his eyes. He felt shaky, but also light and empty inside, as if he had removed some heavy messy burden from somewhere deep inside not just his head, but his body. The whole area of his chest around his heart seemed to have been cleaned out, as if someone had given it a thorough dousing with a hose. Nothing in the external circumstances had changed, he knew that, but the crying had done him good, and the room around him looked cleaner and brighter and simpler than it had before, when everything had pressed in upon him, when the house and the people in it had seemed like a dark dinosaur or monster, pushing into his head.

Brian, an odd sob still breaking from him, involuntarily, watched as David took a strawberry yoghurt from the fridge, carried it to the table, and gobbled it up. This vignette was so normal, so easy, that it seemed beautiful to Brian. This is what he wanted: people to eat yoghurt, to do ordinary things.

When David had finished his yoghurt he looked suspiciously at Brian and Clara.

"When is Dad coming back?" he asked.

"I don't know," Clara answered, deciding that it was better not to lie to him.

"His car is in the garage, he can't have gone far," David said, and repeated it, over and over again, as he went about his business of playing and exploring. It was his mantra and he was sticking to it for all he was worth.

The day passed very slowly. Mrs Moody spent most of it in bed. When she was not resting, she sat in the kitchen and smoked cigarettes, thumbing through a novel which she did not seem to be reading. "*Oh, no no no no! Come let's away to prison!*" she said, over and over again, sometimes interspersing it with "*Howl howl howl howl! Oh, you are men of stones. Had I your tongues and eyes, I'd use them so the heaven's vault should crack.* Clara suspected that her mother was not sure whether Jack was in prison or dead. It was all the same to her.

Brian spent the rest of the day in his own room, listening to his favourite music and writing poems, which were about doors closing and doors opening, about bears sneaking through forests, about thunderstorms and rivers overflowing their banks. David did what he usually did: he played video games with as much enthusiasm as usual, and watched television.

Clara left them all and went for a walk in the afternoon, along the tree-lined road down towards the village. But although she met a few neighbours she did not tell them about her problems. There was nobody in the village she trusted enough to share this terrible secret with. Even Madame Bonne seemed suddenly distant, and strange: she would not understand. How could you tell anyone that your father had been arrested as a dangerous criminal, a drug-smuggler? Who would sympathise with you when you told them that?

They all went to bed early, too worried to do anything else. But Clara found it difficult to sleep, and when she did she woke up every five minutes. At six a.m., however, she was deep in a dream about the river. She and David were sailing on it in a boat that had a parachute instead of sails. The parachute was lifting the boat into the air and carrying it up towards the sun. Suddenly the parachute strings broke and the boat hurtled through the air towards the sea. The air rushed past Clara's ear, making a knocking sound.

Knock knock, knock knock!

"Get up!"

She crept reluctantly from her dream. For a minute she did not remember the events of the day before.

"What?" she asked sleepily, pushing her hair back from her face.

Brian was standing by her bedside, shaking her.

"Get up!" Brian said. "Time to catch the train."

Then Clara remembered everything. She jumped out of bed, dressed in jeans, a T-shirt and cotton jumper, and ran quietly downstairs. Brian was already boiling water for coffee. Clara sighed, looking at him standing by the stove. He was wearing a dark green shirt. Behind him the window was crowded with leaves, morning dark. A bar of honey-gold sun glanced off his dark hair. The birds were in full throttle in the garden. The scene looked peaceful, idyllic almost. It could not have been more at variance with the way they both felt.

"Is David awake?" Clara asked, as she poured water into the coffee-pot.

Brian shook his head. Clara had assumed David would come with them, but Brian didn't agree.

"He'd be a nuisance," Brian said. "It would be bad for him, and bad for us."

Clara knew this was true, but on the other hand they could not leave him alone with her mother.

"Well, he'll be OK, and she should have someone to look after her," Brian said.

In the end, she was forced to agree to this arrangement.

She wrote a note addressed to David and left it on the kitchen table, under a bowl of sugar. Then, after their coffee, she and Brian set off for the station.

They walked as quickly as they could. It was, as usual, a fine morning. The air was crisp and full of the familiar, lovely sounds of the valley. Striding along, Clara felt hopeful. She was certain that her father was not guilty, but she didn't know whether they would be able to do anything to help him. But they would see him. And at least they were doing something, not just sitting around crying "Why me?"

Although the station was small and usually very sleepy, at this time of the day it was quite busy. Many people in the village commuted to the big towns further down the mountains where they had jobs in offices and schools. Brian queued and bought the tickets: he was well known to the stationmaster, who, however, nodded tersely when he saw him, as he did to all the other regulars. He was much too busy to chat.

Clara saw many people she knew, who nodded rather coldly, as they always did; the villagers disapproved of the Moodys, because they didn't go to school and because Mrs Moody acted in such strange and surprising ways. Sometimes their coolness dismayed Clara, but now she was grateful not to have to talk to people. How would she have answered even a normal question, such as "How are your parents?" The father of one of her classmates at school, Monsieur Montbrieux, met her as she was waiting at the kiosk to buy some sweets and a newspaper for the train. He seemed very surprised to see her. In fact, his eyes widened and bulged in astonishment.

"*Bonjour, Clara,*" he said, in a warm voice, and then to her shock he patted her on the head, before rushing off up the platform.

At the kiosk she bought a newspaper and some hard sweets, and tucked them into her bag. Brian rejoined her and they went to the platform, where everyone was waiting for the train. Some people smoked, some read newspapers. A young, very chic woman knitted with quick, deft movements. A long swathe of soft white sweater seemed to grow from her needles. Many people just stared up the track – past the pots of red geraniums and the loops of mauve wisteria – to where it snaked down from the plateau.

Soon the train appeared, a dot of light on the mountainside. The chug-chug of the engine grew louder and louder, until finally at eight o'clock, precisely, the train stopped in the station. Clara and Brian climbed on and were lucky to find a seat. The other passengers alighted. The engine revved up. But a second before the guard blew his whistle a small, plump figure came panting into the carriage.

"David!" groaned Brian.

Clara smiled. She patted the seat beside her and made room for David.

"You nerd!" Brian hissed. "I thought I told you to stay at home!"

"I saw you leaving. Why did you go away without me?" said David, grumpily. He sat down calmly beside Clara. She put an arm over his shoulder and kissed him, whereupon he shook off her arm. He pulled his cyber pet out of his pocket and started to fiddle with it. When Clara tried to talk to him, he refused to answer.

The train moved slowly down the steep hillside.

Clara opened her newspaper.

On the front page was a big photo of her father, with the headline: *Drug Smuggler Caught in Mountain Village*.

"No wonder people were looking strangely at us!" sighed Clara, passing the newspaper to Brian.

"What does it say?" asked David.

"Nothing that we don't know already. Dad was arrested yesterday and charged with smuggling cannabis from the east to here, with the intention of bringing it to Ireland. He is charged with being the ringleader of a gang of drug-dealers who move drugs around various European countries, disguised as part of other legal import and export businesses."

"Like wine brokering," added Clara, sadly. The news report sounded very convincing.

"It might not be true." Brian sighed and looked out the window, wishing he could throw himself out and have done with all of this.

"It's not," said Clara, but a seed of doubt was planted in her heart and she was beginning to believe that her father could be guilty.

The train moved downhill. Initially the gradient was steep. Clara looked out at plunging slopes thick with chestnut trees, at deep gorges and tumbling rocky rivers. Occasionally a brilliant lake gleamed like a winking sapphire in the strengthening sunshine. Every so often the train stopped at little stations, some with peeling yellow paint and crumbling masonry, others chic with potted plants. Passengers got on and got off. Eventually the mountains were left behind and the train raced along through flat fields, covered with vines like twisted mandrakes. In the foothills of the mountains, the vineyards, on precarious terraces, were not in leaf. But as they moved across the plain, drawing closer to the sea, the vineyards became greener. At the same time the towns became bigger:

cities circled by industrial estates replaced the little clambering villages of the highlands.

At first Clara gazed absently at the landscape, seeing little. Her mind was preoccupied with anxieties about her father. This journey was one which she had made seldom enough in her years in France. Its sights were still wonderful in her eyes, but she watched them with a heavy heart and could draw no pleasure from the beautiful scenes. The sun shone, but its beams were not merry. It bathed the lovely country in a watery, tragic light.

"*Oh, for a draught of the sweet vintage that has been cooled a long time in the deep south!*" she said dreamily, aloud.

"What's that?" asked David.

"Oh nothing. Are you all right?"

"He wants to play games all the time," said David seriously.

"What?"

"My pet," said David. "I'm tired. Will you play with him?"

"OK," said Clara, taking the round plastic toy and pressing one of its tiny buttons.

* * *

The jail in Merle was small but forbidding-looking: a low grey building, with bare walls, no windows and a black door. Two armed policemen stood at the gate. Brian explained who they were and after some minutes the children were allowed into a reception area. This was a small glass-fronted office. A gendarme, in uniform, sat behind the glass wall.

"What will I say?" Brian asked, suddenly at sea.

"Tell him we've come about Dad," said Clara. "What else is there to say?" She gave Brian a reassuring pat on the wrist.

He had looked very grown-up at home and on the train, but in this place his tall lanky body only emphasised his youth and inexperience. He was tousled and thin and childish – as much a baby as David who sat on a wooden bench in the hallway and fiddled with his cyber pet.

Bravely, Brian took a deep breath deeply and addressed the gendarme, who regarded him with arrogant indifference.

"We've come to see our father," Brian said. "Mr John Moody."

"Excuse me, I don't understand," said the gendarme.

Brian tried again.

"Why have you come here?" the gendarme asked.

"He is here. A prisoner. Mr John Moody. Or Jack Moody."

The gendarme looked at them quizzically.

"Look!" Clara pulled the newspaper out of her bag and showed it to him. "That's our father."

The gendarme looked at them coldly.

"That man is your father?"

"Yes, and we want to see him."

The gendarme seemed to have no difficulty in understanding Clara. He shook his head. "I will have to consult with my superior."

He telephoned somebody and engaged in animated discussion for five minutes. Then he said, sulkily, "Go through the door on the right."

Clara could hardly suppress a cry of delight. But she did. The three children followed instructions. They left the tiny hot office and went into another tiny hot office, where two policemen sat at untidy desks and shuffled paper around. One of them jumped to his feet and shook hands with Clara.

"Follow me!" he said.

They followed him into a third little hot office, where three policemen sat at untidy desks and talked on the telephone.

One of them jumped to his feet and said: "This way!"

The children followed him.

They found themselves in a small hot empty room, furnished with a few kitchen chairs. Its walls were painted a dull pasty cream. There were no windows, no pictures, no decorations of any kind. The room seemed designed to depress people. A counter topped by a steel grill ran along one of its walls.

"Wait!" said the policeman.

The children waited. The policeman went to the grill, unlocked it with a big iron key, and slid it back. Then he turned to the children and said, with a certain flourish (the only emotion he displayed): "*Voila!*"

Behind the grill, his face half hidden by a screen, sat Jack Moody.

The three Moodys ran to the grill, shouting, "Dad! Dad! Dad!"

"Hi, kids," said Jack.

As far as Clara could see, he looked quite well, and surprisingly normal. He seemed to be sitting on a high stool. All they could see were his head and shoulders, framed as in a passport photograph. However, it was a colourful snapshot. Jack was still wearing his old red lumberjack shirt and his big floppy black beret. With his red moustache and hair the effect was bizarre. Clara felt a desire to laugh.

Jack seemed totally relaxed, as if nothing had unusual had happened. He was delighted to see the children.

"We've been so worried about you," Clara said.

Jack did not look worried at all. He smiled his usual roguish smile, shook his head and asked: "How is your mother?"

There was a moment's hesitation before Brian answered: "She's OK. She'll be down to see you soon."

The policeman was waiting at the back of the room, sitting on one of the chairs. He had buried his head in a file of papers which he was reading or pretending to read. Jack nodded to him.

"No privacy. But I'll tell you the story. I've been arrested and charged with drug-smuggling – a large consignment of drugs was found in a wine case with a cargo I shipped to Ireland a week ago."

"But it's not true?" asked Clara.

Jack was silent for a second and then he replied, "The position is that this is a very serious charge. I will be held in prison until I get a trial. That could happen soon or in several months' time."

"But you're innocent!" David said. "It's not fair."

"No, son, but that's how it goes."

"Have you seen your lawyer?" Brian asked.

"Yes," said Jack. "He is not . . ." He did not finish the sentence, but Clara and Brian could do it for him.

Clara's heart sank. "If you are found guilty what will happen then?"

"I'm not even thinking about it!" said Jack, with a smile. "For now, I'm fine. The prison here looks worse than it is." He indicated the nasty room. "Inside it's nicer than out here. I've got a comfy little cell, a nice bed, a table, a chair. The food isn't great but it's better than some I've had. If you must go to prison go to a French prison!"

"What did you get for dinner last night?" David asked.

"Pommes frites, pork chop, green beans. Ice cream," Jack replied.

"Much better than Chestnut Cottage!" said David. "We had coke and crisps, Mammy's favourite. Can I see your cell?"

"I don't think so, son!" said Jack.

"Ah, Dad! I just want to have a look so I'll know where you live!" whined David.

The policeman put down his sheaf of papers and came over to the grill.

"The visit is over now," he said, looking crossly at David.

David pouted and looked at the floor. Jack glared at the policeman and shrugged at David.

"Is there anything you need?" asked Clara hurriedly.

"Notebooks," said Jack without a second's hesitation. "Pens. Books."

The policeman started to slide the grill across.

"I'll write! *My Years in a French Jail*. Or, I hope, *My Days in a French Jail!*" said Jack, as his face disappeared from view. "Say hello to your mother. Tell her not to worry, everything will be all –"

The grill was closed before he could finish his sentence.

Clara found herself caught between tears and a fit of laughter. The little room was grim and punishing, with its dull paint and its complete lack of any decoration. But the abruptness of the policeman's behaviour was so silly that it made her want to laugh.

"Follow me!" said the policeman, his face as expressionless as a wooden statue's. If he had any human feelings, he was able to hide them completely.

7

Betrayal

Clara came down to the kitchen early the next morning, while the rest of the household slept. It was then that she found the note on the kitchen table. The note was from Madame Bonne and it said that she would not be working for the Moodys any more.

Clara read it with a mixture of dismay and disbelief. Madame Bonne, had been so kind, so motherly, so dependable, that she could not believe she would walk out on them now, just when they needed her most. But the meaning of the note was unambiguous. She said she was sorry, but she would not be back again.

Clara trudged heavily upstairs to her mother.

Mrs Moody lay against her white pillows, reading a novel. Her face was almost as white as the pillows, and her dark eyes seemed to have sunk deeply into her skull. Matted black hair spread around her in a grotesque tangle.

"Good morning, Mother!"

"Good morning," answered her mother, in a weak groan.

"Dad sent you his love," Clara said, suddenly remembering the events of yesterday. She had not seen her mother since then – it had been past midnight when she and her brothers had arrived home and they had gone straight to bed, exhausted.

"I'll need more than that!" said Mrs Moody, her voice a bit stronger now. Clara bit her lip. "I had terrible nightmares, Clara."

Clara did not want to hear about Mrs Moody's dreams, but she had to listen.

"I dreamt I couldn't breathe. I was lying in bed and something blocked my lungs. I called to my mother for help and she came, a little old woman in a grey shawl. Not really like my mother, but in the dream she was. But what did she do? She sat on my chest and blocked me even more. I had to push and push and push . . . to get her off, so I could draw my breath."

Mrs Moody clutched her chest at the memory, and gazed at the ceiling. Clara put her hand on her forehead.

"It was just a dream," she said.

"But what did it mean?" asked Mrs Moody.

Clara sighed.

"I don't know, Mam," she said, feeling sorry for her mother. "Look, I got this note from Madame Bonne." She showed Mrs Moody the note, but Mrs Moody was not interested. "She's left, it says. She won't work for us any more."

"What on earth do you expect me to do about that?" Mrs Moody asked haughtily. She took a packet of cigarettes from under her pillow and lit one.

"Well, did she say anything to you? Did she give a reason?" asked Clara.

"I've had enough of that woman!" said Mrs Moody, with a sudden rush of spite.

"She spies on me. She had the cheek to come in here yesterday and lecture me about my drinking habits! Did you ever!" Mrs Moody made a smoke-ring in the air. It hovered gracefully above her head.

"I see," Clara looked around the room.

It was obvious that Madame Bonne had cleaned it up. The ash-trays were emptied and all the bottles had disappeared.

"I'll bring you up some breakfast," she said, and ran out before her mother could think of some rude retort.

Clara spent the day going up and downstairs with food and drinks for Mrs Moody, most of which she refused to eat. Brian and David slept very late, worn out after the exertions of the day before. When they got up David just slouched in front of the TV, watching cartoons. Brian didn't bother dressing himself, and stayed in his room, listening to music. He didn't write poems today – his mood had swung again, and he felt too weary to lift a pen.

Clara was busy, cleaning the house and bringing cups of tea and food up to her mother. She even weeded a flowerbed in the garden. Seeing her father had given her a boost. She realised he was not coming home, not for a while, but knowing that she could get on the train and go to visit him made her happier than she had been. Work made her happy, too. She wished Brian would realise that if he were more active, he would feel a lot better.

Halfway through the afternoon, Clara was making some tea for her mother in the kitchen, when Brian came in and told her he needed to talk to her. Clara was apprehensive, guessing what was coming. And she guessed correctly. Brian wanted to go back to school.

Clara was getting tired of this discussion.

"Do whatever you want," she said.

"There's no point in my staying here," Brian went on, reasonably enough. "Dad will be stuck in prison for ages. Mother . . . she'll come to herself soon enough."

"Don't worry about me!" said Clara. "I'll skip school and look after her and David. Why should I have a life?"

"You're completely unreasonable!" he shouted. "Why should everyone's life be spoiled? You always insisted on staying here. I told you to get out, didn't I? But my life is different. I go to school. I study! I want to get my exams and go to university and become a doctor, not stew around here doing nothing for the rest of my life like you!" He paused and went on. "Plus I play on a football team – they've a match next week and what'll happen if I'm not there?"

He tramped out of the room.

Clara felt tears come to her eyes. Brian was the one who was unreasonable. She stayed at home to look after David. She would never abandon him to Mrs Moody and her mad ways, and now more than ever she couldn't dream of doing that. But she needed Brian's help. She could not understand his attitude. How could he dream of leaving them? She had no conception of the importance of school in his or anyone's life. Talk about exams and study and football teams was meaningless to her. She did not realise that other young people had goals and ambitions and plans, and that these were harnessed to daily work and planned systems and routines. Clara's ambition, to be a pilot, was as flimsy as a dandelion-puff. She knew she could fly a plane, and it had never occurred to her that she might need to do other things, such as pass examinations, in order to fulfil her ambition. Nobody had pointed this out to her – Mrs Moody, because she wouldn't know; Brian, because he didn't believe Clara would want to be a pilot in the end; and Jack, because he didn't know what she wanted to be. He did not know Brian wanted to be a doctor, either. What he did not know about his children amounted to a great deal more than what he did know.

Clara felt disturbed and distressed after her talk with Brian. She was coping at the moment, but she did not know if she could continue coping if he went away and she was alone, taking care of her mother and David. Brian didn't do much now, but at least he was another sane, sensible head, someone she could consult. Once he went, she'd be alone.

Suddenly, she had to do something. Not thinking about what she was doing, she jumped up, ran out of the house and ran along the road.

She ran and ran, not paying any attention to where she was going. All she wanted to do was run until she reached a state of oblivion. She did not know what she would do then, and at the moment she didn't care.

She ran and ran, and then she came to the river – the river where David had almost drowned a few days ago. It thundered down the valley, swollen from the rain. Its roar seemed to call for her attention; she stopped running. Leaving the road she went down to the edge of the water. On a damp tussock she sat down, and dipped her hand into the river. The cold water poured over it. She kept it there until it was chilled to the bone, as she listened to the river.

The river talked to her, in an old deep sonorous voice, a voice that was not soft, but was soothing in its rhythms, like some ancient song of battles and heroes. The river told a story, of where it had come from, high on the plateau where the wild goats ranged and the snow was still lying in high meadows. It sang a song of where it would go, on its long and varied journey down to the Mediterranean. Clara listened to the music of the river until it soaked into her bloodstream, until the beating of her pulse was in time with the rhythm of the water. And what she had wanted to happen when she had set off on her run happened now, by the river. She forgot about everything. Her mind floated off on the river and visited places her body had never been, and recalled places it had long forgotten. She remembered her first friend, Barbara, with whom she had played "house" and "dolls" when she was three years old in the tiny yard of the house where she had first lived. She could see Barbara, in her red coat and red boots, bossily setting a table on the concrete of the yard. She could see her mother coming out and calling them in for milk and chocolate biscuits, her mother with a round, smooth face like an apple, and soft, hot, comforting hands. She saw the future too, although she did not name it as the future. She saw herself, Clara, flying through the air, she saw herself circling the globe, the countries and oceans of the world drawn beneath her as on a map, she soaring above them, free and in control of her great machine. She saw herself alone, away from her mother and father, her brothers, away from Chestnut Cottage, free and powerful and grown-up. And she knew all this would come to pass. The picture she saw, the image the river's sound painted for her, would become a reality, soon enough, soon enough, soon enough, sang the river. There was only the next few days to get through, only the next few fences to jump over, and there she would be, high above them all!

So Clara sat for an hour, letting her thoughts drift with the flow of the water, until she noticed that darkness was falling. And even then she was reluctant to get up. But she was cold and stiff, and the light was growing dim. So she left the river and her tussock, and she went back to the road.

"I should go home!" she said to herself, thinking of David. She was, she realised, playing the role of David's mother. She had thought Mrs Moody a good enough mother, in a way, but it was a very eccentric way. Before the Moodys had moved to France, she had been more stable. Clara and Brian had been regular school-attenders, for instance, when they lived in Dublin. But although Mrs Moody was fun to be with on her good days, on her bad days she was a disaster. And there had been too many bad days, with the result that David was completely dependent on Clara for everything. He was as good as orphaned.

All of a sudden, as Clara admitted that Mrs Moody was not a good mother at all, a strong scent blew across the road and reached her nostrils. The smell was powerful, and had come suddenly to her, like a swift gust of wind. Wisteria. It was overwhelming, a rich sweet intoxicating perfume that stopped her in her tracks. Clara glanced up. The house she was passing belonged to Madame Bonne. Impulsively she followed the scent, passing through a small gate and under a shady arbour from which the heavy mauve blossoms dangled like bunches of grapes, and knocked on the front door.

Madame Bonne answered immediately.

"*Quelle surprise!*" she beamed. "Come in, come in, my little child! You look frozen!"

Madame Bonne was a widow. She lived alone in this small bungalow, set in a garden full of flowers and vegetables. As well as her prized wisteria, a grape-vine grew around the porch of the house – even more prized, since it was not easy to grow grapes at this altitude. "But it is very sheltered in my garden, the warmest and most sheltered spot in the whole valley!" Madame Bonne liked to boast.

"Sit down by the stove!" she said, pulling a chair up to the tiled stove. She blustered about her strangely cluttered kitchen, getting hot chocolate ready for Clara. Clara always thought this room was the strangest she had ever been in. The walls were lined with cupboards, painted dark blue and dark red, and carved with all kinds of figures, dragons and alligators and tigers and unicorns. There was a bookcase filled with books bound in deep red morocco leather. On top of the shelves perched a huge stuffed owl, with glass eyes which seemed to be alive and stared at everyone below. Other stuffed birds and animals sat on tables or just stood on the floor: two rusty foxes, a hare with a white tail, and, in one corner, a small delicate deer.

"So how are things at Chestnut Cottage?" Madame Bonne asked, as she heated milk on her big old tiled stove.

"Bad," said Clara. "Very bad."

"I know about your father. It is very difficult for you."

"Yes. It is."

"And then your mother . . . ooh!" Madame Bonne threw up her hands in despair.

"She's taken it very badly. She's sick."

"Yes, I know. That's not surprising, is it?"

"I don't know what to do, Madame Bonne."

Madame Bonne gazed at Clara, but said nothing.

"Why have you stopped working for us?" Clara asked. There were tears in her voice, to her shock. If even Madame Bonne had stayed with them, life would be slightly better than it was now. But everyone had abandoned them, every adult in their life had just walked out and left them to their own devices. It was dawning on Clara that adults could be very selfish people. Children trusted them, because they had to, and believed that some adults, their parents, their relations, their teachers, had the children's best interests at heart. Now she could see that this was not necessarily true, at all. Many adults had their own interests at heart when it came to the crunch, and would thoughtlessly abandon children if it suited them.

"Why? I am sorry, dear child, but I have got another job." Madame Bonne threw up her hands.

"But we need you," Clara said, knowing she sounded whining and pathetic. It was how she felt.

"You need me!" Madame Bonne sighed, and shrugged, and patted Clara on the shoulder. "That is very flattering, Clara. But I am afraid your mother has not paid me for many weeks. I can't go on working for nothing for ever, can I?"

"She just forgot!" Clara felt angry at her mother. She was more irresponsible and stupid than she imagined. "You should have reminded her."

"Of course I reminded her many times. You do not think I am the sort of woman who is afraid to ask an awkward question, do you?" Madame Bonne smiled.

"No," Clara smiled. It was hard to imagine anyone as unafraid as Madame Bonne.

"But she forgot and she forgot. And now I do not think she had any money . . . I have a new job. Here! Your chocolate!"

Clara accepted the hot, frothy bowl of chocolate. She sipped. It was delicious. Madame Bonne was the best cook in the valley – as she often pointed out herself.

"So you are in trouble? Have you been in touch with that father of yours?"

"Yes. Brian saw him yesterday. But we don't know what will happen next."

"Where is Brian?" Madame Bonne passed Clara a plate of home-made biscuits, and Clara took one.

"He's up at the house," she said, before biting the biscuit. It tasted heavenly.

"Good. He should stay with you."

"I know. But he doesn't want to." Clara's mouth was full of crumbs.

"Nonsense! You should not be there alone with that mother of yours. She should be in a hospital." Madame Bonne looked serious and thoughtful.

"Yes," Clara said. "That's right." She should have thought of that herself. But she did not know how she could arrange to get her mother into a hospital, which would have to be a psychiatric hospital. That was not something a girl aged fourteen could be expected to organise without help. Madame Bonne knew that, surely?

Clara gulped her chocolate. The heat of the fire and of the sweet drink warmed her heart. She looked at Madame Bonne with longing. If only her mother could have been even a little tiny bit like her! If only she had the gift of making people feel warm and cosy and comforted and loved, the way Madame Bonne had. Madame Bonne was individualistic to the point of eccentricity – as Mrs Moody was. But there the resemblance ended. Everything about Madame Bonne was encouraging. Being in her presence raised your spirits no matter how downhearted you had felt beforehand. She exuded goodwill. Even Madame Bonne's house, with its busy, scented garden, its small crowded rooms, seemed to give a warm welcome to everyone who stepped into it. She had managed to give the inanimate house her own personality. Its furniture and curtains, its many strange ornaments and animals were as interesting and comforting as Madame Bonne herself. Just sitting amongst them made Clara feel happy.

Clara finished her chocolate and stood up, reluctantly.

"I'd better be going home," she said. "I've been out for ages. Brian and David will be worried."

Madame Bonne looked at her. "I want to give you something before you go, my dear child."

Slowly she walked across the room to a long cupboard reaching from floor to ceiling. Clara had always admired this cupboard and sometimes had run her fingers over its ornate surface, but she had never seen it opened. Now Madame Bonne took a tiny golden key from the pocket of her apron and slipped it into the lock. One of the big blue doors opened a fraction. Clara strained to see what was inside, but only caught a glimpse of what looked like a ball of orange twine. Quick as a flash, Madame Bonne took something from the cupboard, closed it and locked the door. The golden key she deposited in the depths of her pocket. She turned and smiled at Clara.

Clara waited, wondering what was coming next. Madame Bonne stood in front of the cupboard, gazing at her with her large dark eyes, which glittered like stars. Clara felt slightly uneasy. The room was absolutely silent. Suddenly, outside, far down in the village, the church bell began to toll. The clang of the bell took Clara by surprise so that she jumped at first, even though she was used to the sound – the bell rang every evening.

Madame Bonne saw her jump, and laughed. She walked across to Clara and stood in front of her, ceremoniously. Then she took a small book from a bag of soft brown leather and placed it in Clara's hand. The book had a dark wine-coloured leather cover, shining and engraved with intricate intertwining patterns. In the middle of the cover was a large amber jewel, set into the leather. It twinkled like an eye.

"There, my dear. This is a precious book. It will protect you and bring you luck."

Clara gazed at the book. The amber shone like the water of the sparkling streams that tumbled down the mountains, and embedded in its clear stone were three tiny insects. "It's beautiful," she said. She opened the book. The pages were made of some thick yellowish material.

"Parchment!" Madame Bonne explained. "The book is made from the skins of sheep, and the cover from the skin of a cow. Both lived once in these very mountains."

Clara looked up. "It's too beautiful," she said. "I can't possibly take something as lovely as this. It must be very valuable."

Madame Bonne opened her hands. "It is yours, Clara. It belongs to you. I am giving it to you because I think you need a precious gift, right now. You are in a dark time, and more dark times are ahead, I'm afraid."

Clara's heart sank. Could it get darker than it was already?

Madame Bonne sat down, probably tired. It can't have

been easy, carrying the weight of her large body on two small feet.

Clara sighed and began to turn the pages of the little volume. It was a very strange book: although it had such an elaborate cover, all the pages were absolutely blank.

"Why are the pages empty?" she asked. Their blankness disturbed her and she was filled with a sudden dread. The owl seemed to stare warningly at her, and the fox bared his white, dead teeth in a grin or a snarl.

Madama Bonne smiled. "I don't know," she replied. "Why, do you think?"

"I don't know either," Clara sighed, suddenly weary.

Madame Bonne stared at her enigmatically. "You will find out, as time goes on. But it is not something you need to worry about. In the meantime, carry the book with you, and look at it from time to time. It will remind you that you have a friend in the Valley of the Springs. I think it will bring you good fortune."

Clara closed the book and placed it carefully in its little pouch.

"I'm very grateful. I will treasure it," she said simply.

There was more to come.

"The book is hundreds of years old," said Madame Bonne. "It was made for a troubadour, one of the great poets who wandered around this part of France in the Middle Ages, singing and reciting their poems. But he never wrote in it. Since then it has been waiting for the right person to come along. And now that person has come."

Clara did not know what else to say. So she said goodbye and left, walking quickly home through the darkening trees.

* * *

When Clara got home, David ran downstairs.

"I thought you'd gone!" he said, throwing himself against her, sobbing. "I thought you weren't coming back!"

"I just went for a walk," Clara said. "Don't worry so much. I'm right back here with you."

"I thought you were gone away!" David repeated.

Clara held him close.

Brian came into the kitchen. He looked penitent again.

"I'm sorry, Clara."

"That's OK. That's OK."

"It's just all been so awful."

"I know."

"And I hate missing school. I love that school. All my friends are there, the people who mean most to me. Plus, I can't afford to miss study. It'll be hard enough for me to make it anyway, to get the marks I need to get into medicine."

"I know," said Clara, understanding that his schoolfriends, his teachers, people whose names she did not even know, meant more to Brian now than herself or David or Jack or Mrs Moody. His ambition to become a doctor seemed remote and unreal to her. She could not imagine him, or any of them, grown up. But clearly Brian could. He already belonged to another world, one she knew nothing about. "You're right. You should go back."

"I'm glad you see it my way," said Brian.

Clara shrugged. "Who knows? Maybe Jack will be released and everything will be back to normal much sooner than we think."

"Yeah. Well, who knows?" Brian did not look very hopeful.

David had stopped crying.

"I didn't get my dinner yet," he said.

"You nerd!" said Brian. "You told me you weren't hungry!"

"Well, I am. I'm starving. I thought you said we were getting spaghetti tonight!"

"OK, OK," said Clara. "I've been up since cock-crow, I'm wrecked. But never mind. I'm your sister, so I'll make spaghetti bolognese for your little lordship!"

"No, no! I'll do that!" Brian said. "Allow me! I insist. You and his lordship sit down and rest your weary limbs. I will slave away on your behalf!" Brian was cheerful, now that he knew he was going to escape. Tomorrow morning he would catch the first train and be back in school for the mid-morning break. He would telephone the school after dinner and let them know he was on his way.

"If you put it like that!" Clara said, sitting down at the table. She pulled her book-bag out of her pocket, took out the book and looked at it again. Brian saw her.

"What's that?" he asked.

"Something Madame Bonne gave me," she said. "A book that's supposed to help me with life's problems."

"Is it a de-luxe edition of *Feel the Fear and Do it Anyway*?" Brian laughed.

"No," said Clara. "It's an old book, hundreds of years old. And it's empty. Nobody has written in it yet."

Brian picked up the book and looked at it.

"It really does look very old!" he said. "It must be quite valuable."

Clara put it back in its bag.

"I'd never sell it, or anything like that," she said, firmly. "I don't know why, but I know it's something I always want to keep."

"OK, OK, only saying," said Brian. He started to boil

water and rummage in the fridge for the ingredients of the spaghetti bolognese. He had never cooked it before, but could guess what it should contain. Meat, onions, garlic, tomato puree.

"Where's the tomato puree?" he asked, as he put the other things on the table.

"In the press, not in the fridge," said Clara. "I'll get it."

She rooted in one of the presses and found two small tins. She handed them to Brian.

"By the way, have you checked on Mother?" Clara asked, suddenly remembering that she hadn't been upstairs for hours.

"No! You bet I haven't," said Brian grimly, peeling an onion and placing it on a wooden chopping-board.

"I'll run up and see how she is," said Clara. "Maybe she'd like some spag bol? Maybe she'll come down to dinner tonight! I think it's time she did that!"

"She won't," said Brian, slicing viciously into the onion. His eyes smarted.

"Oh well! No harm in asking," said Clara.

"You're a glutton for punishment!" Brian said.

Clara walked slowly upstairs. She really was tired. But she felt happier than she had since Saturday. Brian was in good form again. He would be gone tomorrow, and she'd be isolated here with only David and Mrs Moody, but for the moment she put that grim thought out of her mind.

She pushed open the door of Mrs Moody's bedroom.

Then she screamed, "Mum! Mum! What's wrong?"

8

Sacre Coeur

Mrs Moody was lying senseless on the floor, in her nightdress.

Clara knelt down beside her and smelled her breath. It didn't smell very nice, but at least she had one. At least she seemed to be breathing.

Clara dashed downstairs. "Brian! Call the ambulance! Mother has collapsed!"

Under pressure, Brian could act fast. He dropped the knife and ran to the phone.

Clara got a glass of water – she wasn't sure what she would use it for – and ran back up to her mother. She noticed a gash on her forehead: she had cut her head against the leg of the bedside table as she fell.

She put the glass to her mother's lips, which were a bruised purple colour. A few drops of water dribbled down Mrs Moody's chin, but she wasn't drinking. Her breath was so weak as to be almost imperceptible.

Clara decided not to move her mother: she remembered some vague advice that had been given once on a television programme about First Aid. She took the quilt from the bed and laid it over her.

Brian came upstairs.

"They'll be here in twenty minutes." He knelt on the floor and examined his mother's face.

"She's alive," Clara said, flatly.

Brian continued to look at Mrs Moody. But he did not touch her.

"Poor old thing!" he said, in a sad, tired voice. He could have been saying "Poor old me!"

"She's had a tough time."

He did not say, "She's not the only one", but his expression indicated that he thought it.

The ambulance came, as promised, in twenty minutes. The attendants were very efficient and fast. In less than five minutes Mrs Moody was tucked away in the safe white cave of their car.

"Where will you take her?" Brian asked.

"To the nearest hospital – Sacre Coeur. You telephone there in an hour. Your father is here?"

"No."

The ambulance man looked surprised. "You are here alone?"

"The three of us are together."

The ambulance man shook his head. "One of you will come with your mother to the hospital?"

"No," said Clara. "We'll stay here for now. We'll ring the hospital and maybe come tomorrow."

"As you wish," said the ambulance man, shaking his head again. "Where is your father?"

"In Merle," said Brian, quickly.

"OK, it's not my business," said the ambulance man. "What age are you?"

Brian drew himself up to his full height. "Sixteen!" he said, adding on several months to his true age.

"*Alors!*" The ambulance man left, looking disbelieving.

They watched as the ambulance roared off down the road, its blue light flashing and its siren screeching out across the valley.

Soon it disappeared from view and hearing.

Exhausted, the children went to bed without discussing the situation further.

* * *

Clara was woken by the ringing of the telephone, early in the morning long before dawn. She had been dreaming again. In her dream she was walking along a seashore, a seaside promenade in some town on the Mediterranean, full of cafés and casinos and shops. Clara was wearing a hat, in the dream, and a long muslin dress, like a girl of a hundred years ago. She even had a parasol! But as she walked she became aware of a great wave rolling in towards her. She looked and saw the wave, but although she could see it, she could find no way of escaping its onslaught. The wave was as high as ten houses and it gathered momentum as it came, viciously, to the wooden boardwalk. Clara felt, not frightened, but sadly expectant.

That's when the telephone rang.

She knew before she answered it what it was likely to be.

"Yes?"

"Clara Moody?"

"Yes."

"I regret to inform you: Mrs Lily Moody has passed way."

All Clara could say was, "Oh!"

"We did everything we could."

"Can we see her?" Clara asked. It seemed to her that she had been asking this question all her life and on the other hand the question seemed to come from the mouth of another person, a stranger.

"Yes, of course," said the voice. "Come as soon as you can."

"Thank you."

Clara put down the phone.

She sat in the dark shadows of the room, still as a stone, for a long time.

Then she went and woke Brian.

When he heard the news he reacted in quite a different way from Clara.

He screamed.

Clara had not expected this. Somehow she had assumed Brian would be sad and gloomy and thoughtful. But instead he became hysterical. He pushed his head into his pillow and screamed into it. Then he banged his head against the wall.

"*Mammy, mammy!*" he cried. "*Mammy mammy mammy mammy!*"

Clara felt very frightened. But she did not want to cry. What she wanted to do was do nothing – what she would not be allowed to do. Already her mind was forming plans. What to do next. Ring the hospital. Make arrangements for the funeral. She would have to telephone Jack, and Ireland and tell Mrs Moody's only brother, Jim Crabclaw, that Mrs Moody was dead.

First she made a cup of tea for Brian, putting a lot of sugar in it. She had heard somewhere that sugar was good for people in shock.

She brought it up to him. He was lying on his back now, staring at the ceiling, his face streaked with tears. He was completely silent.

"Here's some tea. You should drink it."

"I can't believe it," he said.

"No, no," said Clara.

She was unusually calm. It was as if so many calamities had occurred that they no longer had the power to disturb her. She felt the events of the past few days were a huge dark wave pouring over her. But underneath that wave she was still herself.

"I'll wait until morning to tell David," she said. "No point in waking him up now."

"No no no," Brian shook his head. "Let him sleep. Let him sleep as long as he can . . . poor little thing. What he's going to wake up to!"

"Oh Brian!" Clara felt sadder about Brian's unhappiness than about anything else. "I'm sorry. I thought I should tell you straight away!"

"You did right," he said. "It's just . . ."

"It's . . ."

"Don't say it's better," he sounded angry.

"Not better. But she was very unhappy. All the drinking . . . it wasn't much of a life for her."

"Or for us."

"And where do we go from here?"

"Don't ask. This is enough for one day . . . I can't think about anything else."

Clara went back to bed. To her surprise, she slept for a

few hours. When she woke up again, the sun had risen and the birds were singing in the garden, as cheerfully as ever. She looked out the window and felt amazed, and hurt, that life could go on as if nothing at all had happened. Life in this very garden, where her mother had been sitting drinking coffee a few days ago, was going on just as usual. Why shouldn't it? Clara asked herself. Birds and leaves don't know what happens to people. Grass doesn't know. It doesn't know people exist. It doesn't know anything.

But she felt it was strange, all the same.

She looked in on David, hoping he would be asleep. She did not want to break the news to him, she wanted him to have some more time, believing life was normal, or half normal. But David was up watching television.

"Hello!" he said cheerfully. He was sitting on top of his bed, wrapped in his duvet.

Clara sat down beside him. She took a deep breath and told him as calmly as she could.

"Mammy is dead? Why?" He had not lowered the sound of the television. The high-pitched, tinny voices of the cartoon characters laughed in the background.

"She was very sick," said Clara. "You know that. Maybe it's better this way."

"I'll never see her again?"

"Well . . . not for a long time," said Clara.

"You mean. In heaven."

"Yes," said Clara. "In heaven." Although she was far from sure.

"I want to see her now, I want to see her now!" said David.

"Yes," said Clara.

David put his head on her chest and put his arms around

Clara. He did not cry. But he remained in that position for a long time.

Clara felt she did not have the energy to organise the family for one more day. But she didn't have to. The telephone rang again at about ten o'clock. The voice on the line was familiar and strange at the same time.

"Howareye," a man's voice said. "It's Jim Crabclaw, yer Uncle Jim."

"Oh Uncle Jim!" Clara was delighted to hear his voice. She was also surprised, since she had not phoned him.

"How did you find out? About everything?" she asked.

"Yer da rang me. I hear he's in a spot of bother?" Uncle Jim laughed, to Clara's surprise. That anyone could laugh at a time like this was shocking.

"He's in jail." Clara did not feel like beating around the bush.

"Yeah, well that's too bad. And poor old Lily. What happened to her at all?"

"They told us she had a huge heart attack." Clara hesitated, a lump in her throat. "Where are you?"

"I'm in Dublin. But I'll be over there with you as soon as I can. I've got the flight all organised."

Clara sighed softly. A sense of relief covered her, like a soft shawl. She did not know Uncle Jim very well, but she knew one thing: she and her brothers needed an adult to come and take care of them, at least for a while. Life was too complicated for them to cope with alone just now. Somebody older and wiser had to come to the rescue, the sooner the better. She was under such stress that she didn't care who that person was.

Brian seemed to feel the same. He was also glad to hear the Uncle Jim was coming.

Neither of them remembered much about him, to put it mildly. They had met the Crabclaws now and then when they lived in Ireland, usually at Christmas or some special family occasion. Brian said he remembered going to their cousin Monica's birthday party once – Monica was Uncle Jim's daughter, and she was about the same age as Clara.

"But I don't remember what she was like," he said, with an expression which made Clara wonder if he preferred to forget. "I think Aunty Mary is nice," he added, reassuringly. Aunty Mary was Uncle Jim's wife, their cousin Monica's mother.

"I'm sure they're all very nice," said Clara, optimistically. David widened his eyes and looked hopeful.

Uncle Jim arrived the next evening, full of bluster and good cheer. He was a robust man, short, with a florid complexion and a balding head, also red and shiny. His teeth were yellow and uneven, and there was a strong smell of whisky on his breath. He clapped Brian and David on the back with a plump, heavy hand, and winked at Clara. Although he was heavily built and heavy-handed, when he spoke his voice was thin and reedy. The children found him absolutely alarming in every way. But immediately, without a moment's delay, he took charge of everything, which was a great relief for Clara and Brian. For the first time since Jack was sent to jail they were able to relax.

He set to work as soon as he arrived, making phone calls, visiting the hospital and the jail and the undertaker. He spoke terrible French, but somehow he was always able to make himself understood. Clara, Brian and David stayed at home, reading and going for walks, while he rushed around, contacting people and making plans. They were relieved of every responsibility.

Uncle Jim made the funeral arrangements for Mrs

Moody, and she was buried on the side of a hill outside the village, under a chestnut tree. Only a few villagers, and Madame Bonne, were at the graveside with the children and Uncle Jim. Jack had not been released for the funeral.

"Poor old Lily!" said Uncle Jim. "She had a sad end. But she'd a good life – she made the most of it, and what more can anyone do?"

Clara looked ironically at Brian. After a week they were getting a little tired of the sound of Uncle Jim's voice. But so far they had no greater reason to dislike him.

Back in the cottage, Jim Crabclaw cross-examined Brian and Clara about their father.

"He tells me he could get ten years if they find him guilty," he said, in his thin tones. "Must be very serious, eh?" He chuckled, which he tended to do even at the most serious moments.

"Drug crimes are treated very seriously in France," Clara said bossily.

"Oh they would be, they would be!" said Uncle Jim. "Jack Moody was always one for the big risks."

It was clear from everything he said that Uncle Jim had no pity or fondness for Jack Moody or even for his own dead sister. Whenever he mentioned them he smiled and his smile was never pleasant.

He stayed in the house with the children for a few days after the funeral, making what he called "more arrangements". The main arrangement was that the Moody children would go back to Ireland and live with him and his wife, their Aunt Mary, until such a time as Jack was released from prison or they were grown-up, whichever happened first. The second was putting Chestnut Cottage up for sale.

The children were dismayed at both these plans and did everything they could to persuade Uncle Jim to change his mind. Brian was adamant that he would return to school.

"Who's going to pay for the school?" asked Uncle Jim.

"The state will pay if nobody else will," said Brian. He was almost sure that this was true. He knew there must be some mechanism in the system that would take care of him and Clara and David, once they were in effect orphaned. But he didn't know the details. He didn't know how to tap into the system, and Uncle Jim was obviously not going to help. For some reason which they could not understand he was very insistent that the children leave France.

"Yez can't stay here on your own," he repeated over and over again. "Yez'll be better off at home in Ireland."

He insisted that Ireland was their home, although they had not lived there for years.

"We could stay here," said Clara. "Brian is nearly sixteen. I'm fourteen. We could look after ourselves."

But he just laughed. "Nonsense!" he chuckled. "What would you live on for a start? "

Nothing they could say would induce him to change his mind.

Clara and Brian wanted to go to Merle to meet their father, but he refused to allow that. For some reason he did not want them to communicate with him. "You'll see him soon enough," he said. "They might send him over to Ireland. Then you can visit him in the Joy: sure it'll put in Sundays for you." He laughed. His laughs were as unpleasant as his smiles.

"In the Joy? You mean Mountjoy?"

"To give it its full and true title, and why not?"

"But . . ."

"You're going to ask me now how you'll see him if he's locked up in the Joy while you are here wining and dining in the south of *la belle France*?"

Clara hated that phrase, *la belle France*. She noticed that whenever anyone said that it was heavy with irony, and often had a nasty comment hot on its tail, as in this instance.

"Youse, *mes enfants*, are coming back to Dublino's fair city with your Uncle Jim. As soon as I sort out a bit of business on this side of the water!"

"What business is that?" Clara asked.

Her uncle looked at her mockingly.

"I've to find a buyer for this heap of rubbish," he said, indicating Chestnut Cottage. "Or someone who'll rent the place. Though who in their right mind would want to live here is beyond me. I've a good mind to pull it down and build a decent bungalow on the site."

So that was it, thought Brian. Uncle Jim wanted to capitalise on Chestnut Cottage, and any other property their parents owned. He realised that their going to Ireland was mixed up with this plan: perhaps if the house were occupied by the Moody children, he would not be allowed to sell it.

"Chestnut Cottage is four hundred years old," said Clara in her most superior voice.

"It looks every day of it," said Uncle Jim, with a wry grin. "But we'll soon be rid of it. I'll need the cash to finance your education and upkeep when you're in Ireland."

"Did Jack say you could sell Chestnut Cottage?" Brian asked neutrally. He was quite certain that his father would never have suggested such a thing.

"I don't think he has a lot of say in the matter," said Jim, with that chuckle of his.

"Probably not," said Brian, "since it belonged to Lily and now I think it belongs to us."

Uncle Jim laughed.

"Don't be talking through your hat," he said, and he kicked Brian very hard under the table, reminding him who was boss now. And Brian, although he knew he was right and that Uncle Jim was about to cheat him and his siblings out of their rightful inheritance and their family home, just did not know how he could do anything to stop him.

9

The Crabclaws of Grey Walls

And so, a week later, the Moody children found themselves on a plane bound for Dublin.

They left behind them warm sunshine, the wisteria blossoming and the vines budding. They arrived in a grey, rainy Dublin, with a temperature of ten degrees. Wind whipped across the airport as they walked from the plane to the truck which was bringing them in. Clara pulled her jacket around her.

"The harsh winds of home!" said Uncle Jim. "Not to worry, yez'll soon get used to them. When I bring you home sweet home!"

Home sweet home was a semi-detached house in a suburb of Dublin, called Grey Walls. The Moodys had forgotten what Irish suburbs looked like, but they soon remembered. As they drove through long straight roads lined with little grey-white houses, one exactly the same as they next, with the rain pouring down on them and the leaden sky pushing against the tiled roofs, Clara felt despairing. Her heart yearned for the sunshine and beauty she had left behind her. For the moment, she did not remember all the problems they had had in France.

But her spirits improved as soon as she met Uncle Jim's wife, Aunt Mary. Aunt Mary made the children very welcome. She was warm and friendly, quite different from Uncle Jim, or indeed from Clara's own mother – she seemed as normal and nice as currant buns. She was small and had short black hair, clipped close to her head. Her face was dominated by large green eyes, and she had a big friendly smile. She was dressed in a pink track-suit and lovely little matching pink runners.

"Welcome to Grey Walls!" she said with her winning smile. "You poor poor little things! Come in and warm yourselves by the fire. You've been through the hoops, you sure have!"

She took their coats and gave them seats on a scratchy sofa, in a small room which felt cold even though there was a tiny fire burning in the grate. The room was packed with furniture and ornaments. It contained no fewer than three gleaming coffee tables with embroidered runners on them. In the small fireplace stood twenty-five china dogs – terriers and pekes and many long-eared spaniels, poodles and Alsatians and a few St. Bernards, as well as dogs of no identifiable breed. They stood, some snarling, some barking, some looking meek and pathetic, all gazing out at the roomful of people.

"You sit there and take it easy while I make the tea," said Aunt Mary, with her wide white smile.

"Don't mind if I do!" said Uncle Jim.

"I didn't mean you!" She gave him a kiss. "You can come and give me a hand."

"And me after coming all the way from France!"

"I know. You're real good!" she said. "But you can give me a hand just the same. Right, kids?"

David smiled at her. Clara was glad, when she saw it. Since their mother had collapsed he had been nervous and anxious, crying a lot of the time. This was the first evidence of him beginning to thaw out.

Aunt Mary soon returned carrying a large tray. On the tray was a teapot, five cups and a plate containing five small sandwiches. She deposited this on one of the shiny coffee tables with obvious pride.

"Now!" she said. "You must be hungry after your long journey. Unfortunately you've missed dinner, but I prepared this snack for you."

Brian, Clara and David stared in disbelief at the tiny sandwiches.

"Would you like a sandwich?" Auntie Mary asked, passing the plate around.

"Oh yes!" they all said. One by one she gave them a sandwich. Then the plate was empty. Clara bit into her postage stamp of bread. It was difficult to decide what the filling was. It tasted salty. Brian thought it was sardine, and Clara thought it was ham. David had no idea what it was. All he knew was that, even though he was starving, he didn't want to eat it.

Brian swallowed his sandwich in one gulp, and Auntie Mary, nibbling daintily, gave him a disapproving look. David took a small bite from his, and made a face.

Clara warned him, in French, to say nothing. She had suddenly realised that the sandwiches were a starter. The main course would follow as soon as the funny little salty sandwiches were finished. She told David to be patient and wait for his food.

"Lovely sandwiches," said Clara, politely nibbling. "Unusual. I don't think I've tasted this filling before."

"Marmite," said Aunt Mary. "It's extremely nourishing."

David looked cross.

"Don't want Marmite!" he said.

"That's all right," smiled Auntie Mary. "You can eat it tomorrow!" She took David's sandwich and wrapped it in a yellow paper napkin. "Hunger is good sauce, I always find!" The children looked at her in surprise. They drank their tea and waited for the main course.

And waited. And waited.

But it was not forthcoming.

"There is nothing as nice as a Marmite sandwich after a long journey," said Auntie Mary. "Unless it is a tomato sandwich. Do you have tomatoes in France?"

"Yes," said Clara, hiding her astonishment. Did Aunt Mary really believe that they might not have tomatoes in France? "They make a very good starter," she added, pointlessly.

"Starter?" Aunt Mary smiled and glanced at Uncle Jim. "I'm sure they do. But I don't do starters! I find they take away my appetite for my tea."

Clara realised then that the Marmite sandwich was all they were going to get.

Brian could not suppress a sigh. He was starving and everything in the little room made him feel very uncomfortable. There was so much furniture that there was no room left for people. And the china dogs looked like a malevolent pack, which might come to life at any moment and launch a vicious attack. He could almost hear them barking nasty little china barks.

"Where is Monica?" Brian asked in as friendly a voice as

he could muster, although after a week of Uncle Jim's company it was hard to feel friendly towards any member of the Crabclaw family. Monica was their cousin, as Uncle Jim had told them about a thousand times. Monica Elizabeth Crabclaw.

"Monica is at ballet," said Aunt Mary. "She is a very good ballet dancer and has lessons twice a week. She hopes to become professional one day."

"How interesting!" said Brian in a very uninterested tone. He was on auto-pilot anyway. His life had fallen apart and he still couldn't quite realise what was happening. Mrs Moody was dead, Jack was locked up, Chestnut Cottage was to be sold. School was over. He would never be a doctor. He had had to take two terrifying flights in an aeroplane, which he hated doing more than anything in the world. He had felt violently sick and his tummy was only getting back to normal now. And he was sitting in a cold little room in Dublin talking about ballet with a woman he didn't know. He closed his eyes for a minute. Aunt Mary looked sharply at him and continued.

"The Bolshoi has expressed interest. Or is it the Kirov? Some world-famous Russian dance company. But, to be frank, I don't want Monica to go to Russia. I think she'd catch her death of cold in winter. She is a very delicate child."

"Where are we going to sleep?" David asked, abruptly, reminded by the mention of Monica that there was not a lot of room in the house.

"Oh we'll squeeze you in somewhere, don't worry about that!" said Aunt Mary. "Where there's a will there's a way, right!"

David scowled at her.

Uncle Jim looked quizzically at his wife and shook his head. But she ignored him and poured out more tea. The tea, Clara thought, was excellent – not too strong, not too weak. Sweet and hot. Credit where credit is due.

Monica came home before they had finished their snack.

"Daddy!" she yelled in delight, as she burst into the room. "You're back!"

"Yeah, can't get rid of a bad penny!" said Uncle Jim, giving her a hug.

"I missed you lots and lots!" she beamed at him.

"Not half as much as I missed you, sugar baby!"

"Say hello to your cousins!" Aunt Mary broke up the mutual admiration society.

Clara, David and Brian stood up.

"Hi!" said Monica, staring at them, as her mother introduced them.

She was a very big girl, almost six feet tall, and she looked as if she weighed about fourteen stone. You could imagine her as a good rugby full forward, but not as a ballerina for the Bolshoi. Her hair was black, and long: she wore it in a neat ballerina's bun. She had very large teeth, and reminded Clara of a horse she had known in France.

"They're staying with us now," Aunt Mary said.

"All of them? I thought you said . . ."

"Yes, yes," Aunt Mary rushed in to prevent her saying more.

Clara looked curiously at her. Something was not being said.

"Will you have something to eat? How was ballet?"

"Ballet was fine. I'll have some cake. Where are they going to sleep?"

"We'll soon sort that out."

Clara put down her cup.

"I'm very tired," she said. "Could I lie down somewhere? For a while?"

Everyone looked shocked, as if she had screamed out some terrible insult.

"Yeah, sure," Aunt Mary says. "You must be tired. So much has happened."

"I'm tired too," David started to cry. "I'm tired and I want my mammy."

Aunt Mary came over and kissed him, which made him cry louder. Monica smiled at her father, who shrugged. Aunt Mary held David for a long time, letting him cry.

"There there," she said. "There there!" After a while she picked him up and carried him upstairs. Clara followed.

Aunt Mary brought David into a bedroom, which was obviously Monica's room. It was wallpapered with a pink rosy paper, and festooned with posters of ballet dancers. A white shelf was packed with dolls dressed in frilly old-fashioned frocks and big beribboned bonnets. There were two beds in the room. She put David on one of them and covered him with a quilt. "You can lie down there," she whispered to Clara. Clara felt much too exhausted to ask any questions. She felt she would collapse if she stayed up any longer. So she lay on the bed and in seconds she was fast asleep.

Downstairs, Uncle Jim used the opportunity to have a man-to-man talk with Brian. Brian was also weary; he had said almost nothing since his arrival in the house, but had sat, numb from gloominess, in the chilly little room, while Clara had talked to Aunt Mary. He longed to sleep, for days if possible. What he longed for most was to be back in France, in the house with his mother and father and Madame Bonne. What he longed for was for everything to be normal and pleasant and comfortable again. The house in Dublin filled him with dread. A dark hopelessness had taken root in his stomach. When he looked into the tiny fireplace he wanted to die. He was past crying now. There was nothing to cry for.

"Why don't we stretch our legs?" Uncle Jim said. He threw Monica, who had been sitting on his knee, into the sofa.

"Bring me to MacDonalds?" She smiled brightly.

"You've stretched your legs enough for one day. If you stretch them any more you'll turn into an elastic band and someone will use you in a catapult!" He pulled her hair and looked at Brian seriously.

"Come on! Bit of fresh air will do you good. Knock the cobwebs off."

Brian knew it would be useless protesting that the last thing in the world he needed was a walk or fresh air. He took a deep breath and stood up.

"Sure," he said.

"Thataboy!" Uncle Jim smiled at him, in a way that made Brian's skin creep. Or maybe it was that he felt so cold? He hadn't slept for two days.

They walked down the road, and along several similar roads, all of which looked identical to Brian.

"Your ma . . . it looks bad. And your da is locked up for the time being, it seems," Uncle Jim opened. "I can't see him getting off."

"Why not?" Brian asked. "He could be innocent."

"Think so?" Uncle Jim kicked a stone.

Brian didn't answer. He loved his father so much, but that didn't mean his father was not a crook.

"He's not innocent," Uncle Jim said, cheerfully. "He did well, your da. Too well. I mean, look at me!"

Brian knew what he meant.

"I'm honest. This is what happens to an honest Crabclaw or Moody. He lives in a three-bed semi-d in Grey Walls for half his life, and then, if he's very lucky, he moves to a house with four bedrooms in White Walls. He gets a holiday once a year in the sun, if he's lucky. Yeah. Ten days on a package in the Canaries and that's what they call the Celtic Tiger! Celtic Tiger, my arse!" He scowled for a second, which was most unusual. Then he reverted to his usual cheerful tone. "Well, it all worked out different for your da. He did very well indeed for himself, far too well. Did you ever ask yourself where all the dosh came from?"

"So what's going to happen now?" Brian couldn't bear discussing the problem any further.

"What's the house worth?" Uncle Jim became business-like.

"I don't know," said Brian, realising that Uncle Jim had not seen an estate agent. Good.

"A lot of Euros, I'd reckon. People buy holiday houses up there where youse lived, don't they?"

"Oh yeah, they do," Brian replied. "It's a beautiful place. People like to have a house there."

"So it's probably worth a small fortune."

"Maybe," said Brian. "But we own it, me and Clara and David. I know that," he added.

Uncle Jim looked sharply at him.

"Maybe you do. But I am now your legal guardian. Meaning

I decide how to look after your property until you come of age. Didn't think of that now, did you?"

Brian hadn't. He didn't believe Jim was his legal guardian. He didn't believe a single thing the man said.

"I'd like to talk to Dad," he said. "When can I get to see him again?"

Uncle Jim laughed. "That's a big question. He might be extradited over here, but I doubt it. I'd say they'll keep him where he is and I'm not paying for flights back to the south of France so you can chat with Jack Moody." Uncle Jim gave Brian a sidelong look. "You can see him when he gets outa jail. If he ever does get out."

Brian stopped walking. His legs turned to jelly and his heart thumped like an engine.

"Of course he'll get out," said Brian.

Uncle Jim shook his head and laughed. "Of course he'll get out!" he imitated Brian's accent. "Your faith touches me, it really does!"

Brian wanted to punch him in the face, but he restrained himself.

"So what are you trying to tell me?" he asked.

Uncle Jim was silent for a while. He started to walk again and Brian followed suit, although he didn't want to. After a few minutes, Uncle Jim said: "I was only codding you. He probably will get released. But it won't be tomorrow or the next day. And in the meantime, as they say, youse need a roof over yer heads and a bit of the old readies. So sell the house, is what I say."

Brian didn't want to think about selling the house and he didn't want to talk about it. So he walked along, staring at the grey path. The road seemed to be about a mile long, lined with hundreds of small grey houses, each one almost identical to its neighbour. Overhead the sky was leaden.

"I want to go back to France," Brian blurted out. Suddenly it was what he wanted more than anything in the world.

"I'd say you would all right," said Uncle Jim grumpily, "but you won't be going anywhere."

"So? We're going to stay with you?"

Uncle Jim laughed, a new laugh which was even chillier than the old ones. "In a manner of speaking."

Something in his tone was even more ominous than usual. Brian shivered.

"What do you mean?" he asked, in a shaking voice.

"You've seen the house?" Uncle Jim didn't smile.

"Yeah."

"I couldn't fit a sardine into it."

"Well –"

"We're making alternative arrangements for you and the young fella."

Brian felt tears start to his eyes. Suddenly he felt terrified. He felt more terrified than he had ever felt before in his entire life.

"Alternative arrangements?" he repeated, weakly.

10

Summerlands

A home for problem boys. That's what "alternative arrangements" meant.

Next day Uncle Jim drove David and Brian, and their suitcases, to an institution for homeless and problem children far away in the middle of the countryside, about fifty miles from the Crabclaws' home. Clara was forced to stay at home with Aunt Mary.

Brian was angry, so angry that his skin had become white as a sheet. David curled up in a ball on the back seat of the car beside him. When he had heard that he was to be separated from Clara a light had gone out inside him. He hadn't spoken a word to anyone since yesterday. He'd spent the whole day sitting like a broken statue wherever he was put.

"Sulking!" said Uncle Jim.

"Maybe we should . . ."

"No! There's no room. We're doing our best for them,

for Christ's sake. They could be over there in some godforsaken place in France."

"He seems so . . ." Grief-stricken was the word she needed. Turned to stone by grief. But people do not use such words, especially about little children.

Brian had screamed and kicked. He'd broken cups, smashing them against the fireplace. Uncle Jim found that easier to handle. It confirmed his suspicion that Brian was a Bad Boy, who should be treated harshly and locked up.

"You'll be in jail like your old man if you don't quit!" he said. "You – !" He had punched him in the nose – there was a bruise still, red in the middle of his white face.

They drove along a motorway bustling with trucks and cars, across a flat green plain dotted with great bushes of yellow gorse, big as dragons, and then along narrow country roads which wound between woods and grassy fields. Once or twice they passed through a sleepy town, the buildings painted pink and peppermint and lemon, the shops called "Coffee Stop" or "Foley's Pub". Brian, miserable as he was, looked out and observed everything. He had driven through Ireland often as a young child, but had not been here for years. Everything looked familiar and alien at the same time. But it looked attractive, he acknowledged that. The Irish countryside was much more appealing than the Irish suburbs, there was no doubt about that.

It did not take them very long to reach their destination. The children's home was an old house, not too big, set among trees. Apart from the barbed wire on top of the high wall that surrounded it, it looked quite welcoming and friendly.

The woman who greeted them also seemed warm, but Brian was wary after his experience with Aunt Mary. She had seemed so kind, but all along she had been planning this horrible fate for him and David. The woman in the home was middle-aged, fat, with a head of bubble curls.

"Hi there!" she said, in a round, soft voice. She took Brian's hand in one of hers and David's in the other, and squeezed them. "You must be the Moodys!"

"Yeah," said Uncle Jim.

"Welcome to Summerlands!"

"Thanks," said Uncle Jim. He waited, maybe for an invitation for a cup of tea.

The woman ignored him.

"My names Kate," she said. "Kate Moss. No, that's a joke. Kate Murphy actually. Murphy suits me better, doesn't it? I always think Murphy is a real fat name!"

David looked at her, which was more than he had done at anyone for a few days.

"Is there a form to sign? Paperwork?" Uncle Jim did not know what to do.

"Not today, dear," said Kate. "I could offer you a cup of tea and a chocolate biscuit, but I'd say you'd rather be getting back to the big smog before the traffic. If you don't get away now I estimate it'll take you till tomorrow morning to get into Dublin."

"Ah, sure I know when I'm not wanted!" Uncle Jim gave one of his chuckles. This one did not conceal his annoyance. He wanted Kate Murphy to like him and he knew she didn't.

"It's your choice!" Kate Murphy grinned. "Do these boys have any belongings at all?"

"Yeah, yeah . . . I'll get them." He went to get their bags from the car.

"We'll get to know one another real fast!" said Kate. "As soon as his nibs is gone."

David did not know what to make of this odd woman. Brian liked her, but was still suspicious. Maybe she was a bit too cheerful and nice? He smiled wanly, as she pranced around the hallway, waiting for Uncle Jim to come back.

"Like our elegant hall?" she said. She pointed to a big picture, framed in gold, hanging over the staircase. "That's Lord Banana Skin who used to own this pile before the Health Board shot him and turfed out his widow and ten children on the roadside. He had it coming to him, didn't he? Did you ever see such a smarmy smile? Lick lick lick!"

Uncle Jim heard the last words as he came in. He dumped the two small cases on the floor and said: "Well, I'll be off so! You've got my telephone number if you need me. Nice to meet you!"

Forgetting to say goodbye to David and Brian, he left.

"Nice fella!" said Kate. "Didn't even say goodbye to you! Well, well, it's the nerves. They attack people something terrible when they're dumping their nearest and dearest on the board. Most surprising! Troublesome lot, he told us, you were!"

"What?"

Brian's bruise stood out again, purple as a blackberry.

"They have to say something like that, to get you to the top of the list. I'd say he painted a very grim picture indeed! Otherwise, no room at the inn. And where would you be then?"

"I don't know!" David looked frightened.

"On the streets. Lots of kids are, these days, in dear dirty Dublin, or haven't you noticed?"

"We only came to Ireland a couple of days ago," said Brian.

"Oh, yes! Oh, dear, dear, dear! Come in – leave those cases – come into the parlour said the spider to the fly and let's all have a jolly good cry! Isn't life the pits the pits? Isn't it?"

"Oh yeah," said Brian. Tears started to roll down his cheeks. He kicked himself, but it didn't help. It seemed to him that he had learned to cry in the past month, and once he had learned he couldn't stop.

Kate Murphy hugged him.

"It's rotten. It's unfair. It's horrible. Your mother is dead and your father is in jail and you get an uncle like that fellow! Out of the frying-pan! Oh my God!"

David didn't cry. He'd cried so much already there were no tears left, just for the moment. Also, curiosity got the better of him. He looked curiously around the hall. It was white, with a red carpet, and a table full of old copies of comics: *The Beano, The Dandy*, all of those. At least there'd be something to read.

Brian howled and howled for ages. Half an hour, it seemed to David. Kate held him all that time.

"That's it," she said. "The rotters."

They had tea and sandwiches in the dining-room. It was a big rather empty room, furnished with about eight round white tables. The chairs were red and there were a few posters on the wall, depicting football teams, popular rock groups, and a man on a huge red motorbike. But otherwise the room was colourless and somehow sad-looking – possibly because it was in a basement. A little strip of sunlight fell through one of the tall windows, but the room was rather dark.

They ate a corned-beef sandwich: already they had begun to understand that the food they were going to eat in

Ireland would taste different to what they were used to. They'd have to put up with it, or starve.

"Mm! We have tomato ketchup sometimes. That makes them taste human!" Kate bit into a sandwich herself. "But it gets gobbled up. I don't think there's any just now. Monday! God. None till Thursday when they do the big shop!"

"Is there a shop near here?"

"Sure. There's a village just a mile away. You'll be allowed walk there once a year if you're good."

David's mouth fell open.

"No, no, I'm joking. You can go when you're not doing anything else, if you tell one of us first. Always ask. We're supposed to know where you are. You lived in the country in France?"

"Yes," Brian answered. "In the mountains. David used to walk to school – didn't you?"

David nodded, not expanding on this story.

"So you'll feel at home. And you can walk to school if you like!"

"Do we go to school here?"

"Oh sure! David will go the local national school. And you . . ." She looked down at some papers on her desk. "Mm. You won't have to go to school right now, Brian," she said. Brian detected a change of tone in her voice. "The secondary schools are getting their holidays very soon anyway, it's not worth starting now. But David will have a nice time at the village school!"

"Oh!"

"As nice as . . .you can hope for. Oh guys!" Her eyes softened. "We'll do our best. I'll do my best . . . you'll be OK. Believe me."

"Thanks."

"Thanks! You're gorgeous fellows. You deserve the best . . . it's a bugger."

"Well . . ." Brian felt a tiny bit happier than he had in days.

"All we can do is our best. See *Titanic*?"

"The movie? Yeah." Brian bit his lip. They'd gone with their mother to see it when it was released.

"'Survive!' That's what he tells her at the end, when she's clinging to the scrap of wood and he's freezing to death. 'Promise me you'll never give up!' Do you remember?"

Brian did. He'd liked the line, it had warmed his heart even then.

"That's all there is to say, isn't it? So promise me you'll never give up!"

Brian laughed and did not promise. David looked away, embarrassed.

"Some other day then! I'll show you where you'll be sleeping and then, I'm very much afraid, you'll have to face the music and meet the inmates!"

"Oh!" sighed Brian. He didn't think he could stand that, right now.

"Hell! They're a mixed bunch, let's be honest. Some more savoury than others. But you're going to live with them for a long time. So you might as well get used to them, right!"

"Mm."

"And after your Uncle Jim, they probably won't seem so bad!" she said, breaking every single rule that social workers learn. "Come on, let's get it over with."

She led them out into the hall again, and up the stairs.

"Number one, the Dreaded Dorm!"

11

The Troubadour's Book

Back in Dublin, Clara was fighting with Aunt Mary.

"I can't believe you did this to us!" she said. She was so angry she didn't care what she said, or what risks she took. The worst had happened already anyway.

"What could we do? You can see for yourself what sort of situation we're in." Aunt Mary sat at the kitchen table, her white hands cupped around a mug of tea. She drank tea constantly, to compensate for the fact that she seldom ate a square meal.

"You could have left us alone, where we were!"

"Don't be silly! You'd have been taken away somewhere very quickly anyway. You're much better off here, among your own flesh and blood."

"Own flesh and blood! I never even saw you till the day before yesterday and now you've taken my brothers from me and dumped them in some sort of orphanage. What is going to happen to David? I can't imagine it. He'll die!"

"Of course he won't die! He'll be fine. And he can get in touch with us any time. It's just down the road!" Aunt Mary's tone of voice never changed. She said all this in her habitual calm, pleasant tone.

"I've heard about those places! They can be awful." Clara shut her eyes. She felt her head swim, she thought she would go mad. "They're cruel to the children . . . I just can't bear the thought of him being in a place like that, I can't bear it!"

"It'll do him good!" Aunt Mary stood up. She continued to smile, but it seemed to Clara that the smile was painted on her face and meant nothing. "It'll do him good!" she repeated.

Her smile remained painted on her face, but something strange was happening to Aunt Mary's eyes. They darkened and looked brown rather than green. Her eyebrows were raised over them, widening these dark, angry eyes so that they looked like vats of venom.

Clara found the eyes so terrifying that she paid no attention to her words.

"You pretend to like us, but you don't!" she cried. "You're just as bad as that awful husband of yours!"

Aunt Mary's eyes flashed, but she continued to smile.

"Go upstairs," she said, in her pleasant even voice, her voice that never wavered. "Go upstairs and come down when you've regained control of yourself."

Clara turned and went upstairs to the horrible pink room, which was cluttered to the brim with Monica's dolls and ballet books and size eight ballet shoes, the biggest ballet shoes Clara had ever seen (they had to be made specially, at enormous cost, for Monica, by a ballet-shoe maker in London – no wonder the Crabclaws could not afford to eat properly). Luckily Monica was out somewhere, so Clara had the room to herself. She sat on her little bed and thought. Brian and David in a children's home, herself in this place. Mrs Moody, her strange, loveable mother, was dead. Jack was in prison. How could life be so irredeemably awful?

Clara looked out the window at the Crabclaws' garden.

It was not a sight for sore eyes, but the opposite. Although Aunt Mary was a careful housekeeper, keeping the inside of the house as clean as a pin, so clean that it was very uncomfortable, she hated gardening, because gardens were so messy and filthy, full of soil and worms and nasty weeds. Her fingers got dirty if she did anything out there, she had discovered early in her life, and so she stayed away from the garden. It was a little green rectangle, clotted with dandelions and chickweed and nettles. Through the mess of weeds a concrete path led to a rotating clothes-line, where Aunt Mary hung out all the Crabclaws' underwear – ten pairs of outsize pink knickers, belonging to Monica, a few tiny frilly pink things which were her own, and one pair of red checked shorts and a white vest, Uncle Jim's. These provided the only spot of colour in the garden. By the fence two rusty bicycles were propped up, and at the bottom of the garden was a selection of dustbins. A cat, not of course the Crabclaws', because Aunt Mary hated animals, was nosing around one of the bins, pulling bags out of it and scattering them on the ground.

The garden made Clara cry. It looked like a symbol for her fate – uncared for, ugly, infertile. She compared it to the garden at Chestnut Cottage, that fountain of flowers and fruit, shadow and sunshine. Mrs Moody had been unbalanced, alcoholic, slightly crazy, but at least she cared about her garden. People who care about gardens are different from people who don't, Clara thought. This one, which could have been lovely, made her feel like committing suicide.

"I could jump from this window," she said, looking at the patch of gloomy concrete below, "and it would all be finished."

She stared down at the concrete, grey with a tiny ridge and a shore in the middle, blocked with leaves which had obviously been clogging it up since autumn. There was one terracotta pot plonked on the concrete, containing a dried-out plant, probably, Clara thought, a poinsettia left over from Christmas. It was nothing more now than a blackened stalk with a spiky dry flower that had once been red on top.

"I feel like that poinsettia," Clara said. "Left out in the cold since Christmas, to die of exposure."

She wanted to end it all, but even she could see that jumping out the window might not be the best way of doing it – she would probably just break a leg or, worse, her back, and end up in a hospital somewhere, with nobody to visit or care how she was.

But she could run away.

With this vague idea in mind, she opened her suitcase. Rooting among the clothes there her hand found the leather book-pouch. She had not looked at it since before her mother died, and had forgotten about it. She pulled it out.

It had not vanished. She had not lost it.

Clara pulled the book out of the pouch. The soft leather volume shone softly in her hand and the amber eye blinked. She opened the pages.

They were just as they had been, rich and creamy. And completely empty.

Suddenly Clara noticed something she had not seen before: in the book pouch there was a pocket and in the pocket was a pencil. It did not look medieval. It looked like an ordinary pencil of the kind she had often used in school, red with a little round rubber on top, the kind of rubber that makes black marks when you try to rub anything out with it. She picked up the pencil and wrote her name on the first page of the book.

Clara Moody.

The writing was dark and strong, but it was ordinary pencil writing, in her own familiar hand: round and a bit childish.

She found herself writing more.

Clara and her Brothers.

And then her pencil seemed to take over her hand, and she found herself writing.

Once there was a girl called Clara and she had six brothers. They lived happily with their father and mother in a castle in the mountains. They played all the time in the woods and the rivers that were everywhere close to their home. But one day their mother died and their father married again. Their new mother was unkind to them. She didn't give them enough to eat, and she wouldn't let them play.

One morning, Clara came downstairs to find that all her brothers had disappeared.

Clara stopped writing at this point and closed her eyes. Inside her head she saw the castle and the children playing and then she saw her six brothers in the castle courtyard with their stepmother. But what was happening to them? She hadn't a clue.

She closed the book and put it back in its pouch in her case. From the woods inside her head, the woods and the mountains that looked like the mountains of home, she opened her eyes to this small cluttered bedroom, that had Monica's trademark stamped all over it from the pink skirting board to the frilly lampshade shaped like a ballerina's tutu. Ballet magazines littered Monica's bed. Her ballet pumps hung from their hooks on the side of the wardrobe. The glass-eyed dolls with their elegant figures, huge crinolines, and bountiful blonde tresses stared down from the shelves.

Clara's thoughts wandered back to the castle in the mountains, and the six brothers, vanished without trace. She thought of her own cottage in France, and her own lovely bedroom, and her dead mother, and her two brothers. Vanished.

Suddenly she felt very angry.

Rotten Madame Bonne! Lousy Lily! Stupid Jack! Mean Aunt Mary! Disgusting Uncle Jim!

They had all put themselves before the interests of her and her brothers. They were all just like the stepmother in the story that was emerging in Clara's head and on the pages of the troubadour's book, even though they were, none of them, her stepmother at all. Lily had been her real mother, but she had behaved just as badly as any evil stepmother, concentrating her attention entirely on herself, all her life long.

Poor Brian and poor, poor, poor little David.

What were they doing now?

And what would David do if Clara did not exist? She was far away from him, but he knew where she was. He knew that in a crisis he could reach her. As long as she was alive, he would know that she was there for him, thinking about him, out there somewhere ready to help if she could.

She had to stay around, for David's sake. She was not going to be selfish, like her mother and father, doing what felt easiest to them – drinking too much, peddling drugs. She was not going to be like the Crabclaws. She was going to be different from all of them. She was going to be herself and do what she knew was the right thing to do, now and always.

And committing suicide was not the right thing. Committing suicide would be an out, for her. But once out she wouldn't get a chance to come back in. She wouldn't be able to help anyone. Above all, she would never find out what was going to happen next.

Only someone in whom despair has overcome curiosity could consider the option. And Clara was still curious. She still knew that new things, possibly interesting things, were going to happen, to her and to her brothers.

She lay on the narrow bed and closed her eyes, wondering if the troubadour's story would continue. But it did not. Instead, once more she had a vision of Chestnut Cottage, and of the river that raced through the valley. She saw herself and David playing in the river. She felt the water spraying her face and the sun dancing on her skin. David was jumping from rock to rock, shouting "You can't catch me!". She was chasing him, laughing. She jumped onto a rickety rock and fell into the water.

When she woke up she heard voices.

"Lucky they're not on the streets!" It was Uncle Jim, back from the home. Some hours had passed. Clara rubbed her eyes and sat up. The sun was lower in the sky. She felt shivery because she had slept without any cover.

"It's very hard on them," she heard Aunt Mary say in her creamy voice, "and Clara is taking it badly."

"Tough on her!" he said. "Silly little stuck-up bitch!"

"She's had a very hard time. They all have!" Aunt Mary sounded very reasonable.

"I've done more than enough. Am I my brother-in-law's keeper?" Uncle Jim was getting angry.

"You're not being very understanding, dearest," Aunt Mary countered. "They've lost their mother and their father, and their home, all within a few days. Naturally they feel depressed."

"They damned well haven't lost their home!" said Uncle Jim. "I still can't get me hands on the papers I need to sell the bloody heap of rubble. I'm sick of ringing those cheeky French bastards."

"Be patient. You'll sell it in the end."

"Be patient! It's easy for you to talk! This whole thing was your idea, but you sit on your arse while I go to that bloody country and phone the lawyers. Not to mention all the hassle I had to go through to get the fellas into that home."

"It's only a matter of time," Aunt Mary said. "I know I'm right about the legal position. We are their guardians, and once they live here with us we will have rights to the house. In a few weeks it'll be sold and the money will be in the bank."

"I doubt it," said Uncle Jim. "Anyway I'm going to the pub. I've had all I can take for one day."

The door banged.

Then the sitting-room door closed, and there was silence in the house.

Clara looked across the room. Monica had come in while she was dozing. Now she was sitting on her own bed, her head stuck in a comic. She made a face at Clara and said, "They're hard at it as usual."

"Oh well," said Clara, slipping out of bed and going downstairs.

Aunt Mary was sitting by the fire, staring at her collection of dogs, when Clara entered the sitting-room. Her expression was thoughtful. Clara decided to pretend she knew nothing.

"Aunt Mary, I'm sorry" she said, putting her hand on her aunt's shoulder. "I lost my temper."

"It's not surprising," said Aunt Mary.

"I'm worried about the boys."

"I'm worried about them too. But what can we do? We simply have no space for them here."

"Maybe they'll be OK." Clara had to stop her anger from rising up again.

"Maybe."

They both looked at each other.

"You could telephone them," Aunt Mary said, "and find out."

Clara smiled.

"Can I?"

"Why not? This isn't the Middle Ages, is it?"

Clara smiled. It was not the Middle Ages, but Aunt Mary was so careful about money that Clara knew she wouldn't want her to make long-distance calls.

"Go on, phone them," said Aunt Mary.

"Where's the phone?" Clara smiled.

"Where is the phone in every house in Grey Walls? It's in the hall, of course. You just ring Directory Enquiries and ask for Summerlands."

Clara went out to the hall, and got the number from Directory Inquiries. A few minutes later, she was talking to Brian.

"We're all right," he said. "It's not too bad."

"Can I speak to David?"

"He's asleep," Brian answered. "Maybe you could ring tomorrow?"

"Maybe," Clara wasn't sure if this would be possible. It all depended on other people, not herself. "Now I've got the phone number anyway. It's a start. Did you get something to eat?"

"Chips and eggs and bacon. It was fine. Even David ate some."

"Good. We haven't had ours yet."

"What did you get for lunch?" Brian asked.

"Beans on toast," Clara remembered.

"How many beans?" Brian asked.

"Seven for me," said Clara. Monica had had most of the can and Aunt Mary didn't like beans. She laughed, although she was very hungry. "So they seem nice? Nice people?"

"I've really only met one. And she's very nice. The other, eh, inmates . . . I'm not sure about. They're a mixed lot, I'd say."

"Well, at least the two of you are together. Maybe I'll be able to see you sometime."

"He won't bring you down."

"There must be a bus or something. It's not very far from here, is it?"

"No. It took about two hours. And we were stuck in traffic half the way."

"I miss you."

"Yeah."

"Listen, tell David I phoned and sent my love, and I'll talk to him as soon as I can."

"Will do."

"Bye now."

Clara went back to the sitting room, her face glowing.

"I talked to Brian," she said. "He's all right!"

Aunt Mary was watching television. She looked up without lowering the sound.

"There! Isn't that great. And how about David?"

"He's OK as well. He's in bed. I said I'd talk to him tomorrow. Is that OK?"

"Well, we'll see," said Aunt Mary, not smiling. "Are you happier now?"

"Happier."

Aunt Mary looked at her closely. She turned off the TV and sat down on the sofa next to Clara.

"You're very fond of those brothers of yours, aren't you?"

"Yes," said Clara.

"Well. Let's try and think of something more cheerful. Were you good in school?"

"Good enough. We didn't go all that often."

"Why?"

"It's complicated."

"Your poor mother . . ."

"Yes."

"She had a difficult life too, you know."

"Well, maybe."

"She was always worried about your father. And then she was lonely. She missed Ireland. She loved it here."

This was news to Clara. Mrs Moody always said that she liked Chestnut Cottage better than any place she had ever lived.

"Here?"

"Here in this house. This room. She loved being here with us. We used to have great crack, herself and myself. When he said they were moving to France, she came here and cried. She didn't want to go at all."

Clara found this very hard to believe.

"France was lovely. We had a lovely house. My mother liked it there, I know she did. She never talked about Ireland."

Aunt Mary seemed not to hear her. "She always wanted to come home. When Jack told her they were moving to France she thought it would be like Paris. Chic clothes and the theatre every night. Cafés. She ended up on the top of a mountain miles from civilisation. It never felt right for her."

"It felt right to me," Clara found herself getting impatient with the conversation. She didn't want to remember her mother at all right now; her feelings about her were so complicated that it was difficult to think of her without getting cross, or sad, or upset in some way.

"Yes, it did, dear. But you're Irish, too, and this is where you belong. You'll fit in much better here than in the wilds of France." Aunt Mary paused and put some coal on the fire. The room was quite hot now. She had lit only two lamps and it all looked cosier than usual. Clara thought that the red and orange colour scheme, which had seemed so brash and horrible to her at first sight, was quite warm and stylish, in a way, at least in this light.

"Would you like a bite to eat?"

"Well . . ."

"You haven't eaten all day. What do you really like?"

"Gosh! I don't know." Clara thought. What did she really like? Bread and olives and goat's cheese – she liked that, at lunch-time. And for dinner she liked onion soup, and the beef stew Madame Bonne sometimes made, full of carrots and peppers and mushrooms and wine. She liked baked potatoes with vegetable curry poured over them, or with cheese and bacon . . .

"Lots of things," she said lamely. "Anything really."

"There's a great Indian takeaway in the shopping centre. Fancy a nice curry?"

"That sounds great!" Clara said.

Aunt Mary ordered a curry over the phone. Clara waited, her mouth watering in anticipation. Tonight she would not go to bed hungry, at least. When the man came with the curry, Aunt Mary said, "Give Monica a shout, would you? Dinner-time."

They sat together in the sitting room, eating it and drinking coke, in front of the warm fire, sharing a curry made for one person between the three of them. As usual, Monica had the lion's share.

12

Grey Walls Comprehensive

A few days later, Clara went to school.

It came as a shock to her that she would start so soon. But soon after Brian and David had been dumped in Summerlands, Aunt Mary informed her that she had already enrolled her in the local community school. They would be happy to see Clara as soon as possible, and place her in an appropriate class.

"Ha, ha!" Monica wagged a finger at her. Monica did not like school very much. "Hafta go to school just like me!"

"That's all right," Clara told a white lie. "I'm used to school."

But she wondered what the new school would be like. She doubted if it would resemble the little village school in the mountains much. And she was right about that.

* * *

The Grey Walls Comprehensive was about twenty times

bigger than the school Clara was used to: it looked like a factory to her, when she arrived at its high gates. It consisted of one grey two-storey building with many satellites in the forms of pre-fabs set in a grey yard. The only sign that it was a school were two basketball nets in the yard, and the hundreds of girls who milled around it, all dressed very oddly, it seemed to Clara, in grey skirts and navy jumpers.

"Why are they all wearing the same clothes?" she asked.

Monica looked at her curiously, not understanding why Clara was asking this question.

"It's their uniform," she said, blankly. "They hafta wear it whether they like it or not. Let's go to the office and find out what class you're in."

She led the way to the main door of the school. They stepped into a long corridor, lined with drawings and notices, and smelling of disinfectant. Innumerable doors opened off the corridor. Most of them were pale green, but one was blue, and labelled *Office*. Monica knocked. A voice called "Come in!" They went in.

Clara found herself in the smallest most untidy room she had ever been in.

It was stacked with files, boxes and books. In one corner a stack of navy-blue jumpers was heaped, and in another a little mountain of mobile phones. There were three computers, one on the floor, one on a chair, and one on a desk in the middle of the room. On the desk were ledgers, roll books, pieces of paper, empty cups, packets of cigarettes, and bars of chocolate. Behind this heap of objects a secretary, very small with black hair and a face like a doll, was seated.

"What can I do for you?" she asked, in a surprisingly authoritative voice.

Monica explained about Clara.

"Oh yes!" the secretary said, and Clara breathed a sigh of relief. It came as a surprise that her aunt had really telephoned the school and let them know to expect her. "The girl from France." She stared at Clara for a second, and then extricated herself from her chair. With difficulty, she made her way around to the front of her desk through a mound of papers and shook hands.

"You're in 2X," she said, cheerfully. Then she made her way back to her chair and started to work at her computer.

Monica and Clara looked at one another for a second.

"I suppose we better just go there," said Monica, looking at the secretary for guidance. But none was forthcoming, so they left the room.

"I'm in 2Y," said Monica, "so you won't be with me."

Clara felt alarmed, as they walked along miles and miles of corridor. Finally they came to the green door named 2X.

"See ya!" said Monica.

Clara went inside.

Girls in navy and grey were sitting on tables or chairs, standing or walking around, all engaged in conversation. A symphony of voices, high and low – but mostly high – filled the big, cold room. Clara spotted an empty desk and went to sit there. She opened her bag and took out some bits of stationery. While she was doing this, she noticed something happening. The noise stopped completely. Everyone stopped talking. Clara looked around and saw that twenty-five pairs of eyes were upon her, examining her minutely, from top to toe, or as much of toe as they could see under the desk. She glanced at the sea of faces for a second, then blushed and averted her own eyes. This was a mistake. As soon as she turned her eyes away, the mean, thin, scornful high squeal of a giggle emerged from the silent mass. It was picked up like a telephone by a second girl, and soon the room was punctuated by not quite suppressed giggles.

Clara did not know what might happen next. Luckily a teacher came in and the giggling was turned off as if she had twisted a tap.

Clara survived a morning of Irish, Maths, and History. Then came the hard part: lunch-time. A bell rang in the middle of a lecture on the causes of the Reformation. "One of the reasons for the Reformation was that the Pope lived in Avignon," the teacher was saying, and Clara's ears pricked up because she knew Avignon, quite well. She'd flown there on several occasions with her mother, and shopped in its beautiful streets. "Everything that diminished the papal . . ." The bell rang and before she could finish the sentence twenty-five grey-and-navy-clad girls were leaping out of their desks and clattering out of the room, plastic bags and boxes in hand. The teacher just shut her folder and walked quickly away. Clara was the only one left in the room.

Clara guessed they had gone to lunch. Cautiously she moved to the door and stuck her head out into the corridor. Most of the green doors were open now, and it seemed that all the classrooms had been evacuated. She could not see a single girl or teacher anywhere: the getaway had been very fast and efficient. Where were they? With trepidation, she set off along the corridor. After she had walked for what seemed like several miles, she had found nothing but empty room after empty room. Finding herself near the front door again, she spotted the blue door, the lair of the secretary. Although she did not relish the thought of entering that place again, she decided she'd better make enquiries, since she was feeling decidedly peckish. She knocked at the door.

"Come in!" sang the secretary.

Clara went in. The black-haired secretary was still behind her computer, since there was nowhere else for her to be. But now she was drinking a cup of soup and eating crisps.

"Oh, you again!" she said, not very pleasantly. "What is it now?"

"I was wondering where the restaurant is?" Clara asked.

The secretary stared at her as if she had said something astonishing. She slurped some soup, munched two fistfuls of crisps, and then said, "I'll show you. I'm going that way myself, as it happens."

She burrowed out through the mass of paper and to the door. Clara followed her, expecting another long corridor walk. But the secretary, who was wearing a very chunky warm black sweater, just went to the door and pushed it open.

"There is the restaurant!" she said, indicating the concrete yard in front of the school. "We eat al fresco here!"

Clara gasped. The yard was full of schoolgirls. Three hundred of them swarmed all over its concrete mass, eating and drinking. They wore their indoor clothes, even though the temperature was about ten degrees and rain was drizzling down from the leaden sky.

"You eat out there?" she could not stop herself from asking.

The secretary gave her one of those blank, astonished looks she was getting accustomed to.

"Yeah," she said. "Well, *they*, that is, *you* pupils eat out there. I eat in my own little den. But I smoke out here." She pulled a packet of cigarettes out of her pocket and lit one.

"I've no food," Clara blurted out, suddenly, before she could stop herself.

"Better luck next time!" said the secretary, puffing away. "Sorry I can't help but I've scoffed all of mine." She looked over the yardful of munching human beings. "I doubt if you'll manage to cadge anything off that lot. They're a mean bunch in my experience. You'll just have to starve for today. Ah well, it'll teach you a lesson, one of life's most important lessons, I often think myself: don't forget your lunchbox."

Clara could not think of a reply to this immediately, and decided it wasn't worthwhile exerting her brain to find one. She smiled as coldly as she could at the secretary, and went back into the school. Her stomach felt empty and the rest of her body chilled. She walked very slowly along the pale, empty, interminable corridor. Its half-open green doors looked at her like sneering eyes, and her own eyes became watery.

"I can't bear this," she said to herself. "I just can't take any more of it."

She decided to go back to the classroom, collect her bag and anorak, and leave. She would just walk out of the school and go away wherever her feet carried her. There was no point in staying in this school, in staying with Monica and Aunt Mary. She could not be worse off than she was with them.

The green door proclaiming *2X* loomed before her. She pushed it open. The clouds had lifted slightly and weak silvery sunshine shone through the window onto the shining desks.

"Hi!" a voice said.

Clara could see nobody.

She stared all around the room.

"Hi!" A girl crawled out from underneath a desk and

stood up. She was not quite five feet tall at her full height. She had curly fair hair, cropped close to her skull, and in her eyebrow, nose and ear there were little silver rings. "I'm Sandy," she said, smiling. "And you're Clara, the girl from France. How's it going?"

Clara lied. "I'm fine," she said.

"Would you like some chocolate?" Sandy handed her half a bar.

"I'd . . ." Clara said. "I. . ."

"You what?" Sandy screwed up her eyes, which were a bright green, and looked intently at her.

"Ah nothing," said Clara.

"No, no, you were going to say something. Out with it!" said Sandy, who seemed to be much more mature than anyone Clara had yet met in the school.

Clara was embarrassed to explain about lunch, but Sandy waited for an answer, tapping her foot in mock impatience on the floor, and so she felt she had to make a convincing response. She explained that she hadn't brought any lunch because in her last school lunch was provided.

"You actually get a proper lunch sitting down at a table in French schools? Four courses? Soup and dessert, the works?"

Clara nodded, laughing.

"Jeeze! I wish we had France over here!" Sandy said. "But seeing as we don't would you like to share an egg sandwich with me? I always have twice as much as I need. My dear mother's main ambition in life is to fatten me up, but as you can see she hasn't succeeded and she isn't going to either." She took a sandwich from her bag and handed it to Clara. "If you don't eat it I'll have to throw it in the bin, which is what I do normally."

"Thanks, then," said Clara. "I am hungry."

"You can have the chocolate too!" said Sandy. "If you're a good girl and eat up your sambo."

Clara ate the sandwich, which was quite good, and then the rest of the chocolate.

"Thank you very much," she said. "I feel much better after that."

"I bet you do!" said Sandy. "You won't survive a whole day of Grey Walls Comprehensive on an empty stomach! Would you like me to sit beside you for moral support?"

"Yes," said Clara. "But aren't you sitting beside someone else already?"

"I was, but she dumped me for someone richer and better-looking this morning. You know what schoolgirls are like! See if I care!"

Sandy moved in beside Clara there and then, and Clara could not immediately put into action her plan to run away.

* * *

Sandy walked home with Clara when school was over. She lived a few streets away from Aunt Mary's house, with her mother. "Just the two of us!" she said cheerily. "Father absconded before I was born. Probably couldn't face the prospect of meeting me and having to provide for my luxurious upbringing. I've never seen him."

"Would you like to?" Clara asked.

Sandy shook her head. "What you haven't got you never miss," she said. "Mother and I are getting on very well all by ourselves, thank you very much. She's a schoolteacher. In a primary school – that's the kind of school little kids go to.

We get by. A father would be too much of a responsibility at this stage."

Sandy was very small and thin. Her face was tiny, white and elfin, and her hands were as small as a baby's. She looked quite different from anyone Clara had seen since she came to Ireland. Most people here looked bigger than French people, but Sandy was smaller even than them.

Clara did not tell her everything about her own background on this first day. Although Sandy seemed genuine and kind and appealing, she didn't want to tell her the whole sordid tale until she knew her much better. All she said was that she was staying with her aunt and uncle for a while because her mother was very ill. Sandy accepted this story and made no further enquiries.

They said goodbye at Clara's gate.

"How was school?" Aunt Mary asked, in her bland kind voice, as soon as she came into the house. She had a meal prepared for Clara – half a slice bread and a small tomato. They sat on a pink plate on the kitchen table.

"Great!" said Clara. "It was just great!"

13

Jason and Dean

Brian was woken at eight o'clock by a bell which rang through Summerlands, screaming hysterically like a prison siren. He jumped out of bed and dressed in double-quick time. Breakfast was served at eight fifteen, and then it was time for school for most of the inmates of the house.

This was a Thursday, and David and Brian had been in the institution for a few weeks. Already he felt familiar with the routines, and guessed that they would not change much. Breakfast, school, homework, dinner, activities, television, bed. Weekends were devoted to football, going to the beach, and hanging out. He preferred weekdays, but so far they had survived the weekends as well.

The room he shared with David was narrow as a shoebox. It was painted yellow, and contained two narrow beds, separated by a locker. In a corner was a handbasin, and a rack upon which the boys could hang their clothes. The floor was covered with grey linoleum. There was nothing else at all in the room. It was like a monk's cell.

Brian splashed some water on his face and rubbed his chin. He decided not to shave until later. He went to David and shook him.

David opened his eyes and said, "Leave me alone!"

"It's time to get up, David," Brian said. "Come on!"

David closed his eyes crossly and rolled over.

Brian shook him again. "Come on!" he said, trying to be patient. "Quit the messing. You'll miss breakfast."

David refused to open his eyes at first, but after a few minutes he dragged himself up and pulled on his clothes.

"It's a crap school," he said. "I don't want to go there again."

Brian sighed. "You have to," he said. "It's temporary. Just go along with it for a while and then we'll get out of here."

Although he said this, he didn't know how they were going to get out. He didn't have a clue what was going to happen to either of them in the future.

They went down to the dining-room together. When they got there most of the tables were occupied and they had no choice in where to sit. They found two places at a table at the back of the room.

"Hiya," Brian said to the boys who were sitting at it. Two of the boys he had identified as trouble were sitting there – Jason and Dean. Jason was aged fourteen, blond with an unusually broad nose and a strong Dublin accent. He was tall and burly and had a skull and crossbones tattooed on his arm. Dean was younger, thin and slightly built, with red hair and a face covered with pale brown freckles. The first thing Jason and Dean had done upon being introduced to Brian and David was to say "Frogs!" followed by "Go home, froggie woggies!" Relations had deteriorated since that day, and Brian and David did their best to avoid Jason and Dean whenever possible.

"How's it going, Sprog?" said Jason. Dean stared malevolently at Brian and David.

Brian was not sure whether he should reply or not, but thought it was wiser to do so.

"It's going fine thanks," he said.

"Nicely settled in then?" Jason went on. "Feelin' comfy in your luxury suite? Up to the standards of *La Belle France*? So glad to hear it."

Dean giggled.

Brian poured milk on his cornflakes and passed the jug to David, who was sitting beside Dean. As David picked up the jug, Dean jogged his elbow causing the milk to spill and drench the table and David's trousers.

"So sorry!" said Dean in a high-pitched voice. "Clumsy me!"

David looked as if he wanted to cry, but had the sense not to. Brian went to the kitchen and got a cloth to wipe up the mess and get more milk.

This time, he poured out the milk for David, cautiously keeping an eye on Dean and Jason. But they made no further attempts to spill the milk. Instead they concentrated on taking all the toast which was stacked on a plate in the centre of the table, so that by the time Brian and David had finished their cornflakes, there were only two pieces left. Brian reached out to take those, but Dean beat him to it. With a neutral expression on his freckled face, he swiped the last two pieces of toast from the plate, slowly placed them on the floor, and trampled on them.

"Have a good day!" he said, in a sing-song voice, standing up to go. Jason left too.

"Can we get more toast?" David asked. Somehow he seemed to be able to take Jason and Dean in his stride. It was as if he had experienced so much strange behaviour that nothing could surprise him any more.

Wearily, Brian trekked back to the kitchen. But there was no toast left. How had Dean and Jason known that? He knew they must have known; otherwise they wouldn't have taken the trouble to destroy the last of the toast on the table.

"There's no bread at all left," the young fair-haired girl, Madeline, who made breakfast said. She was very busy, stacking dirty dishes in the dishwasher. She didn't have time to even look at Brian. He glanced at her back, and its long plait of hair, opened his mouth to explain what had happened, but didn't bother. He knew she would not be able to magic up bread out of nowhere. Seeing a few bananas, too yellow, with brown bruises on their skin, in a rack, he took two of them and went back to David. David preferred greenish bananas, but he was so hungry that he accepted one of these ripe offerings. To his surprise the brown spots had not penetrated the skin of his banana, and inside was a sweet, perfect, firm fruit.

Brian walked to school with David. Although he was not attending it himself, Kate Murphy had asked him to accompany his brother to the school gate for the time being. "If it's raining, one of us will give him a lift. But on fine days he'd probably like to walk."

David, being David, grumbled bitterly about having to walk, but in fact he enjoyed the experience. The school was about a mile from the home, and the way was a little-used country road, overhung with beech and oak trees, now in the full flush of early summer. In the shadow of the trees bluebells and wood anemones grew, and brambles were beginning to flower. The boys walked through a green tunnel of foliage all the way to school.

"What do you do there?" Brian asked.

"I sit," said David.

"Do you understand what they say?"

"Some of it," David said. "I don't care if I understand or not."

"Did you talk to any other kids?"

"No."

"Did they leave you in peace?" Brian asked, carefully.

"They didn't call me Frog, or Sprog, or anything like that, if that's what you mean, " said David, flatly.

Brian smiled at him, amused at his stoicism. "Good!" he said.

It didn't sound as if David was enjoying school much, but at least he was safe there. Maybe, just maybe, Brian hoped, David would melt a little in time and begin to participate in school life. He left David in the school porch, handing him over to the teacher who was standing in the hall, and walked back to the home.

He hummed to himself as he strolled along. The sun shone, the little blue road was overhung with eager brambles and hawthorn bushes. Clumps of yellow mustard sprouted from the ditches, and here and there clumps of primroses lingered on. They reminded Brian of cliques of teenage girls, bright, prim and giggling. Close to each lively clump usually lingered a few violets, looking like the quiet girls who don't belong to the in-group. Could it be that nature was a hall of mirrors, he wondered, each kind of species mirroring the other? Flowers were like people. And when he listened to the birdsong in the evenings now, out in the garden of Summerlands, he could distinguish several different sounds – the chatter of the choughs and stonechats, the twittering of the swallows, the sweet tune of the blackbirds. There were many others, which he could not identify. The birds reminded him of a symphony orchestra, and he even wondered if people had got the idea of music and musical instruments, of choruses and orchestras, from the birds?

With such pleasant philosophical ponderings, he passed the time as he strolled from school to the institution.

He felt better than he had in a long time.

So much had been happening that he hadn't had time to sink into a depression. And the surprising fact was that he liked Summerlands, liked it quite a lot. It was a home, its inmates were unknown quantities, but Kate Murphy was lovely and trustworthy. And Brian felt at home in the atmosphere of the place – he liked its tiny cells of bedrooms, its big dining-room, its bells and its rules and its generous gardens. It reminded him of school. He wasn't going to school at the moment, but he believed that he would be, after the summer holidays. It would be a new school, a strange school, but it would be a school; he would study for exams. He would play football. He would be back on track. His ambitions for his future would no longer be altogether in jeopardy. Somehow, Brian felt confident that if he could get back to school everything would be all right. He would study, he would become a doctor – he still clung to this ambition, although the future seemed very remote, like another planet, now, whereas before his father went to jail and his mother died it had seemed like a familiar destination, for which he had already reserved a first-class ticket.

Nevertheless, for the moment, to his surprise, he felt very OK indeed. It was as if he had worried so much that he could not go on doing it. His mother, his father, his unspeakable uncle and aunt – for weeks, although it seemed like aeons, he had had them on his mind all day and all night. His constant obsession was with getting rid of them or changing them or rescuing them or improving them. He had wanted everything to be different from the way it was, absolutely everything. Now, since he had settled into Summerlands, it was as if those worries had slipped away from him. Finally he accepted that there was absolutely nothing he could do resurrect his mother or get his father out of jail, to transform Uncle Jim Crabclaw to a nice nurturing man. Brian could hardly believe that he had ceased worrying. Probably it was temporary, and he would wake up in a day or two and all those anxieties would be there, waiting to pounce on him like a big monster as soon as he opened his eyes. But now the monster was at bay. Brian could relax. He could give himself a break, he could have a holiday, however short.

There was another very definite reason for his good humour.

"But what are we going to do with you?" Kate had asked a few days after Brian arrived in Summerlands. She scratched her head in an extravagant gesture. She made exaggerated, over the top, gestures all the time, dramatising all her thoughts and ideas and problems. Brian smiled.

"May is nearly out!" she said, in her loud voice. She felt

there was no point in starting Brian at school now, since the holidays would begin in a few weeks' time. She did not add that since Brian was almost sixteen, he would probably soon have to leave the home anyway and look after himself. Brian would be on his own a lot sooner than he imagined. But maybe she could get around the problem . . . She didn't have to face it yet anyway, and she certainly wasn't going to spring it on Brian, who had had such a hard time recently. She could see that he had taken to Summerlands. She wasn't going to spoil his precarious contentment. He was in blissful ignorance of the rules and regulations which governed life in state institutions. Little did he know how difficult it had been to give him and David their places in the home. Little did he know how close he had come to being pitched out onto the streets of Dublin, to becoming a bag-boy, sleeping rough in the porches of shops, begging money for a bed in a hostel, like the hundreds of homeless boys who were cast adrift in Ireland. Brian was innocent enough to take it for granted that now the Irish state would look after him. He assumed he would stay with David until something happened at home, until some magic solution occurred and they all went back to France. If only life were so simple, Kate wished. But she revealed nothing to Brian.

Instead she asked him if he would be interested in helping the gardener. Brian decided that he might as well try. The idea of hanging around the house, with nothing specific to do, did not appeal to him. So, even though he had never concerned himself with gardening before, he now found himself being introduced to someone called Charlie.

Charlie was old, at least sixty. He had a red, wrinkled apple face and snowy white hair. His eyes were very small and a very bright periwinkle blue.

"Good day to you, young fella," he said, in an accent which Brian could not easily understand. "What sort of experience have you got of this kind of work?"

When he found out that Brian had none he didn't seem unduly concerned.

"You'll learn soon enough," he said, nodding his head wisely. He stood and stared at the fence. Then he delivered a short but extremely enthusiastic lecture on the gardens of Summerlands.

"We have four acres of lawn around the house," he said. "And there's on top of that the orchard, the vegetable garden, and the football pitch. Not to mention the hedges around the front and the flower-beds. So it's a full-time job and I do it all on my own."

"Right," said Brian, looking dutifully around. There was a lot of grass in evidence.

"I've got the tractor mower this year and that's a great help. Before I used to cut most of the grass myself with an ordinary push-mower. The tractor makes it much easier."

He showed Brian the vegetable garden, where he had peas, cabbages, lettuces, radishes, herbs, as well as fruit bushes, and a greenhouse full of tomatoes.

"Most of the vegetables you eat in there come from this garden," he said. "I do it meself. They didn't ask me to do it. My job was to cut the grass, keep the place looking presentable. But four or five years ago I took it into my head to start the vegetables out of the goodness of my heart so to speak and this is the result. A broken back for me and fresh organic veggies for youse."

"It looks great!" said Brian.

"You can start work here so," said Charlie. He showed

Brian the tool-shed and gave him a weeding spike and a trowel.

"The beds are full of weeds this time of the year, " he said. "You just dig them all up by the roots and put them in that bin over there."

Brian took the implements and set to work on the carrot rills. He encountered chickweed, dandelions, bindweed, and several other weeds whose names he did not know. It was strange, he thought: there was only one kind of vegetable in the rills, but dozens of types of weed. After about two hours, he had rid the carrot rills of all of them and felt very sore and rather pleased with his achievement.

Charlie came along. He was also pleased. His wrinkled red face broke into a smile, and somehow when he smiled it was like sunshine breaking through on a cloudy day.

"You did a good job there," he said, "so you did." He paused and took a good long look at the beautiful, weed-free beds of carrots. The carrot-leaves flounced above the ground, bushy and frilly and freshly green. "They look as cute as bunches of parsley. You could gobble up them leaves with your spuds and roast chicken, so you could." Sighing with pleasure at the sight of the exquisite carrots, he announced that a reward would now be given. "It's time for a break" he said, in the tone of someone saying: "I dub thee knight".

So they proceeded to the garden shed, where, tucked away among the slug pellets, weedkiller, and sacks of fertiliser, Charlie had an electric kettle and the other bare necessities of life: mugs, biscuits, sugar and milk, and, of course, copious supplies of tea. He plugged the kettle into a contact point which was hidden behind a packet of bone meal, and when a ribbon of steam sneaked up over the poisonous-looking pack, he made tea in two big brown mugs. From an old green grass-seed box he pulled a packet of chocolate biscuits.

"A feast fit for a king!" he said, handing Brian a mug and four biscuits. Charlie's hands did not look very clean, but Brian wasn't in a mood to be picky – his own hands were covered in clay anyway. Charlie led him outside, and they sat on a wooden bench to have their snack.

"You've done enough weeding for one day," Charlie said. "It's a never-ending task, but if you do it for more than a few hours you feel very fed up with life. So after the break I'll set you to cutting the grass in the pitch, if that grabs your fancy."

Brian drank his tea, which was sweet and hot. The carrot-tops frothed like green lace in front of him, and beyond them, at the edge of the patch, sweet peas were winding their way along wigwams of green sticks. He bit into one of Charlie's biscuits. It was crispy and chunky with oatmeal and hazelnuts, coated with a thick layer of black chocolate, Brian's favourite – he half-expected Charlie to say that he had baked it himself. The sun was warm on his face and the air scented with grass and compost and flowers.

"I'd like to give it a go," he said, thinking happily of the lawnmower. "I've never driven a car or anything though."

It was true. Clara could fly an aeroplane, but Brian had certainly never wanted to do that, and he had never even had a driving lesson. That was how the Moody family operated – inconsistent to the core.

"It's as easy as riding a bicycle," said Charlie, in his low, calm voice. "I'll give you a lesson and away you'll go, one of Charlie's Angels!"

So Brian had learned how to drive the mower on that first day in the garden.

And every weekday since then, he had worked with Charlie in the garden. He and Charlie had become good friends, and Brian was learning more and more about gardening. He enjoyed the work much more than he would ever have imagined possible. If anyone had told him a month or two ago that he would spend half his day weeding flowerbeds and take pleasure in it, he would have laughed at them. But the fact was that he loved being outdoors, he loved getting his fingers dirty in the soil, he loved helping plants to survive and thrive. He loved learning about plants, their names, their habits, their needs – so much so that occasionally his mind began to wonder if he would not, after all, be as happy working in a garden as working in a hospital. But he didn't spend much time worrying about that – he was happy just to let himself flow with the mood of the moment. He knew, however, that it was thanks to the garden, as much as to Kate Murphy or the Summerlands routines, that he was beginning to feel himself again.

Today he had spent putting compost on the vegetable beds and mowing the soccer pitch – a long but pleasant job. At two o'clock, he said goodbye to Charlie and set off to collect David from school. Hurrying along the country road, he felt light-hearted and happy. It occurred to him that he never even worried about his ears, or any aspect of his appearance, any more. That anxiety, too, he had managed to slough off, thanks to the therapeutic effect of Charlie and gardening and Kate's kindness. Or maybe it had something to do with the bigger problems he had endured. Even remembering that he used to sit in front of a mirror, tweaking his ears, indulging in long sessions of self-hatred, astonished him. What a luxury it had been, to waste time worrying about ears! He hadn't noticed his ears one way or the other for ages. When he glanced in the mirror, which didn't happen often, since there were not many mirrors in Summerlands, he didn't even see them. Was it even possible, he thought, that there was absolutely nothing the matter with his ears? Had he imagined their ugliness all along? The old bat-ear delusion. He gave them a tweak, just to confirm that they were still there.

They were, but, as far as his fingers could tell, they seemed like normal ears. Could he really have been torturing himself about his ears for no reason at all? Had he wasted all that time worrying about nothing? The thought alarmed him. But those ears had seemed so huge. They had looked like elephant ears sticking out for miles on each side of his face. Could that all have been just an elephant-size delusion?

Well, now, he wasn't deluding himself any more. Also, he felt that even if he did have ears the size of dinner plates, he really couldn't devote time to worrying about them. There were so many other more important things to care about.

Such as David, his silly, strange, remarkable little brother.

David was waiting at the school gate when he arrived. He looked happier than he had this morning. And Brian soon found out why.

"Like some sweets?" David asked, opening a cellophane bag.

"Sure!" said Brian.

"The teacher gave them to me," said David.

"Sweets!" said Brian. "Why? Just for being your charming self?"

"No," said David scornfully. He paused and scowled, annoyed at Brian's sarcasm. David could be charming, but he still wasn't, not very often and never in school. Brian gave him time to decide to answer, and eventually David couldn't resist telling him.

"For coming first in the class," he announced, proudly. It was the first time he had ever come first in any class at anything. In fact, it was the first time he had not come last.

"At what?" asked Brian, who was not quite aware of David's dismal academic record.

"French," said David proudly.

Brian laughed. But he congratulated David sincerely, and sucked his sweet, which was a chocolate toffee, tooth-wrenching and very tasty.

* * *

In the afternoon, Kate brought Brian, David and some of the other children to a local swimming-pool. Jason and Dean were not with them; they played football. The swim was peaceful and enjoyable; the group from Summerlands had the pool more or less to themselves, and there were only eight of them. On the way home, Kate stopped and bought them ice creams at an ice-cream van.

Supper passed without incident. Brian was careful to arrive in the dining-room just at the right moment – not too early, and not too late. If you came early, you had to sit at an empty table, and then anyone could come and sit beside you – i.e. Jason and Dean. If you arrived late, you had to sit beside whoever was left – i.e. Jason and Dean, since most of the boys avoided them if they could. By coming two minutes after the bell sounded, Brian and David were able to join a table used by boys who were more or less civilised – much more civilised than the terrible duo anyway.

They were getting to know some of the other boys at this stage. There was Niall, who was twelve, small for his age and quiet. He never seemed to say anything – but that was fine as far as Brian was concerned. By contrast, Dermot chatted all the time, telling everyone everything that had happened to him from early morning. His conversation was punctuated with the word "fucking". But he was OK too. They shared a table with them and two other boys, John and Conor, who were not particularly friendly or talkative. They seemed wrapped up in themselves. But at least they didn't harass anyone.

Dinner was chips, beans and sausages – by now Brian realised that it usually consisted of various combinations of chips and something else: eggs, pork chops, fish. Vegetables from the garden accompanied this food as a rule – carrots, peas or salad. Even tonight, as well as the beans, there was a bowl of tomatoes. Brian and David ate them, but none of the others did. There were big helpings of chips and sausages, and they got a good dinner to compensate for the lack of any breakfast. During the meal, David looked over his shoulder occasionally at Jason and Dean, suspicious that they would somehow interfere with him. But they seemed to be paying him no attention whatsoever. They were busy tucking into the meal, like everyone else, and did not seem to be even talking very much.

Dessert was ice cream and raspberries, which had also come from the garden. They tasted delicious. David licked his lips and so did Brian. At the end of the meal, they both felt very satisfied, and filled with the happy sensation that comes from a good dinner at the end of a long, busy, hungry day.

It was the kind of day that was normal at Summerlands, at least as long as Jason and Dean kept out of your way.

14

Sandy

Clara was also finding that life in Ireland had its compensations.

Just as Brian was finding that he liked Summerlands, she was discovering that going to school at Grey Walls Comprehensive was not the nightmare it had seemed on her first morning there. In fact, going to school at Grey Walls Comprehensive was turning out to be extremely enjoyable indeed.

The main reason for this was Sandy, although there were others, such as the fact that Clara, who had never done a tap of work in her life, was quite clever and, given some stimulation, she enjoyed studying – thanks to some great teachers, the kind of gifted teachers you would expect to see wearing caps and gowns in some ancient ivy-draped academy of learning, but who found themselves operating in the unlikely setting of Grey Walls Comprehensive. Her English and French teachers were particularly good, and

Clara seemed to have a talent for working in both languages. It was going to take her a long time to catch up in other areas, like Maths and Science, but the teachers said there was room for hope, although the Maths teacher wasn't desperately optimistic.

Sandy, however, was the main reason for Clara's state of mind, as Charlie was for Brian's. She and Sandy became firm friends after their first meeting. Usually Clara was first into the classroom – she trained herself to reverse the habit of a lifetime, get up early and run off alone before Monica had finished her breakfast. Clara would sit at her desk, reading or doing homework, for half an hour, before the other students began to trickle into the classroom. Sandy usually arrived one second before the bell, and sometimes later.

"I hate getting up in the mornings," she complained. "I so hate it!"

They continued the share a desk. It was not the only thing they shared. Clara remembered to get lunch after the first day, but since Aunt Mary prepared the lunches for her and Monica, she invariably had an extremely modest repast, beautifully wrapped in a pink or pale peppermint serviette – often the napkin contained two cream crackers, sandwiched together with a scrape of low-fat butter, or two Goldgrain biscuits, dry. On red-letter days there might be a tiny sandwich, of bread and Marmite. Aunt Mary never supplied a drink. "There's a water fountain in the yard, isn't there?" she smiled sweetly. "I think that's much simpler than lugging a big bottle of milk or juice or something all the way to Grey Walls Comprehensive. And water is so good for the complexion. You, dearest, need all the help you can get with those freckles of yours!"

Sandy did not pry into Clara's affairs, but she was not blind and she soon noticed that the contents of her friend's lunchbox were not what you'd call substantial. Without saying a word about it, she began to supplement its meagre contents: she would casually offer Clara an extra ham sandwich, an apple or two, bars of chocolate. After a week, Clara realised what was happening.

"You don't have to feed me every day!" she said, shyly, although in fact she believed Sandy's lunches were probably keeping her alive.

"I know I don't," said Sandy, in her usual carefree tones. Then she spoke more seriously. "But somebody has to do it, and it doesn't look like your Aunt Mary is seriously interested in the job."

Clara was uneasy. They were sitting in the yard, which was bathed in sunshine. The pupils swarmed over the vast concrete area, eating, drinking, talking, playing. Boys kicked ball in the football pitch at the side of the yard. It was late May, a hot day. Soon school would be over, the summer holidays begun. Everyone was in a good mood.

"Yeah. My aunt has a very small appetite and she sort of thinks everyone else has too," she said. It was the first time she had criticised her aunt. It was the first time she had revealed anything about her private life to Sandy.

"Right! Does she have that idea about Monica?" Sandy asked, sceptically.

Clara laughed.

"Monica is different. She needs feeding up, because of her ballet."

"I've noticed that she gets a different sort of lunchbox from you, all right!" said Sandy. "Like, about ten times as big."

It was true that Monica got four sandwiches, filled with cheese or peanut butter or ham and salad, as well as various tasty treats – packets of crisps, bars of chocolate, wrapped chocolate biscuits – in her lunchbox. She also got a flask filled with coffee or soup or a cool juicy drink. Clara was not supposed to know this, but she had peeped into the fridge one morning when she was up even before Aunt Mary and made the discovery, a discovery which made her feel abused and depressed.

"That's how it goes," Clara said. She looked into the distance, not sure if she should say much more. "So thanks anyway. I really appreciate the . . ."

"Grub" said Sandy, helpfully.

* * *

Clara settled in well to the routines of 2X. At first she was abysmally ignorant, but so were lots of kids in the class. And since she was determined to work hard, and did, she found herself catching up, even after a few weeks. Her teachers were pleased with her efforts.

"Your English is wonderful!" the English teacher said. "It's astonishing, for someone who has lived in France for so long. You must read a lot?"

Clara remembered the plays, and her mother's classic novels.

"Yes, I do," she said. "Or at least I did, when I was in France." Because she didn't read at all in Ireland. There was not a single book in the Crabclaws' house, apart from Monica's ballet books, which Clara could not bring herself to read, because they reminded her so much of Monica, and her own book, the troubadour's book.

The teacher noticed her use of the past tense and advised her to join the public library. Clara said that she would.

Apart from Sandy, she did not make many friends, but she was not shy with her classmates and felt secure enough among them. If she returned to school in the autumn, she was sure she would be happy among them.

But would she return?

She had written to her father, telling him everything, but so far she had not received any reply.

And life with the Crabclaws was so strange that she did not have the faintest idea what would happen next.

After a few weeks, she understood how the family dynamic worked. Monica was the centre, the be-all and end-all. Uncle Jim just did whatever he was told to do, by Aunt Mary. Aunt Mary seemed to be rigidly in control, but that was an illusion. Anything Monica wanted, she got, even if it involved an extravagant loosening of the purse-strings.

For instance, on the last day of school there was to be a great rock concert in a big modern music venue in the centre of Dublin. Monica had absolutely no interest in rock concerts, or any sort of music except the scores for the ballets she failed so miserably to perform with any skill: old-fashioned romantic ballets like *Giselle* and *Coppelia*, *The Nutcracker* and *Sleeping Beauty* – the ballets which the characters in the ballet books starred in. Monica's gang at school, or one of the gangs she wanted to belong to, who hated ballet but loved hard rock, were going to this concert. The tickets cost seventy Euro and you had to queue all night outside a shop in the city centre to get them.

Uncle Jim was dispatched to join the queue of thousands. Most people in the queue were aged fifteen, so at fifty he had a certain edge on them. People fell silent when they saw him, large, sad and bald, sitting on the footpath, drinking milk from a carton, waiting. Or they laughed and said, "You haven't lost it yet!"

Two days later Uncle Jim returned, very grumpy and looking bedraggled and half-starved. In his hand was one tattered ticket.

"What took you so long, Daddy?" Monica asked, crossly. She was sitting by the fire, dressed in her purple leotard, a garment which did not flatter her figure. She was drinking a bottle of coke and eating a box of chocolates while she watched her favourite television programme, *Great Russian Dancers of a Bygone Age*.

He could hardly talk, partly due to exhaustion and partly to his bad humour.

"They were sold out at the shop," he said, "but I got this on the black market."

"How much?" asked Aunt Mary smoothly.

"Two hundred," he groaned.

Her eyes flashed, but she smiled at him. "I'll look after it. Thank you, darling!" She took the ticket from his hand.

Monica munched her chocolates and did not say thank you.

This and other incidents in the life of the Crabclaws' household formed Clara's opinion of them.

She had not fallen out with Monica at all. So far, they got on well. Clara asked nothing of Monica; she stayed as quiet as she could when in her presence and she co-operated with her as much as was humanly possible. But she knew very well that if Monica took the slightest dislike to her, she would be in very serious trouble indeed.

In the meantime, she tiptoed around the house as

unobtrusively as possible. Once, she had asked Uncle Jim if he had managed to sell Chestnut Cottage. He had given his nasty chuckle and retorted, "Wouldn't you like to know?" Afterwards he had been very cold towards her for some days, and she did not dare to ask the question again.

She wrote again to her father, explaining what had happened to her and her siblings, and asking him if Uncle Jim could really sell Chestnut Cottage. She apologised to her father for never having supplied him with paper and pens as he had requested, and hoped he had managed to get them anyway.

But apparently he had not – anyway, Clara never got a reply to this letter, either.

Almost every night, if she was alone in the room, she took out the leather book and tried to write in it. Sometimes she could and sometimes she could not. But the story was expanding, very slowly.

Clara's brothers disappeared and she did not see them for months. One night, when she lay in her little bed, she heard a tapping at the window. She went to the window and in the dark outside she saw a big white swan. She was afraid, but the swan tapped again and she opened the window. The swan came into the room.

"Clara," it said, "I am your eldest brother. Our stepmother has transformed all of us to swans."

"Oh goodness!" said Clara.

"We live at the lake in the middle of the mountains," he went on, "and fly around looking for food. You can come and visit us there if you like."

"Of course I will," said Clara. "I'll come as often as I can."

From then on, she visited the swans every day.

15

Homesick

One evening after dinner, Brian decided to go out to the garden and have a walk around what he was now regarding as his own territory. David said he would go up to his room and finish his homework – he was fired with enthusiasm for learning, thanks to the bag of sweets. Never before had a teacher rewarded him for anything.

"I'll come up in about an hour," said Brian. "Then we can watch TV or whatever."

He went out into the garden. The sun was still shining, but there were long shadows falling from the house, which faced west, onto the vegetable patch. Brian looked with pride at the rills he had weeded earlier in the day. He walked through the orchard, where the apple-blossom was still in flower, to the football pitch. It looked lopsided, one side cut close and the other longer. Boys were kicking a ball around, not engaged in real training or a match, just enjoying themselves in the evening sun.

Brian walked around the edge of the pitch and back to the garden where he sat on the same bench he and Charlie used for their morning break. He thought about his situation. Being here in Summerlands suited him, he acknowledged that freely now. It was not so different from the boarding-school he had attended at home, and it was a million times better than life with Uncle Jim. The last thing he wanted was to return to the Crabclaw residence. A pang of worry darted through him, as he remembered Clara. But he knew Clara would be all right. She was the sort of girl who landed on her feet no matter what the situation, and anyway she seemed to get on better with her aunt and uncle than he had.

Brian's thoughts wandered to his father. He would be locked up for at least five years. By the time he got out of prison, Brian would be twenty-one, Clara would be nineteen, and even David would be fifteen, older than Clara was now. They would be almost grown-up.

Grown-up. Brian felt a tear coming to his eye at the thought of that word. If only. If only they could leap over these years and reach the state of being "grown-up" tomorrow, all their problems would be solved. So he thought. David would be able to fend for himself, at least up to a point. Or he would be able to fend for David – he would have a job, he would have a place to live, he would have an income, he would be a student – if he were grown-up, everything would be possible. David could go on to school and college, and Clara too if she wanted to. If only he were older. If only he were nearly twenty-one now, instead of nearly sixteen.

Brian looked around the garden. Thinking of his father made him think of France, and the life he used to have.

When he forgot about this, he was very happy with his present life. But when he remembered, he began to daydream about Chestnut Cottage. He would have loved to go back there, and see the cottage. He would love to be back at school. He would love to see his father.

Like Clara, he had written a letter to Jack Moody. And like her, he had received no reply. However he wrote more than once – he had plenty of money for stamps thanks to the money he earned from his gardening work, and every week he sent off a letter describing what was going on in his life and David's. By now he had given up hoping for a response.

He began to realise that he would never find out what had happened to his father unless he got back to France.

He had never appreciated Chestnut Cottage all that much when he had lived there, and had been delighted to get away from it to the school in Merle. But now he longed for its quaint old rooms, its chestnut trees, its loops of heavy flowers. And he longed too for the school, where life had been so ordered and sane, with its regular routines of work and play. He thought of his friends on the football team, and wished he had stayed in contact with them. He even thought of Louise, the girl who had rejected him some months back, and wondered how she was. He had stopped hating her, even though she had hurt him so badly at the time, and was able to remember her without resentment – well, without too much resentment anyway. He was curious about what she was up to. Would he ever see her or any of his old friends again?

But he didn't allow his nostalgia to get the better of him. For the moment, Summerlands was good enough. And even if he couldn't go back to his old school, come September he'd attend the secondary school in the next town. It would be a new challenge for him, going to an Irish school and studying for the Leaving, but he was looking forward to doing it. And then – the future, that unknown planet, beckoned.

Thinking about what he was going to do in the autumn filled him with jittery excitement. To calm down, he went for a run. He jumped up from the bench and started running. He ran through the orchard, and all around the edge of the pitch, and then around the pitch twice more.

By then, his energy was used up. He was hot and sweating, and tired. He glanced at his watch. It was almost nine o'clock – he had stayed out an hour longer than he intended.

He hurried back to the house. He glanced into the TV room. A few boys, including Jason and Dean, were watching TV and did not look up as he peeped in. David was not with them – not surprisingly. Brian walked upstairs, slowly, since he really was very tired, and went into the bedroom. To his surprise David was not there either. His schoolbag was on his narrow bed, and a few books lay beside it. Other books and papers were on the floor – torn to shreds. Brian felt very frightened.

He called, "David! David!" There was no reply.

He went out onto the corridor. There were eight rooms on this level of the house and eight more on the next floor. Most of the rooms were small bedrooms, just like his and David's. The rest were bathrooms. Brian called out his brother's name, walking along the corridor. Nobody replied. He called his name louder. Niall, the quiet boy, looked out of a doorway. He had not seen David or anyone else. Most of the kids were still outside, or downstairs watching TV.

"Look in the rooms," Niall said. "I'll help you."

They started to open doors and check out the rooms. They opened every door, onto little rooms, some bare and dull like Brian's, others decorated with posters of football teams and rock groups, with stuffed toys and photographs. Some boys, Brian saw, with a wrench, had lived in this place for a long long time. They had had time to collect things, to make their tiny little rooms seem like home. They had no other home anyway.

David was not in any of the rooms.

Brian came to a door at the end of the corridor which would not open.

"It's a sort of storeroom," Niall said. "They keep the hoover and stuff in there."

"If it's locked he couldn't be in there anyway," said Brian.

"You never know with Jason and Dean," said Niall, in his flat unsurprised voice.

Brian looked closely at him. He wasn't as stupid as he appeared to be.

"I'll see if they have a key in the kitchen," Niall clumped downstairs in his slow way. Brian banged on the cupboard door, but there was no response from within.

Niall returned promptly enough with a key. He fitted it to the lock and opened the door.

As soon as he did, about six frogs jumped out on top of them.

The frogs' green slimy legs slid across their faces. Brian and Niall screamed.

The frogs were more frightened than they were, however. They ran slithering on the linoleum down the corridor and into the bedrooms.

"What the hell!" Niall said. He started to peer into the storeroom, which was very dark. He found a light-switch inside one of the doors, and switched it on.

David lay on the floor, crumpled up, his legs under his chin, behind the hoover. He was perfectly still.

16

Frogs

Brian's legs lost their strength. His stomach seemed to collapse and the space inside his head changed utterly, like a vacuum flask which has been suddenly opened. He had a horrible sense of déjà vu: his mother had lain crumpled up on a floor not so long ago. Brian was literally stunned with terror.

But within seconds his paralysis was over. He knelt beside David and listened. He was breathing very weakly, but still breathing.

"Go and get somebody!" Brian said to Niall. Niall ran downstairs.

Brian spoke gently to David, just saying his name over and over again.

David began to come to.

Kate Murphy arrived.

"I think he's OK," said Brian.

"Oh!" David was saying, sitting up and clutching his forehead.

"He probably fainted," Brian went on.

"Have you a headache?" Kate was kneeling beside David now, feeling his forehead.

David nodded. His face was taut and strained. Kate asked Niall to go and get a cup of hot tea, with lots of sugar in it, from the kitchen. Niall ran off.

"Somebody locked him into the cupboard," Brian explained to Kate, "along with a lot of frogs."

"Poor David!" Kate was caressing his forehead. "Poor David! Sit still for a while and soon you'll feel all right."

"Who did it?" Brian asked.

David said nothing.

* * *

"It was Dean and Jason,"

Niall and Brian were in Kate's office. David was in bed, tucked in and sleeping peacefully.

Kate sighed. "It always is Dean and Jason."

She was sitting beside her desk – a big, neat desk. Stacks of letters were piled in a yellow basket on one side of it, and a bowl of freesias stood on the other side. There was a row of little trolls all along the outside edge of the desk. Brian looked at them. He couldn't concentrate on what Kate was saying.

Niall could. He was very angry. "What are you going to do about it?" he asked.

His irritated tone aroused Brian from his dreaminess. He looked at Kate. She was frowning. Her hair was messy. She no longer looked competent and capable of dealing with any crisis.

"What can be done?" she shrugged. "You know the story as well as I do, Niall."

"Yes, I know it too well," said Niall. He turned to Brian. "They're real trouble."

"I'd noticed that," said Brian.

"They mess with everyone. They make life miserable for all of us."

"They've had a rough time themselves," Kate said.

"Who hasn't?" Niall asked, crossly.

Kate sighed again and looked sadly at both of them.

Niall went on. "Having a rough time doesn't entitle you to take it out on the world for the rest of your life, does it?"

Kate shook her head. "You're right. But what do you suggest I do?"

Niall paused before replying. "Get them out. Get rid of them."

Kate smiled sadly. "Get rid of them? Where would they go?"

"I don't care," said Niall. "On the streets for all I care. I'm sick of them wrecking things for the rest of us. They're bullies . . . they're dangerous bullies."

Kate sat in silence and looked at the two boys.

"Brian," she said. "I'm truly sorry for what happened to David and I'll do everything in my power to ensure that nothing like that ever happens again. But I'm not going to turn Jason and Dean out of Summerlands. They have rights too."

Niall scowled, but said nothing. He got up, walked out and slammed the door.

"He's a good guy," Kate said.

"I'll keep an eye on David," Brian said, quietly, wondering how he could manage to do this twenty-four hours a day.

"He'll be OK," said Kate. "Jason and Dean are mischievous,

but they're not really dangerous, like Niall said. Nobody will come to serious harm."

"No," Brian said, politely, hoping this was true. But he trusted Kate's judgement, and assumed it must be. Also, he felt sorry, in a strange way, for Jason and Dean.

* * *

David stayed in bed the next day. The doctor came to visit. She examined him and pronounced him well.

Brian was in the room while the examination was going on. He watched with interest; he wanted to be a doctor himself when he grew up, although now that ambition seemed almost out of reach

"He's OK," the doctor said to Brian. "In fact you're as fit as a fiddle," she said, turning to David, who was sitting up in bed, reading.

"How did he faint?" Brian asked.

"It's interesting how that happens," the doctor said. "Usually people faint due to a lack of oxygen reaching the brain – that's why it happens in an airless room, for instance, or a crowded railway carriage. But in some cases a shock can stun the system so that the flow of blood and of air is suspended temporarily. That's what happened to David."

"I see," said Brian.

The doctor said goodbye to David and she and Brian left the room and walked downstairs.

"It's much rarer than you'd imagine, fainting from shock. Actually, it hardly ever happens. David must have got a bad fright."

"He did," Brian said.

The doctor shook her head.

"There's no harm done, physically," she said, "but he has been severely traumatised. It will take him a while to get over that."

"Is there anything I should do?"

The doctor looked at him curiously.

"He's lucky to have a brother like you," she said. "That's probably the best thing he could have, around here."

Brian smiled, but said nothing.

He left David to his own devices and spent the afternoon in the garden with Charlie. Charlie didn't know what had happened in the house – he seldom went inside, and had little to do with any of the house staff. Brian didn't tell him. It was a relief not to have to think about the problems of the house for a while.

"Do you want to finish off the football pitch?" Charlie asked.

Brian did. He got up on the motor-mower and spent an hour and a half cutting the rest of the grass on the pitch. The loud hum of the mower comforted him, as he drove slowly to and fro over the field. The smell of the newly mown grass filled the air, and soothed him. Concentrating on his work, he was able to forget about David and Jason and Dean; he forgot about his father in prison, and Clara in Dublin, and his dead mother. The only thing he was conscious of was the grass, stretching in front of him, the smell of it, the heat of the sun on his back.

"Good man yourself," Charlie said, when the job was finished. "Grand job. Now it's time for tea."

Brian brought the mower back to the garden and put it in the garage. He and Charlie sat on the garden seat and drank tea.

"Tomorrow you'll be weeding again," said Charlie. "The onions, the broccoli, the lettuce beds, all need a good going over."

"OK," said Brian, drinking his hot sweet tea.

"Is Kate Murphy giving you a decent wage?" Charlie asked.

The question surprised Brian, since he assumed Charlie would know this. But he answered, saying that she was. "She's great," he added. "I'd be glad to do it for nothing."

"Crap," said Charlie. "Why should you? It's hard enough work, isn't it? It's not many of the lads up there could take it on."

"Most of them are at school," said Brian, wondering vaguely why he wasn't.

"Yeah. They'd be better off doing an honest day's work if you ask me. I never had any truck with education myself. You must be glad to be finished with it."

"Oh, I'm not finished," Brian corrected him quickly. "I'm just not bothering to go now because it's so close to the holidays. But I'll be going to school in September."

Charlie scratched his head. "You must be younger than you look!" he laughed.

"I've a few more years to go before I finish school."

Something in Charlie's expression made him uneasy. "Why are you looking at me like that?" he asked.

"Oh, it's just that most of them here are given the boot on their sixteenth birthday," said Charlie. "Unless they're for you know where. Then they move behind bars."

Brian felt frightened all of a sudden.

"I'm sixteen at the end of August," he said.

Charlie looked at him and poured him another cup of tea.

"So you reckon I'll get the boot soon?" Brian asked.

Charlie stared at him.

"I'll give you one piece of advice, " he said, "and it's this. Never look for trouble." He paused and stirred his tea with a stick. "Trouble comes looking for you often enough. No need to go out of your way to meet it. Don't paint the devil on the wall, is what my mother used to say!"

"Right!" said Brian.

"If you're more or less sixteen and you're here, there must be a reason. So say nothing. Sit tight and say nothing. No birthday cake! OK?"

"OK," said Brian.

* * *

Brian tackled Kate about the question of his future.

"Charlie keeps telling me how wonderful you are," she said, not quite answering the question. "I suppose you could always stay on as an assistant gardener." She looked worried. "If all else fails, that is."

"What about school?" Brian asked.

"School?" Kate looked genuinely surprised. She didn't often meet boys who were interested in school. Most of them wanted to get out of it as fast as they could.

"Yes," said Brian patiently. "School, examinations, qualifications. That sort of thing. I need some. I haven't got any."

"Right!" Kate scratched her head. "What had you . . . you know . . . sort of hoped to do? Later?"

"When I grow up?" Brian spoke sarcastically.

"Yeah, when you grow up," she repeated.

"I want to be a doctor," he said, letting the sentence float out calmly into the air of Kate's office. It wasn't a sentence that belonged in Summerlands; he knew that as soon as it came out of his mouth. He could almost see it, floating around the untidy room, looking for a place to fit and not finding any.

"Wow!" said Kate, smiling at him. She was impressed.

"So? What are the chances?" Brian asked.

"Oh God, I just don't know," Kate said. "I've never had a boy who wanted to be a doctor. I've never had a boy who wanted to be anything. We don't really . . . we don't really prepare boys for careers. Or even for jobs to be perfectly honest. You know?"

"I think I do," said Brian.

Kate looked at him.

"But that doesn't mean that there can't be a first time. And it doesn't mean that you're not going to be the first one. The first Summerlands graduate. The first Summerlands doctor."

"No," said Brian politely.

"The system doesn't help us," she said, "but I'm used to fighting the system."

"Maybe I could do better by getting out of it," Brian sighed.

"Oh no! Don't leave Summerlands," said Kate. "You help so much. So many of the kids look up to you already."

"Yeah, right, like Jason and Dean" said Brian, bitterly.

"They'll come round," said Kate. "In the end they will. I know. Remember what Mr Chips always said?""

"Salt and vinegar?"

"There's no such thing as a bad boy."

Brian laughed. He was fairly sure that Mr Chips was wrong about that, profound and charitable as the thought was.

17

Holliers

Clara was sitting on a cushion on the floor of Sandy's bedroom. Sandy was reclining on her bed, painting her finger-nails purple, to tone in with her most recent hair-colour: pink. The strains of Sandy's favourite rock band, Mushroom, thumped from the CD player in a regular *boom-boom-boom*, like a tribal drum. Clara used to hate that sort of music, but she was getting to like it now, after a few weeks' acquaintance with Sandy. She swayed in time to the music.

Clara was doing nothing, absolutely nothing. Just sitting in Sandy's room was an activity in itself. The room had so much going on in it that it was almost like another human being – a strange but charming one.

It was not a teenager's room in the usual sense. Apart from the CD player and the stack of CDs, there was nothing in the room that suggested its occupant was a fifteen-year-old schoolgirl. No posters of rock stars on the walls, no girlie magazines on the shelves. Sandy had painted one wall of her room a deep, mysterious magenta colour. The other walls were papered with paper that looked like oriental tapestries. Her bed was draped with dark blue silky-looking cloth – she had bought it for a few Euro in a second-hand shop in town. The bed was littered with silk cushions in various jewel-like colours: ruby and sapphire, garnet and emerald. There were paintings of wonderful, magical landscapes hanging on the walls, in golden frames. Sandy had painted these pictures herself – she was a talented artist. She had bought old cheap pictures in junk shops and at sales of works and had painted the frames gold, and used them for her own extraordinary paintings. Sandy's interest in painting did not stop at frames, or pictures. All the pieces of furniture in her room had been painted by her, in vivid colours. The dressing-table was dark blue, with gold embellishments: it reminded Clara of Madame Bonne's cupboard. Like Madame Bonne, Sandy favoured reds and blues. The bookshelves were crimson. The wardrobe she had painted a clear sky blue. Clara wondered how Sandy could sleep, surrounded by such lively colours, but Sandy said, "At night all cats are grey, me dear!"

Now Sandy looked up from her nails and announced that she had got a job for the summer.

"Where?" Clara was more than interested.

"In Cave, the music shop down at the centre," Sandy said.

The summer holidays had started today, just as she had become accustomed to school, and now three months of holidays stretched ahead of Clara. She was apprehensive. Aunt Mary seemed to be worried too, at the thought of having Clara on her hands, as she put it, all summer. Clara had overheard her and Uncle Jim discussing the problem last night.

"Maybe we could get a home to take her too," Aunt Mary had said.

"I tried them all. There's nowhere available."

"If we turned her out on the streets they'd have to do something about it," said Aunt Mary.

"We'll think about it," said Uncle Jim. "I don't like having her any more than you do, but I can't turn her out on the streets. She is my sister's child."

"I don't like her," said Aunt Mary. "She's just not a nice girl. If she was a nice girl I'd be glad to have her. But she's not, Jim. I hate to say it."

Uncle Jim turned up the volume on the television and Clara had not heard any more.

"Maybe I could get a job too?" Clara now asked Sandy, wistfully. Somehow she knew that this would be the key to the future for her. Money was a commodity she lacked completely. As far as Clara knew, Uncle Jim was either renting Chestnut Cottage or had sold it, but he refused to tell Clara anything about his wheelings and dealings on that score, and he certainly wasn't planning to give the Moody children a penny. And she hadn't heard a single word from her father although she had written to him three times.

"Yeah, why not?" said Sandy. "I'll ask the lad who manages Cave if there's any further vacancies. It'd be cool if we could work together!" She waved her wet nails in the air and began to hum her favourite tune of the moment, 'I wanna be the moon', swaying in time to her own singing.

"Mm," said Clara, not convinced. She liked music, but not all day long, and in Cave there would be no escape. *Drum-drum-drum* from morning till night, at levels which would burst any ordinary eardrum.

"But even if he can't fix you up, there's loads of jobs going in shops and pubs and things. This Celtic Tiger thing is good news for us schoolkids! My mum says when she was a kid it was impossible to get a summer job."

"The Celtic Tiger? What's that?" asked Clara.

"You meanta say you don't know?" Sandy was so amazed she stuck her not-dry nails into her purple hair. It didn't matter since the dye was the same colour as the varnish, but her hair stuck together messily.

She explained the Celtic Tiger to Clara: "It means we've all got lots of jobs and loadsa money, here in Ireland," she said. "Though there's not much sign of it around the Crabclaws, I guess?"

Clara laughed and shook her head. Needless to say, apart from not feeding her, the Crabclaws never gave her a penny in pocket money or even money for school essentials, although they gave Monica twenty Euro every Friday (money which Monica spent on chocolate, coke, and small stashes of hash, which she concealed in the toe of a ballet slipper; Clara had found it one day when she was hunting for a warm jumper.). Clara still had some money left over from the funds she had had in France. But it was dwindling fast. Even though she hadn't bought any clothes or music or books or anything other than sweets and the bare necessities, such as stationery for school, she was down to her last five Euro.

"You're not sixteen, are you?" Sandy asked.

"No, I'm fourteen."

"You're supposed to be sixteen. But some of them will take you on anyway. You probably won't get as well paid though."

"Let's go there now and check it out!" said Clara.

"Your wish is my command!" said Sandy.

Sandy led the way downstairs. Outside of her own room, her house was simple and plain. It was a smaller house than Uncle Jim's. There were two rooms upstairs and one living-room and a kitchen downstairs. But it was much more attractive. The walls were white, and the curtains plain cream muslin. There was not much furniture, but what was there was attractive – pinewood with hessian cushions, ethnic rugs on the floorboards.

"Your mother has such simple taste!" said Clara. "How come yours is so, hum, shall we say, exotic?"

"This house needs a bit of garishness, in my opinion," said Sandy. "It's far too subdued. That's what comes of being a single mother."

"What?"

"My mum is timid and lacks confidence. Hence all the sackcloth and pinewood. She tries to keep a low profile, to atone for her misdemeanours i.e. having me."

"She seems fine to me," Clara said. It was true that Sandy's mother, whose name was Melissa, was a little more subdued than Sandy. For instance, she did not have pink hair, or dress in black leggings with a purple T-shirt. She did not have rings in her nose, eyebrow and cheeks, confining them to her earlobes. Instead she wore blue jeans and white shirts, and her hair was long and fair, tied back in a ponytail. She was much younger than Aunt Mary, or than Clara's own mother had been. Most of her free time was spent correcting copies from school, reading and meeting friends to go to the movies or to the theatre. She seemed like a perfect mother to Clara. But Sandy found fault with her.

"I wish she'd liven up!" she said. "I mean she's great. But she's only thirty-five. She acts more like a less than active eighty-five-year-old, if you ask me, but then who does?"

Her mother was in the little back garden, weeding.

"Bye!" Sandy called.

Her mother was on holidays from school now too, and spending a lot of time in her garden which was full of sweet peas and hollyhocks, garden seats and pergolas, bees and butterflies and everything that a garden should possess. It was a smaller garden than the Crabclaws, but a million times more beautiful.

"Where are you off to?" she asked, looking up from her weeding.

"We're going to the shopping centre. See you in an hour."

"You'll stay to tea, Clara, won't you?" Melissa smiled at Clara.

"I'd love to," said Clara.

"Good! I'm making something really nice," smiled Melissa.

"Be good!" Sandy said. They set off.

In the shopping centre, Sandy dropped into the music shop. But Cave had no vacancies for another temporary assistant. In the gloomy interior, listening to the loud thumping music, Clara felt relieved. She didn't want to go deaf quite yet.

They walked around and noted several shops and restaurants which had a sign stuck in the window asking for staff: a clothes shop, a supermarket, a butcher's, three cafés and two pubs.

"So which will it be?" asked Sandy.

Clara favoured the boutique, "Crystale". She felt she could contribute something useful there – her French chic – and she also hoped that the boutique could contribute something useful to her – money and large supplies of free clothes.

So they went in.

The shop was quite small, and stuffed with racks of clothes.

There was a boutique smell in the air – that delicious scent of cotton and linen and new clothes that is difficult to define, but belongs to all the best boutiques.

At the end of the shop was a counter and behind it a very elegant woman. She had jet-black hair piled up in a chignon, very brown skin, and very dramatic make-up. She wore a white linen suit.

"Can I help you?" she asked, with an ingratiating smile. Her gold earrings jingled as her mouth expanded to form the smile.

"Yes," said Sandy, in her most confident voice, which was as confident as a fog-horn. "My friend here is interested in working in this shop. We noticed the ad in the window."

The smiled vanished much more quickly than it had come, and the woman eyed Clara coldly.

"Have you any experience?" she asked.

"I haven't had a job before," said Clara. She felt guilty about this, as if it were her fault.

"I see!" said the woman, implying that it was a serious flaw in Clara's character. She stared at her for a few seconds, trying to make her feel more uncomfortable, and succeeding. Then she said: "Why do you want to work here?"

Clara could answer this question honestly – or at least she could say why she had thought she wanted to work here, before she met this woman.

"I like clothes a lot," she said, "and I think I have a sense of style."

"She's French," said Sandy, deciding it was time to play her trump card.

The woman seemed to be marginally impressed. Anyway, she smiled a tiny little smile. The ice in her expression melted slightly.

"French?" she said. Her tone suggested that being French was like having an unpleasant contagious disease. "Are you from Paris?"

"No –" started Clara.

But Sandy rushed in to say, "Yes. She lives next door to Christian Dior and . . . Versace."

The lady looked suspiciously at Sandy.

"Versace is dead," she said. "Everyone knows that." She examined her long nails superciliously before adding. "Anyway, he was Italian."

"I meant Coco Chanel, of course," said Sandy.

The woman raised her eyebrows until they almost disappeared into her hair. "What age are you?" she asked Clara. "You look young."

"Fourteen," said Clara. Sandy gave her an exasperated look.

The woman smiled triumphantly.

"I'm afraid we are looking for someone just *slightly* older than that!" she said, with an expression which suggested that fourteen was a disgusting age to be, rather like a contaminating disease.

"She'll be getting older all the time, *slightly* older," said Sandy. "And she has oodles of good taste."

The woman glared at her.

"Not quite enough for this boutique," she said. "Thank you so much for considering us." She paused to give them an icy stare. "And now . . . get lost, kids!"

They left the shop hurriedly. Outside in the sunshine they laughed heartily.

"No. Crystale is not for you!" said Sandy.

"Imagine working with Crystale every day!" Clara giggled and giggled. "I bet she treats her workers very badly!"

"Probably locks them in a cupboard if they don't sell thousands worth of clothes every day!" said Sandy.

"Probably starves them!"

"Probably docks their wages and makes them pay for things they haven't sold!"

They laughed and then began to look around the centre, seeking inspiration.

"I don't think there's any point in going to the pubs," Sandy said. "That leaves the butchers and Café Condor."

"Café Condor," said Clara.

They went into Café Condor.

It was a modern café, decorated in the minimalist style, with chrome tube chairs and shining glass tables. The staff wore black polo necks and jeans and all had very short black hair to match. Lots of people were sitting at tables, having black and white cappuccinos and café lattes. A thin man wearing a silver earring stood in front of a big mirror, behind the counter. Sandy and Clara went up to him.

"I've come to ask about the job you advertised in the window," Clara said.

"Cool!" The man smiled and looked her up and down. "What sort of experience have you, love?"

"Well, I haven't worked before," Clara said, as Sandy kicked her, too late.

The man made a whistling shape with his mouth. "What age are you?"

"Nearly –"

Sandy kicked Clara again.

Clara blushed. "Nearly sixteen."

The man laughed. "Yeah, right!" He poured mineral water into a gleaming glass and handed it to a waitress. "Sorry, love, you have to be sixteen to work here. Nearly won't do it!"

Clara and Sandy left the shop.

"You blew it!" said Sandy. "Again!"

"I can't lie! They'd find out anyway soon enough."

"It's your funeral," said Sandy. She paused. "In other words, The Corner Café."

They looked despairingly at the Corner Café. There was no attempt to look trendy and up-to-date or old-fashioned and cosy or indeed to look like anything at all, in the design of the Corner Café. It was a strictly functional burger and chips joint. What you saw was what you got. What you saw were tables covered with red plastic oilcloth, a high Formica counter, and steel vats full of chips, sausages, fish and burgers. What you got were chips, sausages, fish and burgers. And also a smell of chips, sausages, fish, burgers. And boiling grease.

A large very fat woman, whose hairstyle resembled Madame Bonne's, stood behind the counter. She was dipping raw pink sausages into pale yellow batter. A large steel tray of battered sausages stood at her elbow.

"I came about the job," said Clara, looking at the tray. A fly meandered lazily across the sausages, and was at serious risk of death by drowning in batter.

"Yeah?" The woman did not smile. Actually she looked very tired. She continued to dip sausages as she spoke. "Well, it's still available. Haw. Five hours a night, starting at six and finishing at eleven. Six Euro an hour."

Clara calculated. Thirty Euro a night! One hundred and eighty a week, minimum.

"Well, I'd like to take it," she said. "If that's OK –" With you, she meant to continue, but did not get a chance.

"Fine," said the woman, impatiently. "So when can you start, haw?"

"Tomorrow?" Clara asked.

"Could you start tonight? Haw?" she picked up the tray and dumped all its contents, including the fly, into a vat of boiling oil.

Clara looked at her watch. It was already four thirty. "OK," she said.

"Great!" said the woman. "My name is Maria. I'll see you at six then. What's your name? Haw?"

"Clara," said Clara.

* * *

"It's funny that she didn't ask you your name even till after she gave you the job!" said Sandy, as they walked home.

"She's obviously desperate," said Clara.

"Yeah. She didn't even ask for your second name!" said Sandy.

"Well, I don't know hers either!" said Clara. "Never mind, we can introduce ourselves properly when we meet this evening."

"You'll miss dinner with us," Sandy said.

"Oh God, yeah. I forgot!" said Clara. She felt guilty again, and also disappointed because she would have enjoyed the occasion. "I'll go around and apologise to your mother."

"She won't mind!" said Sandy.

* * *

Melissa didn't mind, but she was worried about the job.

"What will you be actually doing?" she asked.

Clara had forgotten to ask.

"Serving in the café, I suppose, " she said, wishing she had asked this question.

"Dishing up the chips!" said Sandy. "She'll be a chip lady!"

"Mm," mused Melissa, thoughtfully. "And how will you get home so late at night? Will your uncle or aunt collect you?"

"Yes, they will, I'm sure," said Clara, although she was quite sure they would not. "Listen, I'd better go and tell them about it all. Sorry about dinner. I'll report back tomorrow."

"I might drop in on you tonight!" said Sandy. "Make sure you give me an extra big batter sausage!"

* * *

Uncle Jim was not at home when Clara came to break the news of her job. Aunt Mary was in the kitchen, drinking tea and watching a soap opera on TV.

"You've a job? Good," she said,

Clara told her she'd be coming home about eleven thirty.

This did not seem to bother Aunt Mary. "Take a key in case we're in bed," she said. She turned back to the TV.

Clara went upstairs and picked out an outfit which she thought would suit the café – jeans and a checked shirt.

At six o'clock sharp she was back at the high steel counter.

Maria welcomed her.

"Hi Clara, you're back!" She looked surprised but pleased. "Come on in and I'll show you around."

Maria showed her the kitchen, behind the shop. It was a long, narrow family kitchen, green and cream in colour. On the walls were mirrors framed in gold, a large red picture of the Sacred Heart, and four blue and white pictures of the Blessed Virgin. There was a very large TV set in one corner, with two old comfortable chairs in front of it. The chairs were unoccupied. All the human population of the kitchen were gathered at a huge stainless-steel sink with wide draining-boards, peeling potatoes and cutting pieces of fish.

Maria brought Clara over to them.

"Hey, you guys, have some manners, let me introduce you to our new girl, Clara."

Clara was introduced to three people who looked so like Maria that they must be her children. They were Josia, Mario and Freddo. Like Maria, they were fat, with smooth almond skin and big brown eyes. Like Maria's, their eyes looked glazed with boredom. They had clearly spent too much time staring at raw potatoes.

"Hello," they said, in bored voices, and went back to peeling.

"Don't you mind them, they've got no manners," said Maria. "They're all great fun when you get to know them, haw."

Clara smiled weakly.

Maria led her to a door in the side of the kitchen, and opened it. Clara followed her into a small room, about six feet long and wide. It was almost filled by a huge green machine.

"This is where you'll be working," said Maria.

Clara gasped. The room was like the inside of a concrete block. There were no windows and hardly space to move.

"Doing what?" asked Clara.

Maria was taken aback.

"Haw? Washing up, of course," she said, as if this were the only possible occupation in the world. "Have you ever used a machine like this before?"

Clara had not. Maria gave her a demonstration: load the dishes into a tray at one side, push them into the middle of the machine, pull them out at the other side.

"It's easy," Maria said. "It'll be no trouble to you, haw! The dirty dishes will be pushed in here, through this hatch, on trays. And all you have to do is, haw, scrape them, bung them through the machine, and pack them up over here, for the girls to take out again. Understand?"

"Yes," said Clara.

There was a heap of dirty dishes pushed through the hatch, so she began to work.

Scrape, load, push, pull, stack. Scrape, load, push, pull, stack. Scrape, load, push, pull, stack.

The machine made a very loud noise, much louder than Sandy's CDs. It roared like a monster in pain. Also, it was very heavy. Lifting the lid to push through the trays of crockery gave Clara a pain in her muscles.

At eleven o'clock, the last load of dishes had been cleaned.

Clara wiped the sweat from her brow – there was plenty of sweat left everywhere else, she was dripping in sweat – and made her way through the kitchen and into the café.

Maria and a few of her children were sitting at the tables, eating huge plates of chips and drinking coke.

"Have a bite!" said Maria. "You must be hungry, haw."

Clara joined them for chips and coke. Maria and her family ate heartily, and spoke Italian so that Clara could not understand what they were saying. From the tone of voice, she guessed they were complaining about something or other.

"They're tired, want tomorrow night off, haw. Can't have it," said Maria. "Saturday's our busiest night. They know that."

Clara didn't get involved in the dispute, and wondered how she would cope with Saturday night if it was even busier than tonight. Never had she encountered so many greasy plates, ketchup-stained dishes, and coke glasses, in her life.

As soon as she had eaten her chips she got up and said she'd go.

"Mario will drive you home," said Maria.

Mario, the fat son, looked up, surprised.

"It's not necessary," said Clara.

"Of course he will, haw. You can't haw walk home so late on your own."

Mario stood up lazily and pulled his keys out of his pockets.

"Na, na. I'll take you home," he said, smiling slowly. "Come on now!"

Clara followed him through the long, hot kitchen and out to his car, which was parked at the back of the house on a dark laneway.

* * *

Sunday lunch. Roast beef, roast potatoes, mashed potatoes, boiled cabbage. Aunt Mary had worked hard all morning. Uncle Jim was lashing into the beef. He ate about ten slices, and his face became redder and redder. Clara was nibbling at her thin slice. Monica was refusing to eat cabbage.

"Ah, go on! Please eat it, it's full of vitamins," said Aunt Mary. Monica never ate any vegetables at all, and the cabbage was particularly horrible, but Aunt Mary never lost hope that at some meal her campaign to make Monica eat veggies was finally going to meet with success.

"It tastes like shit," said Monica.

Clara agreed. At least, it tasted watery and rank, like a

weed that grows in a pond, a rather slimy and probably poisonous weed. She nibbled at her cabbage.

"Of course Clara gets fed at the chipper now – she won't want to eat with us any more, probably," said Aunt Mary. She started to nod at Uncle Jim, who was on his seventh slice of beef. He didn't respond.

She kicked him.

"What?" he asked.

"Remember what we said last night?" she said, in an encouraging voice.

"Oh that," he said. He looked at Clara. Then he looked at Mary. "Some other time. Not now, Mary, not at lunch."

Aunt Mary looked aggrieved, and Clara was worried. What bombshell would they drop next?

18

Big Ears

Brian was in the bathroom at Summerlands, examining his ears.

They were sticking out again. For weeks they had been unobtrusive, but now they had flared up. He pressed them to his head and made a resolution to let his hair grow. He hated long hair, but the time had come to make a decision, and long hair was the lesser of two evils. Madeline, the girl with the long fair hair who did the washing-up, had looked critically at his ears for five minutes at least yesterday evening. Brian could read her mind. She was obviously thinking, "I would never, never have anything to do with a boy whose ears stuck out like that, no matter how attractive he was in all other ways." After Madeline had stopped staring at him, she had smiled a strange little half-smile and said, "Mm. Daydreaming again!" But Brian knew better. She had been assessing him and finding him deficient in the ear department.

He looked at his ears again and then consulted a tiny

notebook which he carried in the breast pocket of his denim shirt.

"Hm." He added a few words to a poem he had been writing for the past few days. The poem was about a girl with fair hair who washed up in a hotel kitchen. It was a fictional poem, of course, not based on anyone he knew. He was not sure as yet how it would end, but thought a young man, with black hair to contrast with her fair locks, would probably rescue her from the noisy hot kitchen and bring her to a cool and pleasant garden full of flowers and fruit, where they would be blissfully happy together. For a while. Many of Brian's poems employed the phrase "for a while". He was all too aware of the transience of human joy.

The door to the cloakroom creaked and Niall the Silent came in. Brian snapped his notebook shut and stuck it in his pocket. He left the bathroom, nodding to Niall as he went past. He would bring some supper up to David, who had a slight cold and was taking it easy, in bed. Then he would continue to work on his poem, in peace and quiet.

His mind fingering possible rhymes – carrot/parrot, carrot/dry rot, were some that occurred to him – Brian hummed under his breath as he went down the hallway, into the kitchen, where the beautiful Madeline was doling out the usual evening fare, of chips with something else. He plucked up courage and actually said "Hi" to her, to which she replied "Hi". She did not look critically at his ears, or look at him at all, since she was busily shaking oil off a pan of chips. Her "hi" sounded quite warm, Brian felt, and he followed his up with a "Nice day", to which she responded, "Yeah, hope it keeps up for the weekend". This was one of the longest sentences she had ever addressed directly, or directly if you ignored the fact that she was staring at a pan of chips while she said it, to him. Brian's heart leaped so high he was surprised it did not jump through the top of his skull and hit the ceiling. Trying to suppress his elation, he collected David's grease-sodden ration, arranged it on a tin tray.

He was humming as he decked the tray and Madeline laughed at him and said, "Somebody's in good form!" which was the sort of thing she tended to say to everyone. Cheerful but not easy to respond too. Also somewhat embarrassing. Brian continued to hum, wishing he could think of something clever to say, but he could not. This annoyed him a little, but not much. He was still humming as he left the kitchen and mounted the three steps which linked it to the hall.

Then he suddenly stopped humming.

Jason and Dean were standing at the foot of the staircase.

Most of the boys were in the dining-room, tucking into chips and eggs, but Jason and Dean considered it worth the sacrifice of first go at the food to have a go at annoying Brian.

"Froggie, froggie, froggie!" they called as he walked up the hall. Jason put out his foot, to trip him up. Dean stood on the bottom step of the stairs, blocking his way.

Brian saw them as two big rocks blocking his passage. He didn't feel angry, or even annoyed, but just wholly frustrated. He knew how difficult it was going to be to shift them out of his way.

He managed to avoid obstacle number one, the big foot of Jason. This had the effect of annoying Jason, which was, of course, a dangerous thing to do.

"You effing frog," said Jason. His vocabulary was very limited. In a way this was an advantage for Brian. There was no danger of not understanding what Jason was saying. He only used about four hundred words in total.

"Good evening," said Brian, realising that this was not a greeting likely to endear him to Jason. "Did you have a good day?"

"Effing magnificent," said Jason, laughing. "Thank you very much. Did you have a good day, froggie-woggie?"

"Very pleasant thanks," said Brian, beginning to realise that what he had to do was play for time. Eventually someone would come out of the dining-room – Kate, or one of the other members of staff.

"And how about froggie junior?"

Jason and Dean laughed, remembering David and the frogs.

"He's fine too, thank you. The doctor visited him as you may have been told. But he has recovered fully from the events of last week."

"He has recovered fully from the events of last week!" said Jason.

"He has recovered fully from the events of last week," said Dean, not as competently as Jason.

"Well, that makes me real happy," said Jason. "Send him my regards."

"I will be glad to," said Brian. "Now if you could move out of my way, I'll bring his supper up to him."

Jason laughed and Dean laughed. He did not move out of the way. Brian glanced over his shoulder. The hall was empty.

"Maybe you didn't hear me, Dean. Could you move out of my way?"

Jason nodded to Dean. Dean lifted his foot and kicked the tray out of Brian's hands. Plates, cups, teapot, cutlery, scattered and fell to the floor, with a crash. A puddle of tea and milk appeared on the floor and spread to the edges of the hall like a big inkblot. Chips and beans decorated the puddle, and were scattered all over the floor. One fried egg landed on the floor and another sat neatly on the hall table, like a strange place mat.

The sight of the scattered dinners silenced all three boys for a second. Then Jason started to laugh, a loud, false laugh that didn't sound faintly amused. Dean felt obliged to join in. His laugh rang even more hollow than Jason's.

The noise brought Kate from her office, Madeline from the kitchen, and all the boys from the dining-room, running to the hall.

As soon as people saw the personalities involved, they understood immediately what had happened.

Niall and another boy, John, went to the kitchen and got a brush and dustpan and plastic bag. They cleaned up the mess without being asked to do so.

Kate patted Brian on the shoulder. "Get some more food," she said. "I'll go up as soon as I can." She beckoned Jason and Dean into her office. John kicked Jason as he passed, when Kate wasn't looking, and Jason gave him a filthy look.

Some of the boys laughed, but most of them shook their heads and went back to the dining-room.

* * *

"I've had a long talk with them," Kate said to Brian.

He was in her office now. David had had his tea. Luckily, he hadn't heard the commotion in the hall and was oblivious to the difficulties Brian had encountered on his way upstairs with the tray.

"It seems there's nothing to be done," said Brian.

Kate grimaced and bit her biro. "There is a solution, for us." She frowned.

"What's that?" Brian spoke in a flat, discouraged voice.

"I can get them transferred to another home – a place with higher security."

Brian thought this sounded like an excellent idea. At this point, he felt the best place for Jason and Dean would be Siberia, or Alcatraz.

"I hate to do it. They'd be in a sort of prison situation, with a lot of older men."

Brian said nothing.

"It would mean peace for Summerlands," said Kate. "But for Jason and Dean it would be the end of the road."

"In what sense?" asked Brian, not very interested in their fates.

"If they go to a place like that, they'll never be normal. They'll stay there for a while and emerge as criminals."

Again Brian was silent. It was clear to him that Jason and Dean were going to emerge as criminals no matter where they spent the next few years. In their own small way they were criminals already, if "criminal" meant behaving in ways which hurt other people and endangered their health and safety.

"So you can understand my dilemma!" said Kate. She smiled. "Or maybe you can't?"

"I can," said Brian, smiling too. "Oh well, I suppose as long as they just put frogs in cupboards and turn over plates of chips we're safe."

"This is it!" said Kate, plainly relieved. "They've never actually . . . you know . . . done anything really really terrible."

What was she waiting for, Brian wondered. A murder? Or just serious bodily harm?

He had no doubt that at some stage Jason and Dean, or Jason On His Own, or Dean On His Own, would do something "really terrible". He only hoped that he or David would not be the victims, the catalyst which finally freed Summerlands of its nastiest residents.

"Tomorrow is Friday!" said Kate. "You get paid for your work in the garden and I suggest you bring David out for a treat somewhere. There's a good movie on in town."

"Sounds like a nice idea!" said Brian.

"If it grabs David, I'll drive you in on my way home and there's a bus you can catch when the film's over. It'll take David's mind off things. He should go back to school on Monday."

Primary school, to which David went, did not break up for another week. After that, he would be in the home all day long – at the mercy of Jason and Dean full-time.

19

Battered Sausages

Aunt Mary wanted Clara's money.

"How much do you earn at the Corner Café?" she asked, with a smile.

Clara thought quickly. Aunt Mary might have been motivated by interest or curiosity, but Clara knew her well enough by now to be suspicious.

"Eighty Euro a week," she said.

She had been right to suspect that Aunt Mary had unpleasant reasons for making inquiries. "I think you should contribute seventy-five Euro to me for your keep," she said. Clara gave herself a mental pat on the back for having had the foresight to prevent her taking everything. "I'll allow you to keep five for yourself, for pocket money and bus fares," she added, brightly.

How very generous, thought Clara. She agreed to this arrangement, however, and from then on the behaviour of her aunt and uncle changed for the better. Uncle Jim nodded to her when he met her in the house. Aunt Mary allowed her two cups of tea for breakfast, and an extra slice of bread at lunch-time. She offered to go into town one afternoon with Clara, and Monica, to look at some summer clothes. They went in on the bus. Monica bought several lovely outfits – shorts and cotton capri pants and T-shirts. Clara bought one pair of capri pants and a T-shirt, the pants white and the shirt pink. She had to use the very last of her money for them, but she wasn't worried, because soon she would be rich.

Clara missed dinner every evening, because she had to go to her job at the Corner Café, but breakfast and lunch were pleasant, relatively. Aunt Mary made quite tasty sandwiches for lunch and brought them out to the garden. She had cheered up so much that she actually did some gardening work. The flowerbeds were no longer choked with bindweed and dandelions, and a few roses which had survived decades of neglect bloomed among the rubbish like stars on a cloudy winter night.

Uncle Jim said hello to Clara twice, and once went as far as to ask her how she was.

She considered asking him to take her down to see Brian and David, but thought she would wait just a little longer, until they had melted even more. Soon, her aunt and uncle would be like normal human beings.

Clara went to see the swans as often as she could, and played with them on the shores of the lake. They were happy together for a while. But the brothers said that they were often cold and weary, and that they longed to be real boys again. "Is there any way to break the spell?" Clara

asked. "There is one way," her oldest brother said. He explained that if Clara gathered nettles from the graveyard, and wove the nettles into white cloth, and made six shirts, one for each brother, and put them on the swans, they would become human once again.

"How could I do that?" Clara asked.

"It is impossible," said the brother. "We will remain swans forever, cold and weary, living by the lake."

When Clara went home she thought about it. And she decided to find out how to spin cloth from nettles.

Towards the end of her first week at the Corner Café, Clara was drinking coke with Sandy and her mother, in their lovely garden. They sat on the little paved terrace surrounded by pots of petunias and geraniums, roses and shasta daisies.

"You seem to be in good form?" Melissa, Sandy's mother, commented. Clara was looking relaxed in her new pants and T-shirt.

"Yeah!" said Clara. "It's going fine." She was often tired, but she felt happier than she had for a long time.

Every evening she spent in the tiny scullery, scraping dirty dishes into a plastic bin, loading and unloading the huge dishwasher. She dreamt about the dishwasher when she fell asleep – her dreams were full of its loud clanking noises, and the rattle of cups and saucers.

"Will you have a holiday at all?" Melissa asked.

This hadn't crossed Clara's mind.

"I don't know," she said. "I haven't heard that my aunt and uncle are planning anything."

She couldn't imagine them going on holiday anywhere. And she certainly couldn't imagine them taking her.

"We're going camping in August," Sandy said. "We wondered if you'd like to come with us?"

This was totally unexpected. Clara looked from Sandy to her mother and back again, speechless.

Finally she said, "I'd love to. But I'll have to ask them at home."

Maybe she could, she thought. She'd have enough money to cover her expenses. By August, she'd have enough saved to cover all her school expenses for next year anyway.

"We're bringing the car and an extra person doesn't even cost anything, not for the travel, nor for the tent when we get there," said Melissa, reading Clara's mind.

"We're going to France," said Sandy then.

Clara's heart thumped and she felt her stomach going floppy.

"Near Bordeaux," said Melissa. "Not where you come from."

"But not all that far away," said Clara, trying to make her voice sound normal. She hadn't told Sandy about her father yet. She'd have to, if she went to France with her. Maybe if they found out that her father was a convicted criminal, they'd feel differently about having her as a travelling companion. They might feel differently about having anything to do with her.

"It'll be warm and beautiful," said Melissa. "Sea and sand and sun, I can't wait!"

"I didn't want to go at all," said Sandy. "But if you come, hey, it'll be bearable!"

* * *

Clara took the bull by the horns. That afternoon, she asked

her aunt if she could go on holiday with Sandy and her mother.

Aunt Mary was sitting in her garden at the time, on a plastic chair, surrounded by long grass and dandelions.

"Holiday?" she repeated the word, as if it were a sour slice of lemon that she had to spit out. "That sounds fine, but what about your job in the café?"

Clara explained carefully that the holiday would be more or less free.

Aunt Mary smiled coldly. "Well, there is just one snag about that argument, dearest. As we have agreed, you have to give the money to us, to cover your expenses here," she said.

"So I can't have a holiday at Sandy's mother's expense?" Clara said.

"Of course not," said her Aunt Mary. "And I do not like that tone of voice, Clara."

Clara tried to speak calmly. "I need to talk to you about money," she said. "I was hoping to save up money for when I go back to school."

Aunt Mary smiled glassily.

"I don't think you're going to feel like going back to school, dear, now that you've tasted independence. I'm sure the Corner Café would be very disappointed to lose you. Of course, you may be able to manage to go to school and to work there, but personally I feel the strain would be too much."

"You can't mean that I will never go back to school?" Clara asked, in astonishment.

"That's exactly what I mean," said Aunt Mary. "Naturally I am all in favour of education, even for girls, but I think you'll agree it's a luxury you can't afford, my dear. Beggars can't be choosers, can they?"

Clara did not reply.

"Anyway," added Aunt Mary, with her brightest most cheery smile. "You seem to be very happy there, in the Corner Café, with all those nice fat Italian people."

* * *

Next evening, Clara got paid. She got two hundred Euro – she had worked longer than planned. She put one hundred and twenty in a cup, which she hid behind the dishwasher, and took eighty home with her. Aunt Mary and Uncle Jim were waiting when she got in, although usually they were fast asleep.

"Hello, dear," said Aunt Mary, as she let Clara into the hall. "Pay day!"

Clara nodded and handed her the envelope containing the money. Aunt Mary snatched it, opened the envelope, and counted the notes rapidly. Then she gave Clara a brilliant smile and went back to the sitting-room.

* * *

"I won't be able to go on holidays with you," Clara said to Sandy. It was a sunny day again and they were lying on the patio, working on their tans.

"Crap!" Sandy said. "Why not?"

"They don't want me to," Clara said.

"But why not? I don't understand?" Sandy was almost in tears. Her hair was still pink, and she wore a tiny black bikini top and pink shorts. Her tearful angry face did not match the outfit.

"I . . . don't really know," Clara sat up. She suddenly hadn't the energy to say any more. It was too complicated. She looked around at the lovely little garden, with its pots of trailing flowers, its pergola, its bird table. Sandy had no idea of the sort of life she led.

"Are they going somewhere, is that it?" Sandy asked.

"No."

"Then why won't they let you come with us? You need a holiday!"

Clara made a great effort and collected her thoughts.

"There are lots of things you don't know about me," she said to Sandy. And she explained them all. About her father. About her brothers. About the attitude of Uncle Jim and Aunt Mary.

Sandy was stunned. "God! You poor thing!" she said. "You really do need a holiday."

"Yeah," said Clara, "but I don't know how I'd feel about going back to France anyway. And what I'd really like to do is see my brothers."

"Can't you even do that?" Sandy was puzzled.

"They've never brought me down there," said Clara.

"Who needs them? My mum could drive you," Sandy said.

"No!" said Clara. "Don't tell your mum. Not for a while."

"OK," said Sandy. "But even if she doesn't give you a lift, you could go yourself on the bus. You've got some money."

"I'd have to make up something to get away."

"You'll have to make up a lot of stories just to survive with that aunt and uncle of yours. Tell them you're with me. I'll go with you if you like."

* * *

It was Sunday. Clara and Sandy were getting off the bus in the village near Summerlands. Brian, looking brown and healthy, and David, shivery and worried, were at the bus-stop in the main street, under a sycamore tree, waiting. It was a sunny day and sunlight fell through the leaves, dappling the boy's pale coffee-coloured skin. Brian was looking anxiously at the bus. David was scraping at the sand under his seat, with a twig, drawing.

Clara saw them first. She tumbled out of the bus and flung herself at Brian. "Oh Brian! It's good to see you!" She picked up David and swung him around, which wasn't easy. "David! You're fine. You're here. You're OK!"

David laughed and laughed, delighted to see her.

"Sandy!" said Clara. "This is Sandy."

They stood, laughing and unable to think of anything to say, for several minutes.

Then: "We brought some stuff for a picnic," Clara said.

Brian knew where to go. There was a stream running along the boundary of the Summerlands grounds. They sat on its bank, in the sunshine, listening to the babble of the water.

"It's like home!" Clara said. Brian smiled, but David frowned.

"No, it's not," he said, grumpily. "It's not a bit like home. The rivers at home are bigger and faster and they come down a mountain."

"Well, never mind, it's lovely here too!" said Clara. "Have some crisps!"

David was happy to eat, but he didn't want to talk or to play.

"He's changed," Clara said to Brian. "What's happened to him?"

"Nothing," Brian did not want to spoil the afternoon, and worry Clara. "Nothing that you don't know about."

He told her the home was nice and they had no problems. He told her about his work in the garden, about David's school, about the football pitch, about Kate. But not about Jason and Dean, the frogs, the bullying.

Clara would have liked to visit Summerlands but that wasn't possible. Nobody there knew she was meeting Brian and David. The boys had told Kate they were going for a long hike and had been allowed, since she trusted Brian so much.

Brian asked Clara if she had been in touch with their father. She told him she had written several times but hadn't got a reply.

"I wrote to him once," said Brian. "But I haven't heard anything either. What a wanker!"

Clara felt depressed, thinking about it.

"There's some natural reason," she said, although she couldn't think of one.

"Yeah like he couldn't be bothered," said Brian.

"When will you come again?" David cried when Clara was leaving.

"Soon," she said. "In two weeks, maybe."

"Two weeks!" David sobbed. "Come next week, come next week!"

Brian shook his head at Clara. He couldn't make all the necessary arrangements again so soon.

"I can't," said Clara, "but I'll come in two weeks' time. I'll telephone and let you know in advance."

She got on the bus. David pulled at her clothes and tried to keep her with him. She saw him screaming and sobbing as the bus pulled out of the village green.

"Don't worry." Sandy was distraught by David's sadness,

but tried not to show it. "He'll be fine in a few minutes. Children are like that."

"Yes," said Clara.

"It was great to see them, wasn't it?"

Clara agreed wholeheartedly. But she could not get the sound of David's crying out of her ears. It stayed with her for days.

* * *

She continued to work in the café. The work got easier as time went on. To her surprise, she even found that she was enjoying it – she got some satisfaction from getting the dishes washed as efficiently and quickly as possible, and she tidied up the stillroom, so that it looked much neater than it had when she'd arrived, if not more beautiful. Nothing could make it attractive. By her fourth week, Clara had cut the time it took to wash the dishes in half.

Mario drove her home after work every night. He insisted on this, although Clara protested that she could easily walk. "Na, na!" he said, wagging his finger at her. "Just hop in the car. It's no hassle!" He didn't speak much at first, and neither did Clara, since she was usually too tired to talk at that time of evening. But as time wore on they began to feel comfortable together. Clara noticed that Mario, when he smiled in a certain way, looked a bit like Elvis Presley, of whom there were posters on the wall of the Corner Café. She stopped thinking of him as fat. He was really just well-filled out, she thought – which, considering that he lived on a staple diet of chips and batter burgers, was not surprising.

Aunt Mary collected her money every Friday. She and Uncle Jim no longer went out of their way to be friendly to

Clara, but they were usually polite. Getting the money put them in good humour. Clara could foresee that they would pressurise her to go on working, when school began again. For the moment, she did not want to worry about how she would deal with that. She had no intention of giving up school. If she was ever to fulfil her ambition of being an airline pilot, she would have to do very well in her exams. It didn't seem likely to Clara that she would manage to become a pilot now, but she hadn't given up hope entirely.

Clara gave whatever money was left over to Sandy, who kept it in a special box, covered with gold silk, in her room. When Clara needed some, she dipped in, but most of the money she kept, stored up for next term or for a rainy day.

It was the end of July, a wet Wednesday. Sandy was packing for her holiday – on Friday she and Melissa would go to France. Clara helped her select clothes.

"It'll be hot. You won't need much," Clara said, watching helplessly as Sandy stuffed a huge case full of all sorts of clothes.

"I have to be prepared for every contingency," Sandy said. "Who knows who I'll bump into? I could meet the love of my life over there, and I don't want to find I'm short of suitable gear when that happens."

"I wish I could go," Clara said wistfully, looking at the bright T-shirts and sundresses.

"Yeah, it's a bummer," said Sandy. "You couldn't just come without telling them?"

Clara shook her head.

"It wouldn't work," she said, thinking that the problem was she would have to come back again. It was hard to imagine how her aunt and uncle could behave worse than they already had. But they would find a way. Perhaps they would just refuse to take her back at all? Then . . . Sandy was a good friend, but Clara knew she could not move in and live with her. If her aunt and uncle threw her out, she'd be on the streets. Every time she went into Dublin she saw young people like herself sleeping in doorways, wrapped up in sleeping bags or blankets. They were children who had left home or been thrown out. There was nowhere for them to go in Ireland, apparently. If their families didn't take care of them they were left to their own devices, out in all weathers, sleeping rough. Clara did not want that.

"I'm going to see my brothers on Sunday!" she said. " I talked to Brian yesterday."

"I hope it's better weather than this!" Sandy looked out at the grey garden, The rain dripped down, like tears, against the windowpane.

"It will be," said Clara.

* * *

It wasn't, though. Grey rain poured into the village. Puddles everywhere, cold damp seeping into your skin.

"Where will we go? No picnics today," said Brian.

"The pictures," said David. He wore his anorak, but it was soaked, soaked.

"I don't know . . ." Clara wanted to talk.

"He's right," said Brian.

They sat in the fleapit, watching a bad movie. David ate popcorn and pastilles and drank coke. Clara was bored, frustrated.

Time to go as soon as the picture was over – the boys two drowned rats at the bus-stop, her own hair dripping wet, her coat stuck to her back. David crying.

"Two weeks!" she said. "Two weeks!"

The trip back to Dublin like an underwater drive – leaves like fishes swimming against the windows of the bus, blown off unseasonably, a deluge.

Rain filled her head, filled her heart.

Sandy in France. Driving now along the side white roads. Driving past the woods and the villages down to the south, where the sun shone, the vines groaned under the weight of grapes, the mountain rivers giggled, the swallows darted in and out of the casements.

David unhappy in Summerlands; Brian pretending all was well. Anyone could see David was miserable. Maybe Brian was miserable too?

* * *

When Sandy and Melissa left for France, Clara spent more time than before looking at the troubadour's book, and writing in it.

In the middle of the night, Clara went to the graveyard and gathered a sheaf of nettles. They stung her hands, but she took a large bunch back to her room in the castle. And the next day she began to spin. She was able to make a fine white thread from the nettles. And from then on, every night she went to the graveyard, and every day she span. After many many weeks, she had amassed a large supply for white thread. Only one more visit to the yard and there would be enough to knit six shirts.

She visited the graveyard for the last time. It was dark and eerie, but she had long ago ceased to be frightened. She gathered the nettles, which hardly stung her any more, so

accustomed to them had she become. But as she stepped out of the graveyard with her sheaf under her arm, strong lights suddenly appeared all around her. She was surrounded by soldiers bearing torches.

"You are under arrest!" their leader said. "We have followed you every night for the past week. We know you are a witch!"

20

In the Currant Bushes

Brian was worried about David, but he was not miserable on his own account. He liked gardening more and more with every day that passed. August, and they were harvesting the first new potatoes, carrots and parsnips. The vegetable beds were burgeoning, and needed to be thinned out regularly. The flower garden was in its greatest glory.

He loved to spend a few hours in the flower garden, weeding and spraying, dead-heading roses and tying up delphiniums, first thing in the morning. Then it was good to sit with Charlie on the bench and have coffee and biscuits. Charlie and he did not talk much, and usually their conversation was about the garden – Charlie liked to pass on all his knowledge of plants to Brian. He had seldom had such a receptive pupil. It surprised Charlie, how much he had to impart. He was a greater expert on gardens than even he had imagined.

He liked to quiz Brian occasionally.

"Rhododendrons grow at that side of the field," he said, "but not over here. Now why is that?"

Brian knew the answer. The soil nearest the sea was lime-rich, and rhododendrons could not grow in that. But, curiously enough, at this side of the field it was already more neutral; it was peaty, and they grew quite well there.

"What other plants like to grow in peaty soil?" he asked.

"Azaleas," said Brian. "Blue hydrangeas."

"Anything else?" Charlie looked at him with a laugh in his eye.

Brian didn't know of anything else.

"Heather, of course," said Charlie. "We don't have any heather here, but naturally heather likes a peaty soil. Erica. That's why you call the sort of compost you'd use for azaleas and the like ericacious."

He was always pleased when he found a gap in Brian's knowledge, although since he rushed to fill it, there were fewer and fewer of these.

* * *

David was still frightened of Jason and Dean. Since the episode of the tray, they had not attacked him or Brian overtly: they had been warned by Kate that if they did so again, their days at Summerlands could be numbered. But they were always cold and unfriendly, and lost no opportunity to annoy David in small ways. If they could, they sat beside him at mealtimes, and made sure they took the lion's share of the food. They jogged David's elbow so that he spilled his tea or milk. If they could find nothing worse to do, they liked to stare at him, both of them, for hours on end, in order to make him feel very uncomfortable.

"I hate them," David said. "I want to kill them."

"Don't!" said Brian. He tried to be kind to David, and to

understand him. "They're not going to risk doing anything dreadful again. Kate has given them a warning. I know it's horrible, the staring and all that. But it's just staring. Try not to pay any attention."

"I hate it when they stare," David said stubbornly. "I feel their eyes on me all the time, even when they're not around. I feel their eyes on me now."

"Well, their eyes are not on you now," said Brian. "So try hard to imagine that they're not. Try to imagine that Jason and Dean are far away from here."

"Where?"

"Anywhere," said Brian.

David shut his eyes.

"Jason and Dean are in Brazil," he said. "They're in the jungle. They're paddling down the Amazon river in a canoe. All around are monkeys and parrots and sloths and other animals, growling and screaming. They come to a waterfall and suddenly they're over the edge. They're falling hundreds of feet into the river and it's about forty feet deep at that point. Piranhas shoal up in their thousands and are eating them. 'Stop!' says Jason. 'Aaagh!' says Dean. But the piranhas go right on eating them, bit by bit. They're on Dean's nose now, and have just chewed up Jason's toes. Tastes pretty horrible, but these piranhas are hungry."

Brian looked at his brother strangely. It surprised him that he could imagine such a nasty story. But he really hated Jason and Dean, as he said.

* * *

The next time David encountered Dean and Jason was in the television room next morning. Brian was in the kitchen helping Madeline tidy up after breakfast, before going out to the garden – lately he was spending more and more time in the kitchen, getting to know Madeline. But David had a lot of free time, since he was on holiday from school. He was watching reruns of *The Simpsons* alone in the room when Jason and Dean came in.

Jason immediately turned off the television.

Then he stood at the door, and stared at David.

Stare, stare, stare.

David couldn't leave the room.

He turned the television back on. But Dean turned it off and stood in front of the set, blocking it and staring at David.

David wondered if he should shout for help. But with the door closed it was doubtful if he would be heard.

He thought about the piranha fish, which cheered him up.

Then he had an idea.

He began to stare at Jason.

Stare, stare, stare, stare.

Jason stared back.

They stared at each other.

"What the . . . ?" said Dean, annoyed that he was being left out of this.

Jason indicated with his hand that Dean should stay quiet.

Stare, stare, stare, stare.

It went on for ten minutes.

It went on for twenty minutes.

Finally, Jason's staring ability faltered.

He stopped staring and blinked.

Defeat.

Defeating people like Jason can be very dangerous. He didn't like being beaten by one of his victims.

He'd played by the rules during the staring match. But that was a temporary lapse. In ordinary life he didn't obey any rules at all, except one: do exactly what you feel like doing no matter what the consequences for yourself or anyone else. Now he was furious, literally hopping mad. He lunged at David.

David leaped out of his way and dashed out of the room. He ran out of the house. Jason and Dean chased him. David's idea was that he should find Brian, and Charlie, and seek their protection. He ran across the back lawn. Somebody was moving down among the currant bushes and he guessed it would be Brian.

He made his way down there. Dean and Jason had not given up the chase.

David was in the currant bushes. There was no sign of Brian. One of the cats, Stardust, was among the bushes, hunting for birds who came to eat the currants. That's what David had seen, not his brother.

The currant bushes were in a corner of the garden.

David could not escape.

He started to scream.

But Jason and Dean were on top of him, gagging his mouth. They beat and kicked him till he collapsed among the bushes. Then they ran away.

* * *

Brian had left the kitchen at about ten, and was busy in the garden from then until lunchtime. He staked all the hollyhocks, which had begun to flower and were in danger of toppling over if a shower of rain came. Charlie had about fifty of these flowers in the herbaceous border, and the staking took some time. When he had finished, Madeline from the kitchen came and asked him to pick some tomatoes in the greenhouse. Brian took a basin and began to select the reddest, ripest tomatoes. The greenhouse was hot and humid, and the musty smell of tomatoes gave it an intoxicating, dreamy feeling. Brian felt drowsy and he was tired anyway, so he worked slowly, pulling back the vines, searching for the tomatoes which were ripe among the greenish and orange coloured ones. By the time he had filled the basin, it was almost half past one, half an hour after lunch started.

He put the big basin of ripe red tomatoes in the kitchen – Madeline was going to make soup with them, for dinner. She could make the most delicious tomato soup, a mixture of fresh tomatoes, pepper and salt, and cream. When Brian went into the dining-room, some places had already been vacated. Jason and Dean were nowhere to be seen, and neither was David. Brian assumed that David had gone back upstairs. He was hungry, so he ate his lunch as quickly as he could, before going upstairs to investigate.

The bedroom was empty, the beds made and unruffled, everything in its place as it had been when he had left the room that morning. It was clear that David had not been there at all today. Brian banged the door and ran downstairs. The television room was also empty, dusty and filled with the hot, lazy-looking sun of afternoon. Brian dashed to the games room. A few boys were playing table tennis.

"Have you seen David?" Brian asked.

"No," one of them answered. The other added. "He wasn't at lunch."

Brian ran to the kitchen. Madeline was there, packing the dishwasher. She hadn't noticed that David was missing.

"He's nowhere in the house," Brian said.

Madeline looked anxious, but shrugged. "He's probably out in the garden somewhere."

Brian's heart plummeted into his shoes. Jason and Dean are also missing, he thought. He knew there was a connection. Why had he been so careless?

"Did Jason and Dean come in to lunch?"

Madeline stopped loading the dishwasher and thought for a minute.

"No, they didn't," she said.

"Tell Kate that David is missing!" said Brian angrily, running out of the kitchen and into the garden.

He ran down to the vegetable garden. Charlie was sitting on the bench, smoking a cigarette. "What's up?" he asked.

Brian could hardly be coherent. But he explained that David had gone missing and that he suspected Jason and Dean of having something to do with it.

Charlie made him sit down.

Brian was in tears. He was shaking with angry sobs. "They've done something to him. I knew they would."

Charlie stubbed out his cigarette and put his arm around Brian's shoulder. He let him sob. "He'll be all right," he said. "He'll be all right. Don't you worry."

"I should have kept an eye on him. I forgot about him. I was so busy doing the bloody hollyhocks."

"You can't keep an eye on him all the time," said Charlie. "You just can't do that."

Brian's sobs began to subside.

"When did you last see him?" Charlie asked.

"This morning, before I came out here."

At that moment, Kate came rushing into the garden.

21

Mario the Helper

Clara was in the Corner Café. It was seven o'clock in the evening and she was sitting in the front of the café, having her tea with Mario. The sun was still shining brightly on the square outside, and it was full of people walking about, or sitting outside the pubs.

"It's lovely, isn't it? Like France," said Mario. He was looking dreamy and relaxed. The summer weather made everyone in Grey Walls extraordinarily happy, Clara thought. It changed their moods completely.

"Yes," said Clara, although it wasn't quite. But the square looked very cheerful at this time.

"We should put some tables and chairs outside," Mario said. "Nobody wants to sit in here on an evening like this."

It was true. Business was slack now, at least until about eleven o'clock. When darkness fell, people began to come into the café, but they didn't eat a lot of chips when the sun was shining.

"Why don't we?" Clara looked outside. There was plenty of room on the pavement. They could have half a dozen tables, quite easily. "Maybe you could expand the menu as well? We could make more ice creams, and juices. People would like that in the summer."

Mario was enthusiastic. "I have to ask Mama," he said. Mamma had to be asked about everything. She ruled the roost. You could never be quite sure what her reaction to any suggestion would be, either.

Clara speared two chips and dipped them in tomato ketchup. She loved chips, but was getting tired of them. Every night for six weeks she had had them, sometimes with sausages, sometimes with fish, sometimes with burgers. She wished the café could serve something else. Salad, for instance. But she knew better than to suggest that. Salad was simply alien to the Corner Café world view. They had been in chips for a hundred years and were not going to get into salads now.

Mario looked tenderly at Clara. "I think she will not object. Not to the tables outside anyway. Juices – I'm not sure. She'd feel she was betraying the Coca-Cola company after a lifetime of devoted loyalty."

"It's worth a try," said Clara. She ate a piece of fish.

At that moment, one of the others called her from behind the counter.

"Telephone call, Clara!" he said.

Clara jumped. Nobody ever phoned her here. She ran to the phone.

"It's Brian," Freddo said.

"Hi, Brian," said Clara, knowing immediately that something was wrong.

"Clara, don't be alarmed," he said.

"What is it?" she asked impatiently.

"David is in hospital. He's had an accident. He'll probably be all right but he's . . . " Brian's voice faltered for a second or two, "he's in a critical condition right now."

Clara felt numb. Somehow she remained upright.

"Where is he?"

Brian named the hospital.

"Are you there?" she asked.

"Yes," said Brian. "They're letting me stay here for the moment. I've got a camp bed."

"I'm coming," said Clara.

"I'll give you my number – Kate has lent me her mobile. You don't have to come."

Clara took the mobile number.

"I'm coming," she said.

* * *

Mario drove her to the hospital, even though it was thirty miles away from Grey Walls.

He wanted to stay with her, but Clara asked him to leave. His plump face sank in disappointment, but he smiled.

"You ring me when you want to come home," he said. "Promise? "

"All right," said Clara.

"And ring to let me know how things are. Tonight."

She promised that she would. He gave her a quick, tight hug before he left, and Clara felt warmed by it, even though she was worried sick about David. She stood and watched Mario walking out of the hospital, realising that she had become very fond of him. He was a good friend. "Just a good friend!" she said to herself, aloud.

"What's that?" It was Brian. He looked curiously at the vanishing Mario.

"Oh, nothing," said Clara. "How's David?"

"He's suffering from concussion. He was unconscious for a while, but he's regained consciousness now. He's having trouble with his memory. And he's got a few broken ribs, that's all."

"That's *all?*" Clara asked.

"It could have been much worse!" said Brian. "I thought . . . he was going to die."

They went into the ward. David didn't look as if he were about to die. He was sitting up in bed, drinking orange juice.

"Hi!" said Clara, giving him a kiss. "So what happened?"

"They beat me up," he said. He looked happy.

"Jason and Dean attacked him," said Brian. "They've run away."

"Where's my cyber pet?" David asked.

Brian smiled at him. "He's right here, David, look." The cyber pet was on the quilt.

David picked it up and pressed a button. "They beat me up," he said to Clara.

Clara smiled and said, "Yeah. Nasty fellows,"

Then David said. "Where's my cyber pet?"

"It's right there, David," said Clara, puzzled.

"His short term memory is affected," said Brian. "The doctor said it will be all right in maybe twenty-four hours."

"They beat me up," said David again.

Clara put her arms around David and held him close.

"Oh David!" she said, with tears stinging her eyes. "I love you. I really love you."

Clara stayed in the hospital for a few hours. David chatted

happily all that time, but his memory did not improve. He could talk lucidly about Chestnut Cottage, his life in France, his trip to Ireland. But everything that had happened in the past day, since he was beaten up, seemed to be jumbled up in some kind of stew in his head. He repeated the same questions and comments over and over again.

The nurse in the ward where David was staying reassured Clara and Brian, telling them David would soon be fine. When nine o'clock came, she suggested that they go home and let David sleep, and she promised to monitor him all night. Worried, Clara realised this was probably for the best. So she phoned Mario, who insisted on driving back to the hospital to collect her. He was deeply concerned about David and wanted to bring Clara back to the café.

"You can stay in our house," he said. "I think it would be nicer for you."

But Clara decided to go home and she was in just after one a.m. It wasn't necessary to explain to Jim and Aunt Mary what had happened. Apparently nobody had contacted them. They were slumped in front of the TV, as usual, watching a late-night movie.

Clara did not bother to say goodnight, but just went to bed.

* * *

As the hospital staff had promised, David's memory was restored to him the day after his ordeal, and a few days later he was released from hospital, with his arm in a sling. He and Brian returned to Summerlands. Jason and Dean were still at large.

"I'm very worried about them," said Kate. "They could be in danger."

Brian found it hard to be sympathetic.

David should have felt safe now. But he didn't.

"Have they caught them yet?" he asked, several times a day. The answer was always no.

"They've probably left the country," Brian said.

"How could they do that?" said David. "Where would they go?"

"They're the kind who could do anything. Rob money, go to England or something."

"They could be hiding in the woods down the road," David said.

"No," said Brian. "They're not around here. They would have been found if they were."

Still, Brian did not let David out of his sight. He brought him to the garden when he was working there. David sat on the bench, reading or playing with a hand-held console or his pet, while Brian went about his work. They went to the dining-room together. They went to sleep at the same time. Brian even accompanied David when he had to go to the bathroom, and stood outside, on guard, waiting till he was ready to leave. He wasn't taking any chances.

"Leave the poor chap alone," said Charlie. "Those boys won't be back to annoy him. They're hundreds of miles away."

Brian smiled, but it was several days before he felt confident enough to let David out of his sight, even for a moment.

* * *

Clara did not visit David once he left hospital. She planned to go down to Summerlands on Sunday but not for the rest of the week.

Mario got permission to put tables and chairs on the pavement, but, as he had anticipated, not to serve juice. It had to be tea, coffee, coke and chips. Nevertheless, the tables outside attracted lots of custom.

Clara was sitting outside with him one evening, having a cool drink. Mario was wearing a white T-shirt and blue jeans, which suited him very well. His brown eyes gazed softly at Clara.

"Clara?" he asked.

Clara tensed, understanding that something unusual was about to be said.

Mario looked at her for about three minutes before managing to say it. "There's a good film on in the Grey Walls Cineplex," he stammered.

Clara waited and didn't say a thing. "It's, em, I forget the name of it." He buried his face in his hands.

"I'll go with you," said Clara.

He removed his hands from his face.

"You will?" He was beaming with delight.

"Yeah. If your mother lets us have a night off." Since Clara had not had a night off since she started at the Corner Café, she felt entitled to one.

"She will, don't you worry!" said Mario. "Have another coke?"

Clara nodded, and he went to get it, walking with a jaunty stride. Clara gazed at the Square, dotted with brightly clad people, and felt a strange sensation of happiness. It was as if she were floating above herself, or as if her mind had moved to a new, spacious place, full of air and light. All the colours around her, the red oilcloth on the tables, the pinks and blues and yellows of people's clothes, even the grey of the pavings, looked brighter and clearer than they ever had before.

"Hi there, dream-boat!" a familiar voice shouted. Clara started out of her daydream.

It was Sandy.

"The wanderer has returned!" she said.

Two weeks had passed. Sandy was brown as a nut, and dressed all in white, to show it off.

"Did you have a fantastic time?"

"It was OK," said Sandy, sitting down. "A bit boring. I met a cool guy. We're writing to each other."

She and Clara hugged one another.

Mario came back with the coke and was not at all pleased to see Sandy. He left the coke on the table, smiled at Clara, and disappeared.

"Who was that?" Sandy asked, staring at him.

"Just the guy who works here," said Clara, as casually as she could.

"Hm," said Sandy, screwing up her eyes and examining Clara carefully. But she let it go.

Clara told her everything that had happened. But she did not tell her about Mario.

Sandy left, and Mario and Clara went back to work. Clara sang as she scraped chips and ketchup off plates and stacked them up in the steel teeth of the dishwasher. She sang as she gave the tray a giant shove, and she sang as she pressed the lever which set the machine going. She sang too above the roar of the engine, and she sang when it became silent.

Mario, peeling potatoes and cleaning ray and cod, did not sing, because although he looked so much like Elvis Presley he was tone deaf and knew not a single song. But he smiled, and his eyes were glazed over not with boredom, but with dreams. He dreamed so much that he peeled twice as many spuds as were necessary for the evening's chips. Maria came and shouted at him, but he just stared dreamily at her, and she shrugged and smiled.

"Haw! Something's up with Mario!" she said to her daughter.

"I think I know what it is," the daughter said, slapping batter onto a sausage.

Clara was almost finished with her work for the evening when Maria came to her, telling her Brian was on the phone.

"David has run away," he said, without introduction. His tone of voice was flat and despairing.

Clara could not believe it.

"When?"

"This morning," Brian said. "He's either run away or . . ."

"Are they searching for him?"

"He's nowhere to be found," said Brian. "I thought he might be with you."

"He's not," said Clara. "How would he ever find me? David can't cope with anything . . . buses or travel. He can't have gone far."

"Come down tomorrow," said Brian in the dull tone he had used all through the conversation, a tone which chilled Clara. "Come on the bus. Bring your money and things. I'll meet you in the village."

He hung up.

22

Children of the Greenwood

The trees were dark green, dripping with heavy leaves. They rustled and shivered in the night air. It was warm in the wood and full of night noises – an owl hooted. A fox screamed far away.

David, Brian and Clara were lying on the ground in the shelter of a great oak tree. Brian and David were asleep. Clara was awake, watching them. They were all cosy in sleeping bags. The trees surrounded them.

Dawn began to break in the east. Fingers of rosy light appeared between the tree trunks. Brian and David slept on. Clara slipped out of her sleeping bag.

She was fully dressed, in jeans and a jumper. She shivered as she left the warmth of the bag behind her. It was cold at this time of the morning, and Clara considered climbing back into the hot bag, escaping. But she walked away from her brothers.

The woodland birds had begun their dawn chorus.

Pippits, blackbirds, thrushes, were singing in a symphony of twitters and notes. Starlings picked up the sounds and mimicked them. The wood was full of music.

She walked across the crackling floor of the wood until she came to a stream. She collected water from it in a plastic mug, and then walked back to her sleeping brothers.

Brian was stirring as she arrived back. She started to light a fire – she had twigs, matches, a firelighter. In a short time, she had lit a small fire. She put a tin can full of water on the fire, and waited for it to boil.

Brian woke up.

"Breakfast nearly ready!" said Clara.

"Don't you ever sleep?" Brian asked, stretching and closing his eyes.

"Yes, sometimes," said Clara. But in fact she had not slept much, since she and her brothers had left Summerlands, Aunt Mary and Uncle Jim, the café, and all their strange Irish life, behind them. For four days they had been living rough in the countryside, on the run. They were together for the first time since they had left France. David seemed happy at last, and Brian was also reasonably happy. Clara was worried. She heard voices everywhere. Search parties would be out to get them, to hunt them down, to capture them and bring them back to their prisons. So far, they had been lucky, but she felt it was only a matter of time till they were caught.

"I think we should get out of Ireland," Clara said.

"You're right," said Brian, "and we will. But this is OK!"

The can of water boiled. Clara made coffee – she had a stack of supplies in her rucksack, bought when she was coming down from Dublin a few days before. She had plenty of money, but she did not relish the thought of having to go into a shop and replenish her supplies when they ran out of food. Somebody would be certain to recognize her.

"You worry too much," said Brian.

He bounced over to the fire, not removing his sleeping bag. His hair was tousled, but he looked warm, rested and happy. This life suited him. Maybe someone would catch up with them, haul them back to Summerlands, put him in prison for all he knew. But for the moment he was with his brother and sister. David was safe and happy as a lark. It was a strange situation, but life seemed OK. In the countryside, Brian simply felt safe. It was as if he were an animal, at home with the rabbits and hares and martens, with the foxes and squirrels and badgers who lived like this all the time.

Clara handed him a mug of coffee. Brian toasted a slice of bread over the fire, holding it on a fork. David slept on, his cheeks rosy against the navy blue sleeping bag.

"What will we do today?" Clara asked, in a low voice.

Brian shrugged luxuriously. He sipped his coffee and felt a delightful lassitude in his body and mind. "The same," he said. "Why should we do anything?"

Clara smiled, but she was anxious. "We should have a plan. We can't just spend the rest of our lives here!" She looked around the wood. The long dark tree trunks, the deep green needles on the pines. The silvery grey light deepening and strengthening as the sun rose higher in the sky, somewhere beyond the thick trees.

"Not the rest of our lives." Brian wasn't concentrating on her words. The toast was dark brown now, just the way he liked it. He removed it from the fork and bit into it. He spoke through mouthful of crunchy bread. "Just a while."

"But," began Clara, worries tumbling into her head.

"But we need a holiday," Brian said. "The weather is great. I don't think anyone will find us here, not for a while. We've got enough food to last a week. Let's relax."

David opened his eyes quite suddenly and sat up. He smiled.

"Good morning!" he said. "Can I have some coffee?"

He looked so happy that Clara decided that Brian was right.

* * *

Clara was exploring, looking for something – mushrooms, berries, she did not know what. She had walked for a long time along a narrow path through the forest, and now was in a clearing. Twigs and branches crackled under her feet and the sun beat down, very hot once she was out of the shade of trees. It was mid-afternoon. The sky was so bright it seemed no longer blue, but white, and over the clearing it was huge. She had a strange sensation: she felt she had moved into another dimension, or onto another planet, so different was the clearing, the beating sun, from the shadowy cool shelter of the wood.

She had found some tiny blue berries growing on low shrubs and she tasted one of them. It tasted sweet and tangy and she knew it was safe to eat. She ate a few more, then put the rest of the berries in her pocket. They stained her jeans purple, but she didn't care. Out here, stained jeans didn't matter.

That is all she had found, about twenty purple berries. There were brambles here at the edge of the clearing, but the berries were red and hard, inedible. The only mushrooms she had come across were big spreading umbrellas, under the trees, or toadstools with crimson spots. She didn't want to risk eating either, although she thought the big ones might be all right.

She sat on the ground. She was tired, and it was good to feel really hot sun on her skin. The ground was not hard, but covered with debris – dried pine needles, old crumbling twigs and branches. It was like sitting on cinders. The whole place smelled resinous; it exuded a sleepy, hot, pine-flavoured tang. Toasted tree. Clara, who had been awake, up and about, since early morning, felt sleepy. The sun was a round brass disk far above, the sky was brassy, and earth was like a moonscape. She rested and remembered. The bus from Dublin. Meeting Brian on that village street, late one night. The hopeless, desperate hunting along the little roads, the fields. Then finding David, sitting beside a bale of straw, bewildered, having given up, but not knowing what to do. The moment of joy at the reunion, deciding they would not report back, give themselves up and be separated again. Finding the wood.

She drifted off. The mountains and the house. Her mother was putting on her sun hat and packing the car with swimming gear, a picnic basket. They were going down to the sea, on a hot summer's day. "Hurry up, David!" her mother was calling. Clara and Brian were in the car already, everyone was ready to go. "Hurry up, David!" Her mother was pretty, her hair smooth as honey, under her wide straw hat. She was wearing a pink cotton sundress and white sandals, dark glasses. Perfume, sweet and subtle.

A crash.

"What's happened?" They all jumped from the car, ran to the house. David had fallen, knocked something over.

Crash, crash.

Clatter.

Horses galloped across the clearing, their hooves pounding into the branches, breaking wood, thumping the ground underneath. There were six or eight of them, ridden by young people, dashing across the clearing. Clara lay low, hoping they would not see her, half-covered in twigs. Over the clearing they flew, slowing down as they reached the far side. They hadn't seen her. They slowed down, trotted along the woodland path at the other side.

When they were out of sight, Clara stood up and made her way back to camp.

"We've got to go," she said. Brian was making a toy from wood, paring it with a penknife.

"Why? They won't bother us," he said.

"Maybe not them. But there are people around all the time. I want to get away from here. If we're in another country we'll be safe, somehow. I know that."

Brian wasn't convinced.

But David returned from playing with the news that he had met a man who asked him who he was.

"What did you say?" asked Brian.

"I said I was Shane," he said, laughing.

"And did he believe you?" Clara asked.

"Yeah, of course," said David. "He asked me where I lived and I just said, 'Over there' and then he went away."

Brian and Clara looked at one another and Brian said: "OK, I think it's time to move on."

"I'd better consult my book!" Clara took the leather pouch from her bag, and opened the book.

"Is it a travel guide as well as a feel-good book?" Brian asked. "Does it by any chance include a map?"

"No," Clara laughed and put her hand over the pages, many of which were now filled with her writing.

"So why are you looking at it then?"

"It brings me luck," said Clara. "That's what Madame Bonne said, remember?"

"Madame Bonne! Madame Chancer, more like it," said Brian. "Lucky book indeed! It didn't bring you much luck while you were with the Crabclaws, did it?" Brian joked.

Clara thought of Sandy and Melissa, of the English teacher and the French teacher, of the Corner Café. And of Mario.

"I'm not so sure about that!" she said, sighing and wondering if she would ever see all of them again.

"Can't I see it anyway? You've written stuff in it," said Brian. "Do you write poems?"

"No," said Clara. "It's just a story."

"Tell me the story!" David cried.

Clara told them the story, as she had written it down.

She got to where she had ended, and then she continued to tell the story.

Clara was accused of being a witch, and locked up in prison. After a few days they told her they were going to burn her at the stake, which was what they did to witches in those days. She had managed to bring the thread with her, somehow, and she kept knitting the shirts. All through her trial and imprisonment she was knitting. Finally the day came when she was to be burned. A wooden cart, dragged by a horse, collected her from the prison. By now she had knitted five shirts, and she was working on the last one. She brought them all with her on the cart, and as she was dragged through the streets, she knitted on. All the people

of the town had gathered to look at her and sneer, and shout, "Witch, witch, witch!" She was so busy knitting that she hardly heard them. They took her out of the cart and put her on the top of the huge pile of faggots that would be lit soon, to burn her alive. As they tied her up, a loud flapping noise was heard, louder than the cries of the people. Great wings beat the air, and six beautiful swans landed on the fire, on the cart, all around Clara.

"Burn the witch! Burn the witch!" shouted the crowd.

Clara took the nettle shirts, now white as snow, and placed them on the brothers, one by one. As soon as the shirts were on their backs, the swans turned into big strong young men. They pulled Clara away from the fire and flew away with her.

"They could still fly?" David asked.

"I think so. Yes, they could," said Clara. "They were human, but they could fly."

"Maybe they had a plane," he said.

"Maybe they had!" Clara repeated, thoughtfully.

They slept, and at sunrise they packed everything into two rucksacks, and set off.

"We'll go to Rosslare Harbour," Clara decided. "We can get a boat there that will take us to France."

"Don't you think they'll have warned the ferry staff to look out for us?" Brian wondered. "Or they might just recognize us anyway."

"They might not," said Clara. "I wouldn't say we're in the news any more, would you? We might have been in it for one day, if that. Certainly not more. Most people will have forgotten all about us by now."

"That's not what you said in the woods," Brian realised.

"That was different. The woods were – are – close to Summerlands. Everyone around there will know about us. They won't forget. But once we get away from that district it'll be different."

"We're easy to spot," said Brian, glancing at David. "Three kids."

"One dark, one red, one fair," said David, who was finally beginning to develop a sense of irony. "I think they might notice us, all right."

Clara laughed and hugged him.

"You're not so special-looking!" she said. "I think we'll manage!"

But how? wondered Brian.

Clara waved her hand in the air, dipped into her rucksack, and produced three snow-white cotton shirts.

"What are these for?" David asked.

"For us, of course," said Clara. "We're filthy."

Brian and David looked offended. Brian pulled some grass out of his hair and David fastened a button on the shirt he was already wearing. But like all their clothes, it was rumpled and stained with grass and leaves and food and dirt.

"Let's put them on," said Clara. "They'll make us look a bit cleaner, even if they don't actually disguise us."

"Disguise us? They make us stick out a mile! I hope they're not knitted from nettles!" said Brian, but he was already removing his scruffy black T-shirt and pulling the white shirt over his head. It transformed him completely. He looked like an angel, Clara thought, as she put on her own shirt. And David followed suit.

Then, attired in snowy, clean, soft, fresh cotton, they started on their walk.

They walked in a single file, through the fields, because they were afraid of being seen on the roads. In their white shirts, they looked like swans, making their way across the green meadows.

"How far is it to the harbour?" David asked. They were making very little headway. Walking in the fields slowed them down. They had to cross ditches, or find gates, very often.

"Not very far," said Clara, although she knew it was about seventy or eighty miles. It would take about a week to get there, at least, if they did not lose their way.

"I'm tired," David said. They had been walking for less than an hour.

"We'll take a rest," said Clara. They sat down and drank some orange juice from a carton, sharing it, taking a slug one after the other. Clara glanced at her watch. It was nine o' clock; they had walked less than two miles, maybe less than a mile. She thought they should keep going for another two hours, then eat, rest, continue – where, she did not know.

They set off again.

They had not gone far when David began to complain about the midges.

They swarmed all around them, biting their foreheads, their eyes.

"We just have to put up with them," said Clara. "We must be near a lake or a river or something. They like water."

"They're trying to eat me alive," said David.

"They'll stop after a while, when we leave the lake," said Clara. "We have to keep going, David."

"Tell me more of the story," he said.

So she told him more.

23

The Wild Swans

"Look!"

A flat field, emerald green, dotted with little aeroplanes. They sat like seagulls on the grass, silver and blue and white, gleaming in the sun.

Clara felt her fingers itch and her heart leap. "Bingo!" she said. She knew exactly what to do next.

They had walked for two nights, along the edges of country roads in the depth of night. When headlights suddenly glowed on the road they ducked, tried to hide themselves as well as they could. It hadn't always worked. A few times they were caught, the three of them, in the full glare of light and they felt themselves being stared at with great curiosity. Why were three children out walking at three a.m. in the morning? But so far nothing had happened. The police hadn't caught up with them.

They slept by day, hunting for places that seemed secluded and safe. Clara never slept well – she was wary, expecting at every minute to hear the siren singing, to hear the heavy footsteps, a hand on her shoulder shaking her, bringing her back to her uncle and aunt, putting David away, maybe putting them in prison. She had hardly slept at all, dozed off, opened her eyes constantly, kept an ear alert.

All the time she had worried. Where were they really going, how was it going to end?

Now she knew.

The little planes, something she had never thought of, never dreamed of. With an experienced eye she tried to identify the planes. Even from a distance, she recognised models: there were Cesna 150's and Cesna 172's. A tiny, long-tailed Katana. A big old Skyhawk. There were helicopters, in brilliant reds and yellows, looking perky and confident, like streetwise sparrows among the slender, graceful planes. There was one big luxurious Saratoga Piper.

"I could fly almost any of them, except the helicopter," Clara said to herself, as her eyes took in everything in the aerodrome.

All she needed was a key.

How do you get a key to somebody else's private plane?

Brian was sceptical.

"Let's try it," she said. "I know it's our only chance."

"But we were going to catch the ferry. We were going to stow away. I think that sounds easier," Brian said, nervously. He glanced warily at the aerodrome, wishing they had never seen it. As far as he was concerned, it was very bad luck to have stumbled across what must be one of the few aerodromes in Ireland.

Clara sighed, only half-remembering how much Brian disliked flying.

"How long till we get there, to the harbour? How many

chances of getting caught on the way? Let's give it a chance."

Reluctantly, Brian agreed. They were tired anyway and needed a rest. So they camped near the aerodrome, in the shelter of a small copse of trees.

They were in a new kind of landscape here – they had left the mountains and the pine forests behind them. Now they were in a lush farming landscape, flat and luxuriant. Farms, small woods, big houses behind high stone walls. A wide meandering river. Far away they could see horses, like insects, moving across a heathery flatland. A stone village, its grey spire soaring, nestled into a low hillside not far away.

The area around the aerodrome was flat as a pancake – an easy sort of landscape for amateur flying. Although there were houses in the distance, the little wood was quiet.

Rabbits were their only companions. The aerodrome was home to millions of them – they bobbed about all the time, running and dancing. At first they ran away from the children, but very quickly they became accustomed to them and simply hopped about over their sleeping bags. They tried to share their food.

"What are we going to do?" Brian was getting weary. The trek had been tiring, exhausting, disheartening. Now he wished they had stayed in the forest. At least they could have had a break, a holiday, until they were caught and life took whatever course it was going to take. Clara was getting mad, he thought. They could not fight the world of officialdom, of grown-ups. They could just succumb to its horrible rules and regulations, and bide their time, until they were all grown-up themselves.

"David is only ten," Clara reminded him when he said this to her.

Brian felt sad and angry. David. He was being David's father, forced to that position. And he was not quite sixteen.

"Let's give it a go. I want two days. That's all."

Brian did not know what day of the week it was. They had lost track. Clara thought it was a Friday. She hoped so, because weekends would be a good time at the aerodrome.

Next day she slipped away alone, and examined the surroundings.

A sign on the gate of the aerodrome told her it was known as *Honey Park Flying School*. She smiled. Taking the name as a friendly omen, as she walked up the rough driveway to the offices.

There were three or four fields, each sprinkled with planes. The office seemed to be in an old farmhouse, and a few hangars looked as if they had once been barns. A few men, in work clothes, were hanging around the yard. Clara nodded to them, trying to look as if she had a right to be here.

"Looking for someone?" one of the men asked.

Clara was at a loss for a split second. Then she said, "I've come to inquire about taking lessons."

The man smiled.

"Jenny in there will sort you out," he said, nodding at a door.

Clara had no choice but to go inside.

A girl sat behind a counter, talking on the phone. She saw Clara immediately and indicated with a tiny wave of her hand that she should wait. Clara smiled and sat on a bench by the wall. The girl chatted on, giving Clara an ideal opportunity to get a good look at the inside of the office. Filing cabinets, phones, a coffee machine. On the wall, a chart showing different cloud formations and their names, advertisements for new very luxurious small planes. Behind the girl, Jenny, on the wall directly above her desk, was a flat steel cupboard.

Clara guessed that this was where the keys were kept.

Jenny finished her telephone conversation and smiled at Clara. Clara had prepared her speech: she was interested in taking flying lessons, wanted to know how many she would have to take to have a pilot's licence, how much they would cost, when she could begin taking them. The girl was helpful and enthusiastic, answering all Clara's questions and giving her brochures with the information she desired.

While they were engaged in this conversation a man with a set of headphones dangling around his neck came into the office, opened the steel case, and put a key back there. Clara got a full view of the inside of the safe, and saw several keys hanging there. She had to get her hands on one of them.

* * *

"So what do you plan to do? Break in?" Brian was still very sceptical, as he listened to Clara's account of her visit to Honey Park.

"Maybe," Clara was racking her brains.

"Won't work," said Brian. "Sorry to be a pessimist, but I think that Jenny, or someone else, takes the key of the safe with them whenever they leave the place for the night. Maybe she takes all the keys with her," he added, as an afterthought. "It has probably occurred to them that someone like you might just rob a plane, if they made things easy for them."

"Mm, maybe." Clara didn't think it had occurred to them.

"Plus the place is no doubt alarmed," Brian said, in a sad, discouraging tone.

"I didn't notice," she said. In fact, when she thought about it, she realised that the flying school had not seemed to be alarmed, or very secure. Like the other little aerodromes she knew, it seemed easy-going and trusting.

"I'll think of something," she said, with a smile.

She knew why Brian was being so negative. His fear of flying filled him with thousands of excuses and reasons for not doing it. It was impossible for him to be objective about flying. He didn't even like flying in a large plane, and usually was given some sort of mild sedative before doing that.

It was hot and sunny at their camping place, and Brian liked it. But he was uneasy, and felt they should be moving onwards, on foot, towards the harbour.

"One more day," Clara said. "Then we move on."

"I don't want to walk any more," David complained, pouting. "I won't walk any more."

They slept, Clara more soundly than she had for weeks. She felt safe here, somehow – it did not occur to her to worry about people spotting them from the sky, and on the ground, it was a quieter place than they had seen for days.

The next day, she went back to Honey Park. Nobody saw her this time, and she hid in a bush close to the window of the office. It was Saturday, a busy day at the aerodrome. People were going up in planes all the time, from about ten in the morning. Some went on long flights, others took shorter trips, around the aerodrome, over the nearby fields and back again. There was a constant coming and going in the office.

She got a break at about noon.

Jenny, for once, left the office and stepped outside. Clara saw her walk across the field outside the building to one of the runways – she seemed to want to talk to someone who was sitting in a plane, waiting to take off. The office was empty: for the first time that day, nobody was in it. At any moment, someone could walk in. But Clara took her chance and went inside, walking quietly, trying to look as if she belonged there. Her luck held. She slipped behind the desk. The key to the safe was lying beside the phone. She opened it and took out one key, with a tag saying India June CES. Now she had to hope that nobody would notice the missing key, until she got away.

And she had to hope for many things. That she could manage to take off. That there was enough fuel in the plane to take her across the sea to France. That she could find her way to France.

She slipped out of the office, astonished that she had succeeded thus far. As soon as she got away from the environs of the office she began to run.

"Pack up!" she said. "We're off!" She dangled the keys in front of Brian's nose.

"Now?" he asked. "Shouldn't we wait till it's dark?" His face was white with panic, and red spots began to break out on his neck.

"No! They'll know the key is missing long before then," said Clara. "Also, I don't want to fly in the dark."

"But they'll see us!"

"We have to be quick," Clara said. "The aerodrome is full of people, so we won't look odd. And once we're airborne it'll be too late. They can't catch us in the sky."

"The mind of a hijacker," said Brian, smiling wanly. His neck was itchy. These spots appeared only when he was almost paralysed with anxiety. But he packed their bags in a second.

"Just one," said Clara. "The sleeping bags, the money, that's all. It's probably a very small plane."

"OK, OK," said Brian, crossly, as he pulled things out of one bag and stuffed them into another.

"And we'll put these on!" With a flourish, Clara produced three new white shirts. Their old ones were very disreputable by now.

"Gosh! How many of these things do you have?" David asked, obediently slipping into the clean garment. He remembered how good it had felt before, so white and fresh. Wearing it made him feel renewed and hopeful.

"That's my secret!" said Clara.

Brian put on his new shirt without comment, and then shouldered the one rucksack. They hid the other under the willow tree. Brian felt sad to say goodbye to it – it had been with them for weeks now, and seemed like a friend.

They walked around the edge of the aerodrome, keeping far away from the office. A girl waved to them from a plane and Clara, alarmed, waved back and smiled.

"Do you know which plane it is?" Brian asked, looking at the field of planes with horrified eyes.

"It's called India June," siad Clara. "There'll be a big IJ painted on its side. Can you see a plane with that initial?"

"No!" said Brian. He scanned the field. There seemed to be every initial but IJ.

Planes landed and took off every ten minutes. The blue sky above them was usually clear of planes, but every so often one glided into view, preparing to land after its flight to the skies beyond the aerodrome.

"There's IJ!" screamed David, pointing to a pure white plane, sitting in the middle of the field.

Clara's eyes darted to the plane. He was right. "Fantastic!" she said. "Let's walk quickly towards it, as unobtrusively as we can."

"Everyone will see us!" said Brian.

"If they're looking," said Clara, "but they probably won't be. People at flying schools are usually looking for dangerous things in the air, not on the ground."

They walked quickly, but did not run, across the field towards the plane.

At first they seemed to be undetected.

They gained confidence, as they walked. There were few planes out at this side of the field. Most of them were closer to the office and buildings.

"I won't have time to give the plane the usual once-over," said Clara.

Brian grimaced, knowing what that meant. They were disobeying the first rule of flight, which is to check everything before take-off. They would be taking a terrible risk.

"As soon as we reach the plane, we climb in and I start it," Clara said.

They were within a few yards of the planes when they were spotted.

A shout rang out, followed by a siren. Three or four people ran out of the office and started to run across the field, towards the children.

"Run!" said Clara.

Brian and David ran for their lives towards the plane.

The three of them ran so fast that they were like white horses galloping across the grass.

The men were shouting "Stop!" "Stand still!" The siren went off again.

Clara reached the plane first.

"In!" she screamed.

The boys climbed into the plane. It was a four-seater, a Cesna 172, to Clara's relief. David and Brian tumbled into the back seats. Clara strapped herself into the captain's seat, glanced at the control panel. The men were still a bit away. She turned the key.

The engine fired immediately. She pushed the pedal and turned the plane towards the runway.

It pranced across the grass, and within seconds she was running along the concrete strip of the runway.

If she met another plane, or if a plane were ahead of her waiting to take off, she would be finished.

She looked at the fuel gauge, and sighed with happiness: the tank was full. The runway was completely empty. Which way was the wind blowing? From the north. That meant she should turn and bring the plane back to the hangar area and take off from there. But that would be certain capture. She did a dangerous thing. She accelerated very heavily, sped along the runway with the wind on her tail, and before anyone knew what was happening, soared into the air.

"We're off!" she shouted, as she moved upwards, up into the blue sky.

Brian and David could not hear her. It was very noisy in the plane: they had no headsets, she could not communicate with anyone and the roar was deafening. Brian and David looked down, at the aerodrome. Dozens of people were standing there, gazing upwards at them, some of the shaking their fists in rage.

Clara saw none of this.

She focused on the controls, and gave them the

examination she should have given them on land. Everything was in order.

Up and up and up she went. A thousand, two thousand feet. The plane could go much higher, up to about eighteen thousand feet, but without oxygen they would not be able to stand that. She flew along, at two thousand, for the moment. It was perfectly adequate for this flat, easy landscape, which spread out beneath her, fields and farms, villages and roads, cars and people. She could look down and see it all for a second or two. Then her eyes went back to the controls.

After twenty minutes they reached the coast. Clara had no idea where precisely they were – there was no big city in evidence, so she knew she was not over Dublin. She guessed it might be the Wexford coast, but had no way of telling, since she was unfamiliar with the area, with the country.

She decided that the only thing she could do was to fly due south-east, and hope that eventually they would arrive in France.

Brian's stomach was heaving. The lurching of the plane nauseated him, and made him want to vomit. He felt hot, but at the same time his skin quivered and was covered in goose-pimples. He gripped the sides of his seat so hard that his fingers almost bled. Hating to do it, he looked down. Beneath him spread an expanse of charcoal waves. They were tumbling around, gleaming with a cold-grey sheen. They did not look angry – it was a calm day – but powerful. Powerful and, it struck Brian, indifferent. The sea was there, beneath them. If they fell into it, the sea would not care one way or another. It would support them, until they floated to safety, or it would suck them into its heart and drown them.

But their fate would depend entirely on themselves, on their own abilities, their own will.

We are on our own.

Brian suddenly realised that the whole world was like the sea. When you were a child, you believed otherwise. You believed the world was a nurse, that it was there to protect you and look after you. But as soon as you grew up, as soon as you lost the people who were there to protect you and look after you, your parents, you were then at sea. Other people would step in – relations, the people who ran the children's homes – and try to do your parents' job. But there was no guarantee that they would do it successfully. From then on, it was going to be a matter of chance whether you were looked after or not.

Of course, it was a matter of chance from the start.

He looked at the waves, which seemed to be winking at him in a cruel, cold way. It's up to you, they were saying. It's your life and your responsibility. It's nothing to do with us.

Brian looked at David, for the first time since they took off – he had been too absorbed in his own worries to pay any attention to him. To his surprise, David was comfortably seated, looking happily out at the sea beneath. He smiled when Brian turned to him, and said, "Cool, isn't it?" Brian gave him a friendly, loving punch and David returned it.

He still believed, Brian could see. He still believed that he was being looked after. And he believed that because he had Brian and Clara with him. He believed they were all-powerful, that they could do anything.

David laughed. He saw the sea tumbling beneath him, greeny blue. He saw seagulls wheeling in the sky like dancers. He saw the golden sunlight filling the sky, and felt bathed in it. His heart was full of joy and he felt free and light as a leaf. And he felt safe. High in the air, with his sister as pilot, he felt safe.

The engine roared. Clara sat upright, the control column in her hand, pleased with her progress so far. She was cruising at four thousand feet now, and had ascended this far without difficulty. The compass told her she was flying in a south-easterly direction, which was the way she wanted to fly. As far as she could see there was no other plane close to her: the Honey Park people had not given chase. She could see nothing underneath but the ocean. She hoped she would not sight land until she was over France. What she would do then was a little hazy. But she planned to fly as far south as she could, and land in the small airfield where she had taken flying lessons. How to locate that, in the whole of France, she was not sure. But she had to hope that it would be possible. So far, she had succeeded so well that she was confident that it would be.

24

Allons Enfants!

A ribbon of beach, a strip of green, grey clusters of houses, a town. Clara tensed. Her stomach knotted, suddenly. She looked over her shoulder. Brian was patting David on the shoulder. David smiled brightly at Clara, and Brian smiled, less brightly. He mouthed the words: "*Vive La France!*" They could hear nothing over the roar of the engines.

Clara returned to the controls. The fuel tank was now less than a quarter full. The journey over the sea had lasted more than six hours, much longer than she had anticipated. Maybe she had moved farther south than she had planned? If she were lucky, the land they saw beneath them was the south of France – the town might be Bordeaux, or any of the towns along the southern Atlantic coast. If she were unlucky, it could be the coast of Brittany. Or the coast of Portugal.

It could be anywhere. It could be Wales. There was no way she could know, no way she could recognise it. Nothing to indicate which region, or which country, it was, to the uninitiated. An experienced pilot would be able to tell, at a glance, probably, would recognise the shape of the coastline, the lie of the land, the size of the towns. For her, the minute doll landscape would be filled with clues and identifiers. But not for Clara.

What she knew was, she would have to land as soon as possible. There was no longer any question of seeking out the familiar airfield. Anyway, the sight of that landscape beneath her, its patchwork of burgeoning fields, indicated to her that she would have little chance of finding it. She would have to land wherever she found a suitable stretch of ground, and as soon as possible.

The fields were vineyards. Brian could see that, recognising the small green plants in their long straight rows. He knew they were not in Brittany, but somewhere much farther south, perhaps Bordeaux, perhaps even farther south than that, in Portugal.

Clara did not notice this, although experience told her that the landscape was southern: it was more russet, more burnt, than the deep wet greens of the north. But she no longer cared where she was. All her energy was concentrated on locating a landing place. Beneath her stretched vineyards, olive groves, fields of golden corn. A narrow river, snaking its way through the patchwork of fields. The steep red roofs of farmhouses, the grey walls of a chateau, the dense mass of a town. But nothing wide enough, big enough, to land a plane on.

She glanced over her shoulder, and said: "If you see anything that looks like an airfield, let me know!"

Brian couldn't hear her words very well; the roar of the

engine had become louder. But he understood. So did David. He had been patient for hours, relaxing in his big comfortable seat, playing and looking out the window. Now, when he saw the land underneath and realised that they were soon going to set foot on it, his patience broke. He became excited and worried, and aware of how long he had been sitting in the little cabin.

"Are we going to stop now?" he asked.

"As soon as we can!" Brian shouted back.

"But where are we?" David asked.

"Home," said Brian, with much more confidence than he felt. "We're over France."

"It doesn't look like home!" David said in his sceptical voice.

Thank goodness for that, Brian thought. If they found themselves over the mountains, they'd be in serious trouble. Whatever chance there was of finding a landing place here in this flat countryside, they would have none in the mountainous landscape of home. Clara could never locate the little airport where she had taken her flying lessons.

Suddenly Brian noticed a plane flying high above them. Then another. He had been busy looking at the ground, but the clue to landing was higher up, in the heights where the big planes were flying. Of course they could accidentally have found themselves on a flying route, but the presence of more than one plane might also mean that they were not far from an airport.

He nudged Clara and shouted, "Airport maybe!"

Clara nodded, and looked down. She could see no sign of an airport. But in the distance, there was a blue glimmer. The sea. The Mediterranean.

Landing at a big official airport was not what she had

planned to do. But if a big official airport appeared before anything more suitable, she would have to take a chance and bring the plane down there. What would happen next she couldn't think about.

The smudge of a city appeared on the map beneath them, like a blotch painted on the edge of the blue sea. She guided the plane in its direction. Now there were many planes in the sky, coming and going, and it was clear that an airport was not far away. It would be on the edge of the city, Clara knew, probably on the coastal side.

She was soon able to locate the position of the airport by observing the planes. It was on the south side of the town, at the edge of the sea, so they had to fly right over the roofs and steeples before they reached it. There it was, indicated by lights and flags – a big, green and concrete airport.

Where to land? Clara knew that airport traffic is guided by air-traffic controllers, working from the airport itself, issuing the pilots with directions as to when they should land or take off. Clara could not communicate with the air-traffic controllers. She didn't know how to, and she didn't want to.

Landing without knowing what was happening on the runways could be disastrous, for her and for other aircraft.

But she had no choice.

She was approaching the edge of the airport now. She could see the runways, the greens, the planes, very clearly. A Boeing 747 was about to take off. It was moving down a runway, gathering speed as it went. She watched it gain momentum, and then lift off, rising quickly into the sky, its wings spreading, its flappers retracting.

She understood what she would have to do.

She glanced at the fuel gauge. There was hardly anything left in the tank. The thin blue line was tipping the thick red line, which meant "Empty".

But she tipped back the control column and lifted the plane higher into the sky.

Then she turned and moved away from the airfield.

Brian wondered what was going on. David did too.

"Why aren't we landing?" he shouted. He began to thump Clara on the back. Brian pulled him away and lifted his fist threateningly.

Clara turned and shouted, "It'll be just a few minutes longer!"

A minute later a 147, with the blue Air France logo on its rudder, passed Clara's plane and began to descend for landing. Clara moved away in the opposite direction. After a half a mile or so, she turned, and followed the bigger plane, flying as slowly as she could. She watched the plane go down, land, and run along the runway. Like all planes, it moved quickly at first, gradually reducing its speed until it was going as slowly as a car. By then it was quite close to the terminal, and far from the spot where it had first landed.

Clara did not wait for the plane to stop. As it careered towards the terminal, she descended, decreasing her speed. Before the plane had even halted, hers was hitting the runway almost exactly at the spot where the other plane had touched down a minute earlier. She was hoping against hope that no other plane would land or take off from that runway until the first plane had had time to stop.

Luck was with her. It was a busy airport, with planes landing and taking off every five minutes, but Clara succeeded in landing, careering for half a kilometre and stopping, without colliding. Since her plane was small, she did not need to drive for very long before bringing it to a halt.

Already, of course, she had been sighted, and already she could see men running in her direction. The screech of a siren told her that a car, probably the airport police, had been alerted and were on their way to the small plane.

Clara did not need to give instructions to Brian. Already he was shunting David out of the plane. They all jumped to the ground and ran in the direction of the perimeter of the airport as fast as they could.

The siren screeched louder. Clara turned and saw a white car with a flashing blue light speeding down the runway.

So they were going to be caught, after all.

25

Mediterranean City

They ran and ran, so fast that they felt their hearts would burst out of their skin.

Suddenly the siren stopped screaming.

"Now we've had it," Brian and Clara thought simultaneously.

They stopped running, and turned, expecting to see armed gendarmes bearing down on them.

But they didn't.

Instead they saw a Jumbo Jet coming in to land.

The white car had withdrawn. They couldn't even see it. The huge jet lumbered towards the ground, and hit it with a bump which was audible even from two kilometres distant.

The moment it landed, a flame soared from underneath its right wing.

Clara, Brian and David watched, exhausted and fascinated by the scene they were witnessing.

The flame grew bigger, as the huge plane lumbered along

the runway. It seemed to be going slowly, but in fact it was spinning along at almost a hundred miles an hour.

Sirens sounded all over the airport now. There was a frenzy of sound and activity. Fire engines and ambulances appeared from hangars, sirens blaring and lights flashing. But they stayed outside the hangars, close to the terminal, for the moment.

"It'll explode!" said Brian, going white.

"We should run!" said Clara.

They turned and continued to run to the fence that surrounded the airport.

They ran for about ten minutes until they reached the fence. It was a high chicken-wire fence, electrified on top. Brian had anticipated this. He took a pincers from his pocket and snipped the wire, making a hole big enough for them to slip through.

When they were outside the airport, they looked back.

The jumbo jet was partly on fire. But it had stopped and passengers were being evacuated through several exits. The fire engines were surrounding the plane and dousing it with water.

Brian said, "It's all right. Let's go!"

They ran again, until they reached a wood about half a mile from the airport. The wood was a pine wood, and it stood on the edge of a beach.

"Let's sit down and decide what to do!" Brian said.

They sat down, in the cover of the trees, but with their eyes on the sea.

* * *

Half an hour later, they were in a bus, making their way

along the coast towards, they hoped, the city nearest their village.

"This is nicer than flying!" David said, as he looked out at the blue sea on one side of him, and green fields and rugged mountains on the other.

"Much, much nicer!" agreed Brian. It had been his idea to catch the bus. He had seen a bus stop, outside the airport, and when moments later a bus marked "MERLE" arrived he could not believe his good luck. They were not far from home, not too far. He looked at this watch. Already it was eight o'clock. They wouldn't catch the train to the Cevennes tonight.

"It's a pity !" said Clara. "By tomorrow they may have identified us and alerted the railway stations."

"It's possible," said Brian, "but not all that likely. Was there anything on the plane to indicate that it was Irish?"

Clara shook her head.

"Not that I noticed – but there could easily be something that I wouldn't be aware of, and that an expert would notice in seconds."

"If they discover it's Irish, it won't take long to trace the plane," said Brian. "But they still won't know who flew it, will they?"

"They probably would have noticed at the airport," Clara responded. "When we were running across the airfield, they might have observed that there were three of us, one a lot smaller than the usual private flier."

Brian smiled. He had managed to survive the flight. Somehow he thought it unlikely that they would be identified so quickly.

"Where will we sleep?" he asked.

Clara laughed. "Under a bridge! In the public park! On the street! We've slept in so many strange places over the past month, a night out under the stars in Merle won't do us any harm."

"Yeah," said Brian doubtfully. "You know Merle's reputation!"

It was the sort of town where murders were reported almost every week. Being murdered in Merle was so commonplace that it hardly got reported at all in the newspapers or media. From time to time, articles informing you that the murder rate had gone up or gone down, fractionally, from last year or last month, appeared. Usually it had gone up. But although this was regarded as unfortunate, the local attitude was that murder in Merle was simply a phenomenon you had to learn to live with, like rain in the autumn. You could do your best to avoid being rained upon, or murdered, yourself, but you couldn't hope to actually stop the clouds or the murderers moving in and doing their damnedest.

"Yes," said Clara. "Well, we'll have to take our chance."

David pouted. "Stop talking like that!" he said. "Is there any food? I'm starving."

Brian and Clara had been so busy, flying and bussing and organising the great escape, that they had forgotten about their base appetites. But as soon as David mentioned the word food they realised they were starving too. They hadn't eaten in about fourteen hours.

"Let's scarper then," said Brian. The bus pulled to a halt, at the harbour side in Merle. They scrambled out and walked very fast along the dock towards the lights of the town.

"France!" said Brian, looking around him. It was a far cry from the place they had left behind them, the abode of the Crabclaws. They were walking along a quayside street. On one side was a black finger of harbour, or the mouth of a river. On the other, was a strip of restaurants. Outside on the pavement people were sitting, eating and drinking. In front of each restaurant was a tank full of lobsters and a window displaying a vast assortment of fish – oysters, mussels, langoustines, every imaginable kind of fish.

"Let's go inside," said Clara. "Let's have a decent meal."

Brian hesitated. He examined Clara and David. Their white shirts were streaked with dust and oil. They had been sleeping rough for almost a month, and, although they had done their best to maintain their high standards of neatness and chicness, they had definitely lost the battle. Their hair, in each case, was dirty-looking, unkempt, too long in all the wrong places. Their skin was clean – they had washed in streams and rivers. But washing in that sort of water produces an effect quite different from washing in water that comes from a shower-head or a tap, and is hot and accompanied by soft scented soap and soft springy sponges. (Brian yearned for a bath, as he thought of bathrooms). They looked like things which had been left out in the dust and rain for too long – as they had been. And all this before you even considered the state of their clothes.

"It's a good idea," he said diplomatically. "But we'd have to clean up a bit first. I think. Do you have any more white shirts?"

Clara looked at him and agreed.

"I've three more in my bag," she said triumphantly. "Maybe we could slip into the cloakroom of a restaurant and wash and change?"

"It's not so easy to slip past a waiter in one of these places," Brian said. " They've eyes in the backs of their heads, and they hate scruffy-looking people. Plus, the toilets are always at the back of the establishments, usually downstairs, so they can make sure people like us, who really need them, don't use them. I don't think it'll work."

"Maybe there's a public loo?" Clara suggested.

"That's where seventy per cent of the murders take place. For some reason the public loo is the most sought-after spot, by murderers."

"We've escaped from the Crabclaws and Summerlands. We've evaded the Gardai and the Gendarmes. We've stolen a plane. We've made it, alone and unaided, from Ireland to France!" said Clara. "Surely we should be able to wash ourselves!"

Brian shrugged and thought for a minute.

"Why don't we just book into a hotel? I think we'll get away with it."

Clara was so tired now that she agreed, although in a normal frame of mind she would have assumed that that was a sure way to get caught very quickly.

But it was easy.

They found a small hotel, a pension, just around the corner from the quay.

Brian introduced himself as Pierre Lafontaine, and Clara as his partner, Mary. He claimed David as their child.

The concierge looked suspicious. But when he said he would pay in advance, she gave him the key of a room, with bathroom.

"Whoopee!" said Clara, bouncing on the bed. "Sleeping in a real bed! I can't believe it!"

"Let's wash and get some food," said Brian.

One by one they made use of the facilities – hot water

and a bottle of body shampoo. There was a hair-drier. Clean, and with their hair washed and combed, attired in the last of the white shirts, they looked beautiful.

"I'm tired," David said. "I don't want to go out. I want to go to bed." He looked longingly at the bed, with its snow-white duvet and plump pillows. He had not slept in a bed for weeks.

Clara and Brian felt disappointed, and annoyed. Everything was going so well. They wanted to celebrate.

"We could buy some stuff and eat it here," Clara said.

"You two go and eat. Bring back something for me," David said. "I just want to have a nap now. I'm so tired."

He had lain down on the bed and was almost asleep as he spoke.

Clara covered him with the soft duvet. Then she and Brian left, locking the door behind them.

A little worried about David, they walked along the street and around the corner to the quayside.

"He'll be fine," said Brian. "Let's not worry about him. It's just for an hour or less."

Nothing could spoil the sense of well-being which filled him. Feeling clean was a marvellous sensation, after being dirty for so long. He felt as if he had sloughed off an old, anxious, grubby skin and put on a shining new hopeful one. He felt as if he had grown up, completely, irrefutably, and that from now on nobody was going to tell him what to do. From now on, he would trust his judgement, make his own decisions.

Clara was pleased to have had a chance to shower and change, but physically she was tired, and did not feel as exhilarated as Brian did. The flight had been exhausting – that she had succeeded in bringing the small plane on such a long journey and landing safely at one of the biggest airports in the south of France, was, she knew, a great achievement. In one part of her brain, she realised that she was now a fully fledged pilot. She knew the theories, the basics of aerodynamics. She knew a lot about small planes. And now she knew she had enough practical sense, enough sensitivity to the plane, to handle any kind of aircraft. She would have to train and become a real pilot.

She knew that. But in another part of her head she was feeling sad, tired, despairing. There were so many obstacles to be overcome. They had achieved a lot, by dint of doing one thing at a time, taking one step at a time. But their life was a mess. She could not think of the future. She could not think of tomorrow without feeling faint.

"A penny for them?" said Brian.

"I'm thinking about tomorrow."

"Don't worry, it'll be OK," said Brian. "You'll feel better about it when you've had something to eat."

"I don't think I can go on. Fighting everything."

Brian took her hands in his.

"Listen. You've done something that nobody of your age could dream of doing. You've flown from Ireland to France, you've brought us safely here. The worst is over. It's going to be a cinch from here on."

"I wish I could believe that," said Clara.

Brian shrugged. Clara was sounding like one of the Crabclaws now. But he felt certain that food would restore her to her senses.

They sat at a table at the back of a restaurant, and ordered chowder and a seafood salad. Brian drank wine and Clara coke, which reminded her of Mario.

The restaurant was cosy with candlelight, and the food

was perfect – crispy bread, delicious soup. The waiter seemed to believe they were adult. Brian wondered how grown-up he really looked.

"Do I look eighteen? Nineteen?" he asked Clara.

She pretended to scrutinise him. He was tall, so maybe some people would take that as in indication of age.

"You look very grown-up," she said. In fact it seemed to her that he had looked exactly the same since he was about four, but of course he had grown. If he had better clothes, he would look like a real grown-up man.

"You could pass for sixteen," Brian said, very pleased.

"You too," said Clara.

"I am," said Brian.

"You are what?" she said.

"I am sixteen. Today. It's August 31st, my birthday!"

Clara clapped her hands and laughed out loud.

"Congratulations! Happy Birthday! How could I forget? Why didn't you say? You are sixteen!"

"Sh!" said Brian. "Don't let them hear. Yeah, I'm sixteen." He looked around the restaurant, and smiled. "I'm grown up!"

"Sort of," said Clara, but she did not deflate him.

"I am," he said. "I really am."

The waitress took away the soup plates and brought their plates of seafood. Big white platters, on which prawns, salmon, swordfish, and crab were arranged with lemon slices, were placed before them, along with a basket of fresh bread.

"Oh, goodness!" said Clara. "I'd forgotten what this tasted like."

"Better than fish and chips?" Brian chuckled.

"Yeah. But they were good too. And the folks at the chipper – what good people!"

Clara's eyes were dreamy.

"You'll see them again," said Brian, reading her thoughts. Would he ever see Madeline again, he wondered. "Some day. Some day when you can travel over there legally, on your own, independent of the Crabclaws."

"Yeah," said Clara. "I might write to Sandy in the meantime. I should let her know that we're OK." She hadn't contacted Mario since he left her outside Summerlands in the middle of a warm July night four weeks ago, although she had promised to get in touch as soon as she could. He had wanted to stay and help, to drive all of them wherever they wanted to go, but Clara had insisted that she was staying at Summerlands with the boys and that there would be no room for him. Sadly he had gone home – to hear the news next day, on the TV in the corner of the café kitchen, that Clara and her brothers were missing.

"Don't write," Brian said. "Phone. Phone from a phone box. Don't tell Sandy where you are . . ."

"She'd never report me," Clara said.

"She might come under pressure. Don't risk it!" said Brian. "Isn't this sauce lovely? I wish I could send some to Madeline. She'd love it."

"Send her a bottle," said Clara. "From a false address! Put it afloat on the sea and maybe it'll reach her!"

At that moment, Brian saw something that took his breath away.

"What?" Clara had noticed a change in his expression. He looked alarmed and shocked.

"Dad!" Brian stood up and shouted. "Dad!"

In the doorway of the restaurant a tall man with a red moustache, wearing a big black beret, stopped, turned around, and then walked away.

Brian jumped up.

"It's Dad!" he said. "I've got to follow him."

"But . . . leave some money. Come back!"

Brian tossed some notes onto the table, and ran out onto the street.

26

Sparkling Rain

Clara couldn't eat any more. She paid the bill.

"Hein!" said the waiter. "A quick departure!" He smiled sympathetically at Clara, thinking that Clara and Brian had had a lovers' quarrel. Clara smiled back, trying to look wistful, which was not difficult for her. Then she left.

It was raining now. Light rain bounced against the footpath. It fell in gleaming veils in front of the shop windows, and sparkled like diamonds around the streetlamps. People walked up and down the street, holding their arms out to feel the rain against their bare skin. A girl laughed and turned her face to the sky, opened her mouth and drank raindrops.

Brian was nowhere to be seen.

Clara walked slowly back to the corner, looking out for him. She stopped at a late-night shop and got bread, cheese, juice and chocolate, for David. Then she continued around the corner, checking all the time for a sight of Brian. But she couldn't see him.

She let herself into the guesthouse.

The concierge was still at her desk. She eyed Clara up and down.

"Alone?" she said.

Clara nodded, then went upstairs.

David was still asleep. Clara lay on her bed, and using the remote control turned on the TV, keeping the volume low.

The late-night news was on.

Trouble in the Middle-East. A strike on the railway. A murder in Merle. A fire in a Boeing 747 at the airport at Nice. Clara watched, fascinated, the footage showing the plane on fire. It had not been a big fire and had been put out very quickly. All the passengers and crew escaped, some with very minor injuries.

The newscaster went on.

"Minutes before the Boeing 747 landed, a small unauthorised plane landed without permission at the edge of the runway. Police and airport officials attempted to detain the occupants of the plane, but without success. The plane was abandoned at the airport. The plane is a Skyhawk, and thought to originate in Great Britain. It was occupied by three men, two of average and one of below average height. It is believed that there may be a connection between the occupants of this small illegal plane and the fire on the Boeing 747. Investigations are continuing."

Three inaccuracies at least, in one short report! Clara turned off the TV, too tired to feel worried. She was in France, she was in France. She had got her brothers back home – almost. Exhausted, she closed her eyes and fell asleep.

The sky was full of flowers, purple and crimson, pink and

saffron. There were long flowers with iridescent stamens like peacock's feathers, and big circular daisy flowers, their glowing pink petals distributed evenly around a nub, like wheels. Names were attached to the flowers. Puya, Corunus, Euronima – names Clara had never heard or seen before. But there they were, in the dream, clearly labelled on the flowers. The flowers floated in the sky, flew in the sky like birds or planes, with their names tagged to their stalks.

"Clara, Clara!"

She stirred. The purple flower remained, central, glowing like a star, then dimming. Its name was Puya, but it was fading . . .

"Clara, wake up!"

She opened her eyes.

What was that name? Gone.

"Brian!" She roused herself from her dream and began to remember recent real events. "Dad," she said. "So was it him?"

Brian shook his head emphatically.

"No," he said. "It was just a man who looked like him."

Clara felt deeply disappointed. She had not really believed the man in the black beret was her father. But she was so tired that she wanted to believe it. She wanted a fairytale ending now; she felt she had done enough. It was time for someone to step in and solve the family's problems.

"But," said Brian, smiling, "I went to the prison. I met Dad and talked to him."

Clara looked questioningly at him.

"He's fine," Brian shrugged. There were black rings under his eyes and his skin was white with exhaustion. But he looked lighthearted and carefree. "The good news is, his case is coming up next week and he feels sure he'll get off.

We're to stay here until the trial. He's getting in touch with somebody in Ireland to sort out all that stuff over there."

Quite a lot of stuff.

"As long as he doesn't get in touch with Jim Crabclaw, that sounds fair enough," said Clara, closing her eyes. She felt a burden floating away from her, her bundle of worries sprouted wings and flew off into the ether. There were problems ahead but her heart was light.

* * *

Clara, Brian and David remained in Merle, at the pension, until the day of the trial. They did not attend, but, as he had expected, Jack Moody was found not guilty, and was set free straight away.

Next day, he hired a small car and drove up into the mountains with his children.

"I was acquitted," he said in answer to David, as he wound his way expertly along the narrow roads.

"What does that word *mean*?" David asked happily. Naturally he could guess what it meant, since his father was a free man, driving a hired car up the winding roads of Languedoc in the direction of home.

"It means I got off," explained their father. "The evidence against me was found to be insufficient. The judge decided that maybe I hadn't done what I was accused of."

"Smuggling drugs," said David. "Maybe? So was the judge right? Did you?"

His father did not answer.

Clara had a question, too.

"Why didn't you contact us when we were away?" she asked. "We had such a terrible time. We needed help."

Her father paused before replying.

"I wrote to you a few times, in reply to your letters. I sent the letters care of Mary and Jim."

"He would have made sure we didn't get them," said Brian. "What a great guy!"

Clara felt a pang of terror, all of a sudden, remembering the Crabclaws and Grey Walls.

"Didn't they even get in touch when we ran away?" she asked.

"No, they didn't," said her father. "But someone else did, a woman from the home where David and Brian had stayed. She telephoned me."

"Kate," said Brian.

"She was very nice, and extremely worried. But what could I do? I was locked up. She promised she'd let me know if anything happened . . . she phoned a couple of times."

"You must have been worried?" Clara asked, happily.

"Very worried," said Jack. "What you did was very dangerous. Outrageous," he spoke slowly. "Running away, stealing a plane . . . how could you?"

"We had no choice," said Clara. "Or so it seemed."

"I am proud of you, I have to admit," said Jack. "You've got courage. But I want you to promise never to do anything like that again, ever."

"I won't go around stealing planes," said Clara, "and I won't run away. But you have some promises to make too."

"Yes, I know," said Mr Moody. "I have promises to make and keep. And we know what they are."

There was silence in the car.

David wasn't one to give up easily.

"So did you smuggle drugs?" he repeated.

And Mr Moody repeated his answer.

"There was insufficient evidence against me," he said.

It wasn't a great answer. Brian and Clara glanced at one another. Was their father innocent or guilty? Would they ever know? They did not feel like asking him right now, but both of them privately decided that at some stage in the future they would persuade him to tell them the truth. The strange thing was, Clara thought, that although smuggling was a serious crime, she hardly cared just at the moment, if her father had done it or not. One way or the other she loved him. She wanted him to be at home with his family, not locked up in prison in Merle. It seemed that when a parent got punished for a crime then his whole family had to take the punishment as well. She did not understand why this should be so. Even if Jack Moody had hidden boxes of hash with his boxes of wine and sent them from one country to another, she and David and Brian, or their mother who was now dead, had not done that. But they had been punished as badly as Jack – even more severely. He had stayed in the prison in Merle, but their mother had died and the children had been shunted all around Ireland.

"So why did they put you in prison?" David persisted.

"I'll explain to you sometime," said their father.

"Explain now," said David.

Their father sighed.

"You're right to ask these questions," he said patiently, "but I'm going to ask you to do something now, something very hard."

"What?" David countered quickly.

"I'm going to ask you to be what you find hardest of all: be patient."

"Yuck," said David.

Their father went on. "I'll explain everything. Later tonight, or tomorrow, when we've settled in. Now I want to concentrate on the road."

"OK," said David, making a huge effort. Clara and Brian looked at one another in surprise. Could David be growing up at last?

Not quite yet.

"I want you to be innocent," David said then, "but I don't know if you are or not."

The car was filled with a nervous silence. Clara listened to the hum of the motor. Jack kept his eyes fixed on the road.

David spoke again.

"*The quality of mercy is not strained*," he said loudly.

Clara and Brian gasped. He was quoting one of Mrs Moody's favourite speeches, but they had not heard him doing anything like this since she died.

"*It droppeth as the sparkling rain from heaven.*"

Shouldn't that be gentle rain? Thought Clara. But she didn't correct him. Instead she continued the quotation: "*Upon the place beneath.*" The lovely words came back to her, like birds flying into a garden. "*It is twice blessed. It blesseth him that gives and him that takes; Tis mightiest in the mightiest.*"

"*It becomes the throned monarch better than his crown*," Brian joined in. He remembered this speech too, because Mrs Moody had quoted it so often. He saw her in his memory, standing in the middle of the garden under the chestnut trees, proclaiming it in dramatic tones:

"*His sceptre shows the force of temporal power,*
The attribute to awe and majesty
Wherein doth sit the dread and fear of kings;

But mercy is above this sceptred sway
It is enthroned in the hearts of kings."

"*It is an attribute to God himself,*" Jack Moody entoned, along with Brian. He repeated, "*It is an attribute to God himself.*"

He drove along the road. It was narrow and winding now, as they climbed into the Cevennes. The flat vineyards had disappeared and given way to rugged mountain faces, deep gorges. Trees clung tenaciously to the steep slopes, clinging on against all the odds.

There was silence in the car again. Each member of the family drifted off. David remembered the Play Days, when he had dressed up and pranced around the house, shouting out lines from plays he half understood. Clara thought of Mrs Moody, dressed in her outrageous clothes, directing *The Merchant of Venice* in the kitchen of Chestnut Cottage with as much enthusiasm and seriousness as if she were working for the Royal Theatre. Brian thought of the rain falling on the garden at Summerlands. He remembered Madeline's fair hair, and Charlie's blue eyes, and wondered if he would see either of those people ever again. "Gentle rain," he said to himself, looking at the hot, windswept mountainside. "Sparkling, gentle rain is what we all need a lot of."

* * *

Chestnut Cottage was right where it always had been, hidden behind its stone walls and chestnut trees. There was no *Sold* or *For Sale* sign outside, and no new residents within. Uncle Jim had not managed to sell the cottage, although he had tried hard. Jack knew all about his efforts to do so, but his solicitor had ensured that the Crabclaws' unscrupulous plans had come to nothing.

The chestnut trees were darkly green now, and heavy with spiky nuts, and the grass was as high as David's shoulders. The house seemed buried in grass and foliage. The Moodys made their way along the winding stone path to the front door. When they opened the door, the house smelled musty and damp. But everything was in its place: the red rugs, the comfortable old furniture, Mrs Moody's bizarre paintings on the walls. The children ran from room to room, checking the furniture, the toys, the crockery, the books. A layer of grey dust covered everything, but not a single thing had been disturbed.

Clara opened all the windows to let the cottage breathe. The swallows had not yet left the valley, and their musical twitters floated into the rooms. And as soon as she opened the windows the bells in the village began to ring too. She could hear the streams babbling, faintly, in the distance. A chorus of joyful sounds welcomed her home.

"Are you going to stay here and look after us now?" David asked, when they were seated at the kitchen table, having a makeshift supper of soup, bread and cheese. Clara had lit some candles, and poured a glass of wine for Jack and Brian, and the supper was the most delicious any of them had had in months.

"Yes," said their father, "I'm going to stay here and look after all of you now."

Brian looked at him questioningly.

"Of course you'll go back to school, Brian, as soon as it can be arranged," Jack said, answering his question, "and Clara will have to go away to school now too."

Clara looked surprised, and David was dismayed.

"Clara? Clara has to stay here with me!" David pouted.

"Yes," said Clara, "I want to go to school, but why does it have to be boarding-school? The school in the village is good enough."

"I think so too," said Brian. They all stared at him.

"What I mean is, I don't want to go back to the boarding-school. I think the village school will be fine."

"But what about being a doctor?" asked David.

"People from village schools get to be doctors too, if they want to," said Brian. "I can still be a doctor, if I work hard enough. But I'm not sure if I want to be one any more. I'd like to study botany, maybe, or just be a gardener. There's more than one way to live your life."

"Well, you can make up your own minds about which school you want to go to," said Jack, "but you don't have to worry about David. I'll be staying here with him."

"Do you mean you won't go travelling again?" David persisted.

Jack laughed. "No. I'm going to find another job, something I can do from home on the Internet. I've had enough of imports and exports for a while."

David slurped down his coke, and seemed satisfied for the moment.

"Now, I think we should relax and have an early night," said Jack. "And tomorrow I want to go and visit Lily's grave. I want to plant some roses on it. She always loved roses."

"We'll all go," said Clara.

* * *

Next evening, before dinner, Clara paid a visit to Madame Bonne.

Madame Bonne was delighted to see her.

"*Mon enfant!* You are back!" she said, embracing Clara in a big hug. "How are you? Tell me everything!"

Clara followed her into her kitchen. Nothing had changed there. The fire, the table with its strange bowls and cups, the red and blue cupboard, were exactly as they had been. The stuffed fox and the stuffed owl stared down from their shelf, and the same golden light danced over the floor. Madame Bonne was wearing identical clothes – her navy and red overall, her strapped black shoes. She bustled about and whipped up a cup of chocolate, and produced mouth-watering cookies from a tin. Clara told her story. She kept the best for last – her father was innocent, he had been released from prison, he was living with the children at Chestnut Cottage.

"*Merveilleux!*" said Madame Bonne. "All along I knew he was innocent!"

Clara let her rejoice in the happy turn events had taken, before asking the burning question. When every detail of the story was told, she dipped into her big pocket, and pulled out her book-bag.

"Thanks for the book," Clara said, taking it from the bag.

Madame Bonne raised her black eyebrows and clapped her big hands. She laughed and her brown eyes danced.

"It helped, did it not?" she asked.

"Not in the way I expected," said Clara.

"What was that?" Madame Bonne asked.

"I thought it would just make me lucky, or happy, or something."

"Ah, my dear child," said Madame Bonne. "You thought it was magic? But you don't believe in that sort of magic, do you? The genie and fairy and leprechaun sort?"

"No," said Clara, who thought it might be nice, after all, to have the occasional genie or leprechaun around to help solve the serious problems of the real world, the problems which she had encountered all too many of over the past summer. It would make life so very much easier.

"Of course you don't, my dear, because such creatures do not exist. They are figments of the human imagination, are they not?" said Madame Bonne, wagging her finger to emphasise the point.

Clara felt forced to agree. She had never come across a leprechaun or a genie, or any kind of supernatural being, herself. If they existed, where were they?

"I didn't mean that I expected the book to perform magic tasks," she said, "but I suppose I thought it would bring me good luck or something like that. And in fact all that happened was that I wrote a story in the book. Maybe having it encouraged me. But maybe I could have written it in any sort of book, or on a notepad, or scrap of paper."

Madame Bonne smiled and stared patiently at Clara, as if she were a little dim.

"And did writing the story help you?" she asked.

"It made me feel better, usually," said Clara. "I don't quite know why. And sometimes it gave me an answer to a problem. I got the idea for the shirts from it. They cheered us all up. And I got the idea about flying from it, too, which is how we got here."

"There! It was magic, after all!" said Madame Bonne.

"No, it wasn't," said Clara. "It was nothing like magic. It was quite hard work actually."

"Each time you wrote in the book you thought of a solution to your problem, didn't you, Clara?" Madame Bonne stared at her, serious now. The kitchen was dark even though outside the sun was splitting the chestnut trees.

"Sometimes. Not each time." said Clara.

"Sometimes is as good as anyone gets," said Madame Bonne. "A bit of magic, sometimes. And," she tapped Clara's forehead, "it's in here. It is in our heads. It is what we know. It is what we can do. That's magic. It is sometimes called imagination, and it is sometimes called wisdom, and it is sometimes called knowledge or experience or initiative or independence. It is the ability to look at a problem and figure out a way of solving it, it is knowing how to leap across a stream, something you have always been very good at. Isn't it a kind of magic?"

Clara nodded, remembering the times when she had opened her book and longed for a solution to her problems. The time in the Crabclaws' bedroom, when she had decided not to commit suicide. The time when she had decided to leave everything and join Brian and David in the woods. The time when she had decided to return to France. The time she had seen the aerodrome and known how she would bring everyone safely home.

"Well, maybe," she said. "I didn't always get the solution."

"Of course you didn't," said Madame Bonne. "What do you expect? Life is not a jigsaw puzzle. You can't assemble all the pieces and solve the puzzle in an afternoon. It's a bit here and a bit there, it's sometimes you understand and sometimes you don't."

"So where's the magic? Or whatever?" asked Clara.

"This and that," said Madame Bonne. "Work and imagination and understanding and luck. And something else as well. Something that helped you and your brothers on your flight across the sea. And what was that?"

"Friendship?" asked Clara, thinking of help she had received, from Sandy and Mario, and all the others.

"Yes, my dear. And finally magic is the thing that gave you the strength to undertake that journey, the strength to stick together in spite of all the difficulties. It is what gives you the strength to forgive your father, in spite of what he might or might not have done. *L'amour*, Clara. Love."

"The quality of mercy is not strained," said Clara. *"It droppeth as the gentle rain from heaven. It blesseth him that gives and him that takes."*

"Yes, yes, yes," said Madame Bonne, who did not particularly care for quotations from Shakespeare. She smiled and slowly heaved herself out of her carved chair. She walked to the far side of the room.

Clara closed her eyes and tried to figure out what Madame Bonne had said to her. But instead she relived all the episodes of the past few months: the crisis in France, the journey to Grey Walls, her friendship with Sandy, the Corner Café, the time in the woodland, the flight across the sea. They unrolled before her eyes like a video, one after the other, blending into a seamless adventure.

She fell into a reverie. In her daydream she was soaring over the stream, like a heron in flight, like a ballerina. On one side of the river was her father, sitting on the bank, fishing, his black beret perched sideways on his red hair. On the other was a blurry figure that might have been Mario. She couldn't make out his face, but he had the same thick brown wavy hair. The bank on which he sat was green, grassy, dotted with buttercups. There was a big tree, like a chestnut tree, behind him, but its branches were bare and chip-pans dangled from them instead of chestnuts.

Clara jumped. The church bells were ringing through the valley. The sound startled her and she awoke from her daydream and opened her eyes. The kitchen had grown mysteriously dark while she had drifted off. She must have been asleep for hours. The day was gone and the evening shadows were falling into the kitchen.

Madame Bonne had disappeared. The troubadour's book was still lying on the table by Clara's chair, opened on the story, which still needed to be finished. Clara closed it and put in back in her pocket. She would finish it off tonight, after dinner. And maybe she would start another story then.

Slowly she got up and walked to the door. It was ajar. She went outside. The sun had disappeared behind the mountains and Madame Bonne's garden was shadowy and dark. The swallows had gone to bed; the great trees whispered in the evening breeze. Above the plateau, the moon was rising – a wheel of amber, a full moon.

"Madame Bonne! Where are you, Madame Bonne?" Clara called sleepily.

The sun had set, and shadows filled the leafy garden. Clara searched under the arbour and behind the shrubs and chestnut trees. She looked in the vegetable garden. Madame Bonne was nowhere to be seen.

Clara didn't like to be rude, and go away without saying goodbye. But it was getting late and she was feeling hungry and she wanted her dinner.

"Goodnight, Madame Bonne!" she called, as loudly as she could, to the trees and the rooftop. "See you soon!"

See you soon, see you soon. The happy words floated around the garden. See you soon! They floated around like birds, like birds whose song was "I love you, you know!"

Clara closed the garden gate behind her. At that very moment a flock of white swans flew across the evening sky, their necks stretched, their wings beating the mellow air.

She watched them until they were out of sight. They were not three swans, or six swans, or seven swans, but a great flock, of twenty or thirty. "It is true," she said, aloud. "The world is not a jigsaw puzzle. It is quite a mysterious place." There was a great deal she did not understand. She patted the soft leather of her book-pouch, safely nestling in her pocket. Then she began to walk along the road through the trees, on her way home to Chestnut Cottage.

THE END